About the Author

Claire Handscombe is a British writer who moved to Washington, DC in 2012, ostensibly to study for an MFA, but actually, let's be honest, because of an obsession with *The West Wing*. She was recently longlisted for the Bath Novel Award, and her journalism, poetry, and essays have appeared in a wide variety of publications, including *Bustle*, *Book Riot*, *Writers' Forum*, and the *Washington Post*. She is the host of the Brit Lit Podcast, a fortnightly show about news and views from British books and publishing.

UNSCRIPTED

UNSCRIPTED

CLAIRE HANDSCOMBE

First published in the United Kingdom by Unbound in 2019;
this edition published 2021.

© Claire Handscombe, 2019

The right of Claire Handscombe to be identified as the author of this work has been asserted in accordance with Section 77 of the Copyright, Designs and Patents Act, 1988. No part of this publication may be copied, reproduced, stored in a retrieval system, or transmitted, in any form or by any means without the prior permission of the publisher, nor be otherwise circulated in any form of binding or cover other than that in which it is published and without a similar condition being imposed on the subsequent purchaser.

This book is a work of fiction and, except in the case of historical fact, any resemblance to actual persons, living or dead, is purely coincidental.

ISBN (eBook): 978-1-91261-895-8

ISBN (Paperback): 978-0-9975523-5-5

Cover design by Mecob

*For my own Cambridge friends –
How lucky I am to have shared such formative years
with such wonderful people.*

Thom

On the cover she is hand in hand with him, the two of them shadows against the sunrise. Thom picks up the book, turns it over and over, reads the words on the inside flap. Nothing about him. Of course nothing about him. This is not a book about him. It's a book about Ebba, and he was a mere parenthesis in her life before she dumped him and moved on to the handsome man on the cover. He knows this. He has always known this.

'Excuse me?'

He looks up from the book, from the page he has turned to and begun to read there in the 'memoir' aisle. He has done this enough times to know to smile as he looks up.

'Yes?'

The girl can't quite meet his gaze. She's late teens, early twenties at most, and she fiddles with her necklace. 'You're not who I think you are, are you?'

'I guess that would depend on who you think I am.'

'Well. Um. It's just. Um.'

Her friend rolls her eyes and steps in to rescue her from the awkwardness. Steps in quite literally, that is, shoving the other girl forward a little, more directly into his line of sight. 'She thinks you look like Thomas Cassidy, and she's a big fan of his, so.'

'Oh,' he says. He is tempted to play a game of some kind – *yeah, I get that a lot* – but the girl is so sweet. So nervous. This is probably a big moment for her, bigger than he can appreciate. 'Then yes. Guilty as charged.'

'Can she get a picture with you?'

She shuffles in and he puts his arm around her, careful as always where he puts his hand.

'Thank you,' she says, and that's all she says. Later, he thinks, she will kick herself for not having had a hundred things ready to say, prepared for just such a moment. They're in Pasadena, after all. A stone's throw from LA. She probably even knows he lives here. She might have been lurking with exactly this intention, of bumping into him. And she had nothing to say. She will be mortified.

He tries always to be gracious. To remember he is where he is, living this improbably charmed life, because his fans put him there. But sometimes, sometimes it's hard. Sometimes he just wants to be able to browse his favourite bookstore and not worry about hearing that voice behind him, those whispers. 'Is that Thomas Cassidy? I think that's Thomas Cassidy. From that show, you know? The one from the early 2000s about the school in New York City? He was the visionary English teacher all the girls had crushes on?'

'Oh, right, right,' the other person tends to mumble, unconvincingly. 'I remember you liked that show.'

In his moments of greatest self-awareness, Thom wonders if that is really what pains him, this half-fame, this has-been fame, this maybe-one-day-again fame. He wonders if he would, in fact, prefer a life where he couldn't go to bookstores at all because everyone, but everyone, knows him, is eager to take pictures of him in unguarded moments and plaster them all over Instagram. And there would be very few of these unguarded moments, these moments without make-up, and this would make them all the more precious, all the more Instagrammable.

It had been big, his show. Its inexplicable cancellation is still mourned in some quarters. It is the kind of show that appears regularly in lists of Top Ten Best Written Series or Best Romantic Pairings or Most Inspirational Moments on TV. More than a few young teachers, even these days, quote lines from it in job interviews – he knows this because they write and tell him – half-hoping the lines won't be recognised as borrowed, half-hoping their interviewer will smile and say, season two, episode one, right? That character was my favourite too.

People said that a show about teachers would never work. No one would care about the internal politics, or the esoteric debates about the merits of phonics versus the whole-word approach in teaching children to read. Only it turned out that when you wrote something well enough and treated the audience like they were actually intelligent, when you tapped into their ideals of what education was, what it could be, what it could do for people, for the country, for the world, when you appealed to their better natures, viewers did care very much. Office workers discussed phonics at the water cooler. Real-life teachers wrote blogs analysing the pedagogical issues raised in the latest episode. Even some of the fan fiction rose to this level, though most of it – it has to be said – centred on Thom's character's will-they-won't-they relationship or non-relationship (or whatever it was) with a beautiful blonde colleague. Seven seasons they drew it out for. Thom is proud of the chemistry they had.

But it is over. Very much over. He's been in other stuff – plenty of other stuff – but no one ever opens interviews with him by mentioning the other stuff. He is, will forever be, 'the guy from that teacher show'. He tries to be gracious about this, too. *The Classroom* has definitively saved him from playing minor villainous characters in TV movies, and, crucially, from anonymity. It has shown the world that he can act. Really act. His Emmy nominations year after year saw to that – with finally, finally a win in season six. (It turns out these things matter a whole lot more to the general public than his Juilliard degree does.)

Three years later, he is ready to move on. He is ready for another success after a bunch of ratings-boosting guest appearances on all the cool TV shows. He's been in one of his own; it only lasted a season. He had a lot of fun shooting it, but still. Steady work and a steady income are not things to be looked down upon.

***

Later, in bed with his wife, he brings up Ebba's book. He isn't sure why.

'I knew it,' he says. 'I knew Ethan was going to break her heart. I knew it wouldn't last.'

She laughs, Thom's dynamic wife. Says, 'So, what? You want to me to congratulate you on your prescience?'

'No,' he says. 'I just think it's interesting, is all.' But he is relieved. Yes, that must have been why he has told her. For affirmation. Encouragement. He is relieved she understands this where he could not.

'You're going to divorce me and marry Ebba now?'

It's a joke, he knows it's a joke, but still he feels the need to say what he has always said when things get tricky with Jenny. Like when they were both working so hard on their shows that they barely saw each other, let alone their children. Or like when she was at home with their newborn, watching her husband kiss the blonde on TV. Or like when she woke up the morning after they got back from their honeymoon and wondered, what now? We've had the party; what now? She'd expected to feel changed but she didn't: she'd been so focused on the wedding that she had not thought about the marriage, and this scared her suddenly. Was she meant to be different somehow, now she was a wife?

'Marriage is for life,' he says now, what he has always said since that newly-wed morning. 'We are committed to each other. I am committed to you.'

This line, he has been repeating it for so long. But he realises now that what he really wants to say is: if we get divorced, it won't be because of Ebba. It terrifies him, this realisation, terrifies and chills him, and the most terrifying and chilling thing of all is that it feels like a thought that he has thought many times, though he was not aware of having done so.

As if! Jenny is his wife, his love, the mother of his four fantastic children. (Four! Whatever were they thinking? No one in Hollywood has four kids, except for the crazy people, and even the crazy people don't have four: they have nine, adopted from five different countries.) They have built a life together, a life he (mostly) loves, a life he is pretty sure she (mostly) loves too, though maybe he should ask her sometime. Stop assuming.

He assumes so much. Has assumed, for example, for so long that this marriage would last till death would them part, like they promised on that beach fourteen years before. They were so young, not even thirty, and for that, too, people thought them crazy. Not their Midwestern families, who considered them slightly past their sell-by dates, but their friends in the New York theatre scene, where they worked hard and partied hard and everybody had a lot of sex because that was just what you did in the New York theatre scene in the

1990s. They would still have a lot of sex, just with each other all the time and he was crazy about her so that was okay with him, and from the way her body responded to him it seemed that was okay with her, too. But now, this. This stray thought, interrupting his assumptions. Burrowing, worm-like, first into his consciousness and then into his responses to Jenny, until over the months the marriage begins to splutter. He holds Ebba's book in his hands, turns it over and over, and wonders if he might find something in its pages that will help him understand himself, help him move on. A clue as to why the most precious things in his life can't seem to last.

Libby

The book. Finally, the book. Months, she has been waiting for the paperback to come out (because shelling out twenty quid on a hardback for some terribly written celebrity memoir, I mean, come on!), and now here it is, on the first day of the summer holiday. No more lessons to plan. No more overachieving teenagers to think about. Six blissful weeks of lie-ins ahead. The timing couldn't be more perfect.

It's a sign.

She found out about this book because of the Google Alert she has for Thomas Cassidy. It's probably awful, and she prides herself on never touching awful books, but this one matters. It's by an ex-girlfriend of his, and she wants to read everything about him. Everything. So even if there's only a paragraph, it's worth it. She flips through, passes over childhood, adolescence, the ballet classes, the career-ending injury. Finally gets to the section on college. Reads the description of Thom. Smiles.

The author's name is Ebba Brown. Her initials are the same as Libby's – Elizabeth Bolton. Another sign.

There have been so many signs on this journey, signs others refuse to see because hers is an impossible dream, something that only happens in fairy tales and novels with glittery pink covers. She doesn't tell many people the dream – or The Plan, as she prefers to call it – because the words sound crazy as soon as they are out of her mouth. She is not unaware of this, and therefore she cannot actually be crazy, can she? Crazy people don't think they are crazy. They think they are perfectly sane, and the world just doesn't understand them.

But, oh.

That is mostly how she does feel.

Never mind. She'll show them, and they'll all be sorry. All the naysayers. She'll write a novel, name the main character after Thom, and find a way to get it to him. Intrigued and flattered, he will read it, fall in love with her prose, contact her and ask to turn it into a movie. She'll pretend to think about it for a week or so, then say, sure, but can I work on it with you? Their eyes will meet over the script, and… fade to black.

It is a fail-proof plan.

Except.

Except for the fact that he is a Hollywood star – not A list, perhaps not B list, but certainly C-plus – and she is, well, not. She has never been in a play (or, well, now that she thinks about it, she did get to be a sheep in the nativity at nursery school). She is slightly overweight. She has never had her teeth whitened.

Except, too, for the fact that he lives in America. And as if that didn't make things difficult enough, he lives on the West Coast. California. Even further away. Even more of a time difference.

Except, too, for the age gap.

But – it's not even twenty years! Tiny, in the grand scheme of things. Totally overcomable.

All of the obstacles are totally overcomable. Although, there is one flaw in her flawless plan: there is no novel yet. There is this elaborate Plan revolving around the novel, but no actual novel. Like eleven-year-olds who decide what they are going to name their children before they've fully developed the physical ability to produce them.

So, yeah.

She should probably start by writing the novel.

Which, again: perfect timing. Six glorious weeks of glorious freedom. No money for any holiday to speak of, unless you were counting five days' camping in the Lakes. The rest of the time she will write the novel.

The novel that will change her life for ever.

The novel that will make her famous.

The novel that will make her Thom Cassidy's wife.

First things first: a notebook. And pens. Just the right notebook and just the right pens. These things are of paramount importance. A computer is not the same. A computer is for researching which pens are best, and which notebook. Extensive research. Important things.

'They're for my novel,' she says to the cashier upstairs at WHSmith in Victoria station. She likes the stationery department, spacious and quiet and almost classy (they even sell Filofax refills!), away from the crowds downstairs buying bestsellers and chocolate for their train journeys. The woman behind the till wears a name badge: Susie. Something like a smirk passes over Susie's face. But Libby is probably just imagining that. Susie probably just has an odd-looking smile.

'Seventeen forty-six,' Susie says. 'Would you like a bar of Cadbury's Dairy Milk with that?'

Ordinarily, Libby is tempted to snap. Tempted to say, 'I can see the bars are there, and I can see their enormous price sticker, so I think it's probably safe for you to assume I've already decided I'm going to pass on the chocolate, thanks.' In her defence, when you spend all day every day with snarky teenagers it is difficult not to turn into one yourself.

But not today. Today, Libby says, 'Yes, please. Brain food for the novel.'

Susie smiles again, the weird, smirk-like smile. 'Good luck,' she says as she hands over the notebook and the pens in the flimsy plastic bag the shop has the nerve to charge five pence for, despite the fact that it will disintegrate as soon as it is in Libby's hands.

'Thanks,' she says, and thinks: *Luck?* This has nothing to do with luck. Writing, like everything else in life, is about determination.

***

Determination, yes. But something seems to be missing. Inspiration, perhaps? Yes. Yes, that's it. But she knows you can't just wait for inspiration to strike. You have to start writing. Something. Anything. Thom, she writes, was—

And then she stops. Was – what? What is she going to make him? A teacher, like in the series? She isn't writing fan fic. She is moving beyond that now. She is writing Serious Literature. Something with the potential to be made into an Oscar-winning movie. Not that films about teachers can't be: look at *Dead Poets Society*. (Although, *what* was with the missing apostrophe there?)

She closes her eyes, pictures Thomas with his reddish-tinged blond hair, his freckles, his green eyes, his boyish smile. Those round glasses his character wears in *The Classroom*. A 'cellist? Her friend Dan from uni plays the 'cello and she's always thought it sexy. I mean, Dan is just Dan, you know, but a 'cello, on the right person? Sooo sexy. Okay. She closes her eyes and imagines it. Thom could be a 'cellist. (Not least so she could smile a little smugly while adding that old-fashioned apostrophe: 'cello. Short for violoncello. Missing letters, ergo apostrophe. Just like in 'phone.)

But is that his job? Concert 'cellist? Or is that just his hobby, and, really, he's a—

The sudden onset of thrumming outside breaks Libby's concentration. She looks up from her desk and out at the communal courtyard, the patch of grass she likes to lounge in with a book on sunny Saturdays. It looks perfectly tidy to her. As tidy as her desk: piles of textbooks and endless photocopies have been shoved in the cupboard back at school, to be dealt with on the last possible day in August. In front of her now are the essentials: just the right pens, just the right notebook. Nothing else. Uncluttered desk; focused mind. All tidy. Like the courtyard, which is not in need of any mowing whatsoever. And yet, today? They choose today? She can't think with that going on. She certainly can't close her eyes and imagine Thom playing Elgar's 'cello concerto.

She may as well make a cup of tea. She stands, stretches, glares out of the window in the vague direction of the lawn-mowing noise. The tribulations of artists. She remembers a quote by Thom from a speech he gave somewhere a few years ago. Great artists persevere no matter what. And she will. She will persevere. As soon as she has had her cup of tea and the lawnmower has shut up.

Vicky is in the kitchen, making her lunch. It must be later than Libby thinks. She must have been visualising Thom playing the 'cello for a long time.

'How's the novel?' Vicky asks, and again Libby thinks she sees a smirk there. What's with all the smirking? Don't people *know* she is serious? Don't people think she can do it? 'Cause (apostrophe!) she can totally do it. She'll show 'em.

'It's going really well,' she says, forgetting for a second that Vicky will not be fooled. Vicky can read her as if she were badly written fan fic that spells everything out and leaves zero to the imagination.

(Not that Vicky would read such things; she's far too level-headed. Or boring. Whichever way you want to look at it.)

Vicky and Libby have known each other all their adult lives. Which, granted, is only six years, but for three of those years they were at Cambridge together and even in their mid-twenties they both intuit that those three years at King's College were some of their most formative, will bond them for life. They've seen each other in tartan PJs from Marks and Spencer, hair unbrushed, hungover from the previous night's Formal Hall. They've helped each other into and out of ball gowns, navigating stuck zips and safety pinning slightly-too-revealing necklines. They've got lost amid the Sixties concrete of the Sidgwick Site looking for the language lab, Libby crying with frustration at the newness, the complicatedness, the overwhelmingness of it all, Vicky furrowing her brow and applying herself to following the map she had Pritt-Sticked into her diary. They've laughed together at the cognitive dissonance of carrying their plastic trays of industrialised, nondescript curries into the dining hall that almost resembled a church, or at least a temple to the ancient men in their gilded frames on the walls. They've delivered each other's Valentine's cards into pigeonholes at St John's and Clare Colleges, hugged each other when nothing came of it. They've met each other with champagne after the last exam of their final year and they've wept with relief and a tiny hint of disappointment at their 2.1s.

And even if they had not done those things, even if Vicky did not have the equivalent of a BA and a PhD – six years! – in Advanced Libby Studies, it isn't as if you need any kind of advanced anything to know what Libby is thinking, or, more crucially, feeling. Her face tells you, and her demeanour, and her voice. She is the definition of wysiwyg: what you see is what you get.

Which is to say that when she tells Vicky that her novel is going really well, there is no chance that Vicky will believe her. But nonetheless, Vicky plays the game. She smiles, and asks, 'Do you know what it's about yet?'

'A love story, basically.'

'Of course. Hopeless romantic that you are. Let me guess. The hero looks like Thom Cassidy?'

'Perhaps a little.' She omits to mention the name of the character.

'And the heroine looks like you.' Not even a question.

Libby hasn't got that far. But that seems like a great idea. What's wrong with a little wish fulfilment? Nothing. Precisely nothing. Some might argue that's what writing is all about. Jane Austen, for example, giving her sister and herself a happy ending in *Pride and Prejudice*. Writing as an antidote to life: its pain, yes; its uneventfulness; its disappointing lack of romance, too.

'He likes brunettes,' she says. 'So yeah.'

'The character in your novel, or the real Thom?'

'Both. His wife's a brunette. His ex-girlfriend, the one with the book: she's a brunette. The woman he thinks his character should have ended up with in *The Classroom*? All brunettes.'

'Don't do this, Lib.'

'What?' she says, though she knows perfectly well what is coming.

'*He likes brunettes, and I'm a brunette, so he's going to like me.*' Libby has to admit Vicky has her down pat, complete with the twirling of her hair between two fingers. 'He's not even real!'

'Of course he's real!'

'No. His character is who you're in love with. You don't know *him*. You only know the character he plays.'

'I've seen a ton of interviews.'

'He's not real,' Vicky says again.

'Well, anyway. The kettle's boiled.'

Libby stalks back to her room, but the spell is broken: no matter how much she closes her eyes and tries to concentrate, she can't see Thom playing the 'cello.

Ebba

From the time she spends talking to other writers, and browsing online authors' forums, Ebba knows that reading reviews of your own book is seldom anything other than a mistake, and a destructive one at that. Not the ones in the papers – such as still exist – no: those are okay, for the most part. They are, at least, thoughtful and intelligent. It is never pleasant to hear criticism, however mild, however couched in gentle language. But from the professionals, she can take it, just about; she has learned to, from her many years on the stage. She copies and pastes the negative things into a file labelled 'Notes For Next Time' and she will read them more closely, analyse them, when it comes to the second book, a novel, she thinks. For now, she skims them, protecting her own heart.

The reviews that are to be avoided at all costs are those by ordinary readers, many of whom have no sense of aesthetics. *Shrug*, writes one such reader, and Ebba thinks: shrug? I pour out my soul to you and spend two years crafting this book, and all you can do is shrug? So she has stopped reading reviews on Goodreads. She was forewarned, but apparently needed to learn the lesson for herself.

Still, though, curiosity gets the better of her sometimes. She has not yet had any destructive or discouraging run-ins on Twitter and it seems to her that it cannot be too dangerous a place. How much damage can really be inflicted in 140 characters?

She should have known. Shrug, after all, consisted of only five characters, and that was the one that stung most of all.

Still, this tweet kicks her in the stomach. *I still don't understand how anyone can break up with Thomas Cassidy*, it says. *Beautiful book, though.*

The truth is, she still doesn't completely understand it herself. She'd hoped that her memoir made clear the wrenching nature of the decision she'd wished she didn't have to make. On a primeval level the answer is simple enough: she needed Ethan. Somewhere deep in the reptilian part of her brain she needed him, had always needed him, would always have wondered about him, about them, if she didn't go get him. Was it the right decision to leave Thom for him? Who knows. But was it inevitable? Yes. It saved her from the what if that would always have lingered over her life like a cartoon question mark in a thought bubble.

Except that now she is left with a different set of what ifs. What if she had stayed with Thom? Would she have been happy? Would they have lasted? Her gut tells her yes; his history tells her yes too: fourteen years married to the same woman. Granted, they have filed for divorce now, but nonetheless, fourteen years – fourteen years and four kids! – says something. It says something about his willingness to work at his marriage. To change diaper after diaper (she has read in an interview that he did his fair share). To talk out disagreements. To make up for passionate fights with equally passionate sex. (This she does not need to read about; this she well remembers for herself.) He would have worked at making her happy: this too she remembers. The throwaway comment she made about too many takeouts and when she came back from acting class, Thom was scattering basil over a chicken and squash bake. Ethan did not work at their relationship that way. Ethan knew that Ebba was deeply, irresistibly attracted to him, that it almost did not matter what he said or did, that something in her would always draw her back to him. Sure: he was not above the odd romantic gesture. He swept her away on vacations to exotic destinations, but the gestures were for him as much as they were for her. There was an inherent, pervasive selfishness in Ethan that she did not perceive in Thom.

In Thom, there was also sweetness, and a sense of humour that made her smile sometimes even when he was not with her. He could turn anything into a pun, would sometimes launch into a themed series of them that had her groaning at first and then laughing until her stomach hurt and she begged him to stop and he replied no, never, I am addicted to the sound of your laughter. Laughter has been his enduring gift to her; most of the theatre roles she has are comedic ones, a balm for her sometimes hurting soul. They were his legacy to her, these moments of pure joy, moments she treasures now in the aftermath of Ethan's death, moments she thinks sometimes that she would have liked a lifetime of.

So the tweet kicks her in the stomach, because there is an element of truth there, a judgement on her life and decisions that is correct if incomplete. She thinks hard about how to respond. She wants to defend herself. She wants to deliver a lecture about stone-casting. But instead, she takes a deep breath. Instead, she decides to be calm. *Thank you*, she writes, and that will be the end of that.

Libby

Libby has never been much of a partier. Dinners out, yes, absolutely, the more the better, the longer the better, and, of course, the posher the better. Glasses of wine, yes, definitely. Pinot Grigio Blush, preferably. So long as she's home before half past ten on a weeknight, because the day isn't complete without half an hour of reading. Half an hour every night during the school year, no matter how exhausted she is and how much later than ten-thirty it is in reality by the time she has marked all the essays, planned all the lessons, stuck all the colour-coded Post-Its on the textbooks in preparation for tomorrow's photocopying. Reading is what keeps her sane; she gets grumpy if she doesn't do it. It is thus even more important than sleep, since being grumpy before the day even starts is not a good thing when you're a teacher, even a teacher at a school full of relatively well-behaved kids like those at Greycoat. Even well-behaved kids are capable of being obnoxious. Sometimes the best-behaved are the most obnoxious of all.

But during the holidays, she reads for more than half an hour every night. An hour, if she stays awake long enough. More, sometimes. She saves the books she suspects she will fall in love with for the summer, so she can indulge them, indulge herself, allow herself to be drawn entirely within the world of the book without having to sneak glances at the clock on the wall.

And this, this book of Ebba Brown's, it has captured her heart. She did not expect this. She expected to skim it looking for references to Thom. Celebrity memoir, let's face it: hardly the stuff of Great Literature.

But.

This.

Book.

The writing is elegant, eloquent. It has a rhythm to it, the melancholic rhythm of a love song written by someone whose heart is yet to fully heal. Libby wants to write like this, to be able to lay bare her own romantic soul with such subtle musicality. The story is, in many ways, a simple one, of young love lost and mourned, of two men and only one lifetime, but it makes Libby want to hug Ebba. To go and find her in Santa Monica and hug her. Ebba's decision – to leave Thom for Ethan, the hot-shot screenwriter, the subject of the memoir – was inevitable; the book makes that clear, but Libby cannot accept it was the right one. Who is she to judge? People are complicated. Relationships are complicated. She judges a little bit nevertheless. This is Thom, after all: the very best human being that exists. Ebba has said nothing but complimentary things about him. He didn't deserve the heartbreak. Libby wants to reach into the pages and hug this younger version of him, too. She wants a happy ending for both of these broken people. In the moment, she wants it for them almost more than she does for herself.

She has to do something with this emotion building inside her. Once upon a time, she might have made a poem of it. Before social media. Before it was possible to send your thoughts into the universe and by some mysterious alchemy have them transformed into a conversation that transcends huge distances and national borders, and sometimes, through the wonders of Google Translate, even language. So Libby reaches for her iPhone and condenses her thoughts into 140-characters-or-less. (Fewer! she always wants to scream at Twitter. It's fewer, not less!) *I still don't understand how anyone can break up with Thom Cassidy. Beautiful book, though.* Then the hashtag that would make her tweet searchable, and thus findable: #NotMeantToBe, the title of Ebba's book.

Which proves to be something of a mistake. The next morning, when Libby sleepily opens her Twitter app, Ebba has replied: *Thank you.*

Her stomach lurches. What has she done? Why did she think it was okay to pronounce judgement on someone's choices – someone who is a real person, who can read tweets, who has written a book that has brought to her readers, to Libby, an exquisite combination of joy in the beauty of its language and heartbreak on behalf of its author? Who has made herself vulnerable on the page in such a way that Libby has begun to think of her as a friend? Who is gracious enough not to argue with Libby's incomplete view of her personal history?

I'm loving your book, she types eventually. *And I shouldn't judge; I'm sorry*. Maybe the deftness of her semi-colon use will make Ebba smile. It certainly will if they are kindred spirits, as Libby suspects. Kindred spirits who love language, who live with passion, who take refuge in fictional characters – Ebba in embodying them on the stage, Libby in reading about them.

And after the mortification, after the disappointment at herself – this, after all, is the person whom only eleven hours ago Libby wanted to hug – something else occurs to her, too. Not only has she been hurtful, she has also been careless. She should have gone about this entirely differently. She should have written, or found a way to email. Because if there is anyone who can lead Libby to Thom, it is Ebba, and now she has alienated her.

Damn social media, mysterious alchemy and all.

***

When Libby begins to write, to get past those first hesitant sketches of the hero in her book – *Thom was... Thom was* – a strange thing begins to happen. A thing that she did not expect, a thing that has sneaked up on her like some kind of predator. The thing is this: as she writes, she finds herself thinking about her sister. Writing for her sister. Her favourite sister, the eldest, Iona. In the story she is writing, she finds herself wanting to say, you don't need a man to be happy. You don't even need a man to be fulfilled and live a meaningful life. She wants so very much for Iona to get this.

It's been nine years since Jeremy died in the car crash on the way to visiting them in their new home in Suffolk. Surrey to Suffolk: a difference of just a few letters; a three-and-a-half-hour drive, assuming the traffic on the M25 cooperated to a reasonable degree and you could get around London without too much hassle. Three and a half hours in a north-easterly direction, and it would be less if Suffolk was the kind of place that even had motorways, but those three and a half hours were more than enough to upend everything, upset everything that was good about life.

Iona had been stoic when they moved. Not like Libby. Stoic was not something Libby really understood, let alone exhibited. When it came to this move, she had plenty of emotions. It was wrong. It was unfair. She had just been invited to her first sleepover with the popular girls. She had worked hard at the entrance exam for this grammar school; she had earned her place there, the chance to wear the green tartan skirt and the tie and the blazer that said: this girl belongs with the high achievers. She had always known – or at least hoped – that this was true. But for two and a half years now she had dressed every weekday morning in the incontrovertible evidence of that fact, and she had brought excellent mark after excellent mark home, to less familial acclaim than she would have liked (such was the fate of a middle child). And now they were going to move to a part of the country that didn't even *have* grammar schools. And she was going to go to a comprehensive? She'd checked the exam success rate there and dissolved into tears. And, if that weren't bad enough, the uniform. If you could even call it a uniform. Black trousers, black sweatshirt and if you really, really wanted you could have the sweatshirt with the school's logo on it (a logo with no Latin phrase, no phrase of any kind), but no pressure. I mean really, was there any point in even having a uniform?

And this, all this, because her parents had decided to be all worthy and civic-minded and help 'elevate' crappy schools, instead of cruising along in the Surrey private schools where they had been teaching, as any reasonable person would. A promotion: her father to head of the science department, her mother to deputy headteacher. At the same comprehensive school. What were the chances! A 'chance' like that would not come along again. A promotion and yet still, somehow, a pay cut. They wanted a challenge, apparently. They wanted to do some good in the world, or something. You work hard, you work hard, you work hard, and then one day you get to stop working hard: isn't that the point of working hard in the first place? Yet her parents, supposedly intelligent people, had failed to grasp this most basic of truths.

So stoic was not Libby's attitude to the move. Iona, on the other hand. Iona, who had even more reason to throw a fit, or, since that was not really her style, at least sit the parents down and calmly and with logic and well-thought-out arguments talk them out of this decision, Iona took it, yes, stoically. Jeremy loves me, she said to Libby. A few miles aren't going to change that.

This, if Libby had been capable of fury towards Iona, would have infuriated her. This spectacular failure to get riled up at so great an injustice. But, she said. But. Fury was one of the few things that rendered Libby speechless.

'We'll be apart for a couple of years. And yes, it's a long drive. But it's do-ably long. We're not moving to Scotland, Lib. He's got a car.' And then Iona dissipated Libby's fury with her most effective weapon: 'Want to know a secret?' And of course Libby did. Libby always did. 'I think he's going to ask me to marry him.'

Libby thought it was meant to be a surprise when the guy asked, but that didn't seem like the right thing to say. Nor did it seem quite right to ask what colour the bridesmaids' dresses would be.

'Wow,' was what she went for.

I know, Iona said, and Libby thought in that moment that this must be what it means in novels when someone is 'beaming'. Iona was grinning with all her teeth, in that way she did which showed her gums a little and Libby wished it didn't because it marred Iona's beauty, like a crossed-out spelling mistake on the first page of a new exercise book. But today she almost didn't mind, because look how happy Iona was. How beaming.

***

But then, the horribleness of that day. This is still how it's referred to in Libby's family. That Horrible Day. Iona in her pale pink cotton dress, her hair curling on her shoulders, sitting in the window seat, as she always did on those Saturdays, waiting for Jeremy to arrive around twelve, as he always did, in time to take her out for lunch. Waiting a little too long. Waiting till quarter past twelve. Half past twelve. Refusing one cup of tea, accepting another. No news, nothing. Why don't you call him? their mum asked, but over and over Iona shook her head. I don't want him to pick up his mobile when he's driving. It's dangerous. Unaware that danger was irrelevant now. That he was being cut out of his wreck of a car, that he was no longer breathing when he arrived at hospital.

Whenever Libby reads words like forlorn or misery or heartbreak, her mind races back to that day, digs up the image of Iona, her hands clasped around her bent knees, waiting at the window for the boy she loved, or thought she loved, because at eighteen, who knows? And when Libby reads of helplessness, she pictures herself on that day, those weeks, those months, having nothing to say, no way of making her sister laugh the way she always had. She longed to see the gums above Iona's teeth now. She offered hugs, and sometimes Iona took them, but often she didn't, and each time this happened Libby's soul ripped a little. Libby was outwardly angry, angrier than anyone in the family, so angry that it almost didn't hurt when she made her mother cry: see what this stupid move has done? See? I told you it was all wrong, she'd shouted. It did hurt, though, when she realised Iona had overheard her telling Karen, the sister between them, I'm never falling in love. Look what it's done to her. She heard Iona's bedroom door click shut and the phrase came to her fully formed: irreparable damage. To herself, to Iona, to their relationship? She is still not sure, all these years later, but all these years later Iona is still single, still more mopey than she should be, still missing Jeremy. Libby worries about her. Iona is beautiful, thoughtful, accomplished, in much the same way as a Jane Austen heroine might be. She plays the piano, speaks French; she has never – as far as Libby knows – tried her hand at needlepoint but would probably be brilliant at it if she did.

And so as Libby writes, she finds herself wanting her sister to know: there is hope. You can have a meaningful life. Even a happy life. She wants the lost love not to define her heroine in the way it has defined Iona. She finds as she writes that her heroine carries deep sadness within her, melancholy, nostalgia, but that these things drive her to achieve greatness. It's what she wants for Iona. She wants her, of course, to find joy with another man, but she wants this book to tell her: it's okay if you don't. Life is still worth living.

***

Week three and Libby is getting somewhere. Not far, and certainly not fast. But somewhere. She's filled in character profiles. She's brainstormed plots and subplots. And most importantly, she's even started to actually write: put actual pen to actual paper. And it's not terrible. I mean, it's not Proust – not that she wants to be Proust, not even remotely; she doesn't know why he popped into her head for comparison – but it's not terrible. It's something she would read (and she's fussy). It's something she can see on the cinema screen already: every scene she visualises as a scene in the film. Thom, of course, playing the hero, she playing the heroine, though she knows it can't really be her since all she has in terms of acting experience is the sheep thing.

But is it something she could see in Waterstones? Why not? It's as good as *Fifty Shades*. Better, arguably, if considerably less raunchy. Still, it couldn't hurt to get a professional opinion. She wonders if Dan could help. Dan, her university friend, her supervision partner through much of the Cambridge years, with whom she'd climbed creaky spiral staircases on their way to having their respective essays picked apart and examined and argued spiritedly about the fallacy of Proto-Indo-European as a concept. Dan, who after a couple of years' worth of false starts and almost giving up on his dream of working in the publishing industry has finally landed a job as a literary agent's assistant. He is the gatekeeper; he is the one who after a cursory glance at a couple of pages of someone's supposed work of art decides whether to keep reading, to recommend it for the eyes of someone more powerful. He knows what is good. Or at least what sells: avid reader that she is, faithful peruser of (usually) independent bookshops, she knows better than to equate the two. It would be good to have Dan's opinion.

It would, now that she comes to think of it, be great to see him. The gang from King's College meets relatively often: most of them have ended up in London, and those who haven't have stayed in academia in Cambridge or ventured no further away than Oxford. (Traitors.) Aside from Vicky and Libby in Pimlico and Dan in Putney, there is a shared house in Lewisham (Libby cannot quite fathom why Lewisham), with the result that it is relatively easy to meet for coffees in Costa (never Starbucks, because of American capitalism) or for a glass of tepid rosé at the Chandos. Why the Chandos, no one is quite sure – and there are those amongst them who wrinkle their noses at the very mention of the pub's name – but it is a tradition that seems intent on sticking, perhaps because of its proximity to Covent Garden Tube station smack-bang in the middle of London, its non-chain-ness, and a lack of strong enough argument to back up a veto.

But Dan, like Libby, likes nice things, and he prefers his rosé cold, so perhaps that is why he is coming out for those drinks less and less often. A new venue may have to be sought: Dan won't come if it's the Chandos seems like a good enough reason to veto. In the meantime, she misses him. Three years after graduation she still finds herself working with her door open, as she had in the final year, on echoey S Staircase. Working on the same essay on the history of the English language, they would lean back on two feet of their chairs and shout across the corridor at each other.

'Page seventy-six, David Crystal, good quote, halfway down the page.'

'Mark it for me? I think you got the last copy out of the college library.'

The first thing Libby had noticed when she got out of the taxi for her interview at King's was the lamp post just outside: iron, and ornamental, just like the one in *The Lion, The Witch and the Wardrobe* that indicated where one world ended and another began. She knew the Narnia stories inside out, had listened to Iona read them to her over the course of one Christmas holiday as they huddled together under a blanket in the window seat of their chilly dining room in Surrey. Eight-year-old Iona had needed reading practice, and Libby, four years old, wide-eyed, and delighted at the attention from her favourite sister, was the ideal audience.

Libby had wanted ever since to find her own wardrobe, her own alternative universe, and she had found it in books, and then in *The Classroom*. But here, in Cambridge, right in front of the college she had chosen, was an actual lamp post, a portal into the new life she hoped was ahead of her. Not for her, she knew already, the frequent visits home or the protests against elitism and archaic structures. To protest against these would be like protesting against the White Witch and Turkish delight, Aslan or the place where it was always winter and never Christmas. If you went through the back of the wardrobe, if you willingly slipped into that other reality, you embraced it all: it was a choice, and one Libby made without hesitation.

Because how could she not? How could she not choose to live in a world where champagne corks floated past punts full of tourists admiring what would be her home? Where even just to walk on those perfectly manicured lawns was a hard-earned privilege? Where the night-time air, chilly and filled with the music of an organ scholar's practice, was cinematic and almost a little creepy, so that she was never quite sure what it was that was making her shiver? Where the sepia-toned buildings had housed great scholars, men and women who had gone on to be eminent in their fields, or famous, even. Where she would make new friends who did not think it sad to work as hard as she did, who would understand she couldn't stay at the bar too long because she had an essay to write. The bright red hexagonal pillar box on the uneven cobblestones in front of King's: she had seen the photograph of it in the Cambridge prospectus that her school had eventually managed to find for her, and here it was, so real she could touch it, so real she could post letters into it and they would make it back into that other, less real world, back past the lamp post and through the wardrobe.

She was right all along – they all were – when they speculated that there would never again be a time in their lives like their time at King's, that life in that other world was bound not to measure up. Perhaps that is why they now huddle over their lukewarm rosés as often as they can, creatures clinging to habit as they did back then: dinner in Hall at six-thirty, finishing in time for *The Simpsons* in the TV room. They are grown-ups now, grown-ups who own TVs and record *The Simpsons* if they feel the need to, and who have learned not to get excited about four-pound bottles of wine, but the rituals they shared and those they still share – tepid Chandos wine included – are part of the bonds that will keep them allied for life, or at least Libby certainly hopes so. Only, Dan is there less and less and she misses him.

Two birds, one stone: she texts him. *Hey, stranger. Want to do lunch sometime?*

On a rainy Thursday, she meets him on the South Bank, at their favourite Pizza Express, and wonders why she bothered blow-drying her hair. He, however, shows no signs of having walked through the sodden streets, aside from his dripping umbrella and the slightly damp hem of his beige trousers. Granted, they are round the corner from his office, but still, it just goes to show: he always looks so good, so neat and tidy, so well put-together. In a suit, especially; his sandy-blond hair is newly cut – after years of nagging from her he has finally learned not to get it cut *too* short. They hug, sit, order olives without having to consult with each other: it's a familiar routine, the enjoyment of which would be enhanced by the consuming of wine, but alas, that is not advisable in the middle of Dan's working day. They comment, as they so often do, on the incongruous name of Pizza Express that implies fast food rather than, as Libby thinks of it, 'class on a budget'; on the fact that even in the rain the view from their window seat is remarkable: the angry-looking Thames, the formerly wobbly Millennium Bridge, the dome of St Paul's Cathedral. They exchange pleasantries, news of the others: Liam's been promoted again at Merrill Lynch; Matt's broken up with his latest girlfriend, which is probably for the best. They didn't like her much anyway.

And then Dan gets that look in his eyes, the look that signals a shift into a more intentional, more meaningful part of the conversation. (It would usually be accompanied by a topping up of wineglasses.)

'So how *are* you?' he asks. 'Really. What have you been up to this summer?'

'Well, I—'

She has promised herself she will say it confidently. She will not fumble it or sound unsure of her newfound vocation. But she finds herself embarrassed. She finds herself a little too desperate for his approval, or desperate at least for him not to mock her. She finds herself blushing, but to her credit she does not chicken out.

'I'm actually writing a novel.'

'Hey,' he says. 'That's great! You've always said you wanted to write a novel.' He gets it! He will not be one of those people who think it's all because of 'the actor guy'. He understands about books, their power to transport us to other times, other places, universes where all is right. Or where nothing is right: equally comforting in its own way, so that real life feels like escapism when you close the pages.

'Wait a minute,' he says. 'That's not why you wanted to have lunch, is it?'

'No.' But she is a terrible liar. She knows it, and he knows it, and has known it for ever, or what feels like for ever, and she knows he knows it. 'Well,' she says. 'In part. But I miss you, Dan.'

He smiles. At least she thinks that is a smile she sees flirting across his lips. 'Uh huh. But you also want me to take a look at it when it's done, don't you?'

'Well, I was hoping.'

'It's a bad idea, Lib. Like your dad teaching you to drive. We're too close.'

Admittedly, the driving lessons had been a disaster, though she slightly embellished the story she told her new friends during freshers' week. There had been no actual wall in the way, and she had only scraped the paint on the car a little. Over port at matriculation dinner, before forks tapped on glasses and the provost spoke about showing the rest of Cambridge what a college mostly made up of state school students could do, Dan had said, 'There was no wall, was there?' and she'd thought, I'm going to have to watch that one. Then almost simultaneously, I'm going to enjoy being known by him, and maybe that was why she kissed him later that night in the dark cellar bar, sweat dripping down her back and down the walls. A rite of initiation of sorts, that kiss: it was never spoken of again. At least not that she knows of. At least not between the two of them.

'We're too close,' he says again. 'Nothing good can come of my getting involved with your book. Conflict of interest, blah blah.'

He waves his hand dismissively but he still has the serious look in his eyes.

'Really?' she says. She can't quite believe he is saying no to something that would mean so much to her. 'Not even for me?'

Dan drops his eyes. 'Let me know when it's done,' he says after a swig or two of water, as though the water were the Dutch courage that the conversation had lacked. 'And I'll think about it.'

Dan

The novel is not very good; it is somewhere between burnt ochre and beige. It is only October, of course, only three months since she started writing, and so he knew it wouldn't be very good, though Libby is not unintelligent, and no one knows books better than she does. In the laity, anyway: that's what his boss calls the world outside the publishing industry. The people outside, their fists red-raw from knocking, their desperation-contorted faces pressed against the window. (Dan feels vaguely guilty about this, this gentle mocking of the not-yet-published and the unpublishable.) For one of those people, Libby knows her stuff. Though it is not so much the publishing world that she yearns to enter; it is, in fact, possible that it doesn't interest her at all. It's all about Hollywood for her, an even harder club to gain access to, although no: that is not quite true either. It's not the whole of Hollywood. Just this one person, this one man, this actor guy she wouldn't shut up about all the damn way through college. Dan might have suspected that the hero in Libby's novel would bear a striking resemblance to Thomas Cassidy, though he did not expect that she would go as far as to give him the same first name.

It occurs to him for the first time that she really might believe that all it will take is this novel, and *voilà*, she will be swept up in the hero's warm embrace, leave behind the unglamorous London teacher's life where the only available men are people like Dan, though none of that will matter any more because she will have her man. Her man who in actual reality does not even know she exists and would run as fast as he could in the opposite direction if he did. The plan is glaringly apparent to Dan, as is the speed with which she has written the novel. This smacks of First Draft Syndrome – too many adjectives, unresolved subplots, fuzzy timelines – yet she clearly believes all it needs is some tweaking, a few line edits. She did not say this; she said, rather, that she wanted his honest opinion, but her eyes said please love it, the way they sometimes say please love me, a call he'd heard and responded to so long ago, to her obliviousness and the detriment of his own heart. And he suspects that were he to give her his actual honest opinion, that would be the end of their friendship, never mind hopes for anything beyond that.

'Hi,' she says, sliding into the seat opposite his at Costa and putting her enormous latte in front of her.

He looks up from her manuscript, and her smile does to him what it always does to him.

'Hello,' he says back, and takes a deep breath.

'Did you like it?'

'It has potential,' he says, and hates himself. For the blandness. For the cliché. For not being able to give her, at least not yet, what it is he knows she wants: pure, admiring wonder.

'Potential,' she repeats. She takes a sip of her coffee and licks the foam from her top lip.

'Yes,' he says. He has a speech ready for such occasions. He does not have to deliver these speeches often: a book like hers would be rejected, by email if she was lucky, but more likely by auto-reply followed by silence: if you have not heard from us within three months, you may assume… It's harsh, but it saves everybody time, and at least it has the merit of being clear, of sparing him exactly this kind of awkwardness. When he meets the agency's clients face to face it is usually with the expectation of delivering happy news – a French publisher is interested in acquiring rights; a long-worked-on manuscript is at last ready for submission – a handshake confirming what has already been decided through a long string of emails dating back, sometimes, as much as a year. But Libby is not the first of his friends or acquaintances who has asked for a favour, for his professional opinion; far from it. Usually he reads the first couple of pages, ascertains the basic issue preventing successful replies from other agents, then has coffee with them and recommends two or three books on particularly relevant aspects of the craft of writing, sending them off with a cheerful platitude or two.

So he knows just what to say to Libby, or he would if she were anyone else. He has read the whole thing, made copious notes in the margins in case she ever asks for more than the banalities he is able to summon today. But the copy he is returning to her today is clean, save for the occasional tick where a turn of phrase has particularly pleased him. She shows flashes of talent, of brilliance, even, but they are not enough, these flashes, to carry even a casual reader. If she works at it, he believes she can get there. But he believes she can do more or less anything if she puts her mind to it, and there is the rub: six weeks of single-minded work at her desk is his Libby all right (well, okay, not *his*). But years of honing her craft? Not so much. She'll be on to the next thing by Christmas. Learning the oboe, maybe. With just as much gusto.

'How serious are you?' he asks her, and she seems hurt that he feels he has to ask.

'Really serious,' she says, frowning. 'Why?'

'I'll lend you some books,' he says. 'To help.'

'So it's not very good?'

'Writing is hard, Lib.'

'Oh,' she says. She scoops up the froth at the bottom of her latte cup with her spoon and refuses to look at him.

'It's good,' he says. 'It's really good. I just think you can make it even better.'

'Oh,' she says again, and this time she looks up and she smiles. But her smile does not do to him what it always does to him. Instead, something curdles inside him.

Libby

Libby loves Pimlico for many reasons. She loves the Tachbrook Street market with its fabulous choice of olives, the Oxfam shop with its basement full of bargain books, and she loves, too, the surprising quietness of this central London enclave, so worth the sacrifice of what the price of rent is doing to her bank account. She can walk down Belgrave Road with its tall, elegant, shiny white houses and almost forget that she is in a big, noisy, smelly city. But if she walks far enough down this street, she'll find Victoria station, and be reminded: this is London, central London, busy, ebullient central London, full of people and possibilities. After the sleepiness of four and a half weeks of the summer holiday, this is what Libby needs. She needs to be bumped into; she needs the noise.

There is a new issue of *Writing Magazine* out and Libby wants to buy it in the WHSmith at the station, the nearest place which stocks it, the place she goes for stationery though not for books. There is so much to learn when it comes to making a novel; she is hungry for knowledge. The other day, she jumped on the Tube to Green Park and marched past dawdling tourists taking selfies in front of the Ritz to the giant Waterstones at Piccadilly Circus, a tall building full of natural light and potential discoveries. Wow, she'd said, the first time she'd bought books there, on a family trip more than a decade ago. Is this the biggest bookshop in the UK? It's the biggest in Europe, she'd been told by the proud, smiling man behind the counter. And when she'd got the teaching job in London, one of her first jubilant thoughts had been of the Waterstones, of the hours she'd spend there, walking reverently among the themed tables of books, taking the lift up to each of the upper five floors, then sitting down in the café on the basement level to page through what she'd just bought. But on her visit a few days ago, Libby didn't dawdle in the fiction section at the front as she usually does; she didn't take the time to mourn the old three-for-two tables or the now-absent apostrophe in the shop's recently rebranded logo; she didn't run her hands over the covers or write down titles of the books she'd buy later. Instead, on a mission, she went straight to the lift, up to the fourth floor, and emerged two hours later, arms full of writing prompts, guides to novel structure, advice on characterisation.

She can't get enough. She reads incessantly, the books Dan has lent her, and the books she has bought, and she does exercise after exercise, learning to use different voices, learning to write descriptions.

It's not rush hour today at Victoria station, but nevertheless there is plenty of bustle, plenty of life. People walking faster than they do in any other British city, diagonally across the concourse, the precise angle of the most direct trajectory. Women in hijabs pushing small children in buggies. Gaggles of French teenagers, their rucksacks firmly anchored onto both shoulders. A ceaseless stream of tannoy announcements about platform numbers and delays and projected arrival times and don't forget to take all your belongings with you when you leave the train and if you suspect it report it. The tempting smell of pseudo-Japanese noodles from Wasabi. In WHSmith, the tiny aisles are clogged by the luggage of the many people who pop in to page through magazines while they wait for their trains, with not the slightest intention of buying anything. The narrowest of all aisles – the most clogged of all – is the one towards which she is headed, the one with the writing magazines. Still, it's life, London life in all its messiness, and it's what she wants, what she needs.

She has brought her highlighters and her pens and her notebook with her, so on the way home she stops off in Caffè Nero. She has been there many times and it is always thrumming with activity. The coffee is flavourful and full-bodied and has a bit of a kick to it. She likes to sit at the table in front of the counter, to look out of the window at London rushing past, to hear the accents of the servers and the customers, coins being left in the tip jar, the coffee machine fizzing and frothing. But today the noise, rather than energising her, distracts her. She can hear a private French lesson over in the window-seat leather sofas: the tutor, a few years older than her, is visibly wincing as her American student attempts a few basic phrases. She watches a mother with her three children, each of them demanding attention in their own way. The little one, leaning on her clenched fists, is crying for reasons best known to herself. The eldest is intent on telling a story that seems as if it is never going to end. And the middle one? The middle one sits impassively, almost bored, as she sucks on the straw of her Frappuccino or her hot chocolate and swings her legs back and forth, back and forth. Desperately wanting someone to notice her. To pay attention. To notice the silence above the noise. But of course nobody does. The nose of the youngest is wiped and the older one is listened to and the middle one sits, and this makes Libby so sad that she drinks her coffee without even opening her magazine.

From earliest childhood, she had longed to be taken into Iona's confidence, and the longing was only increased by Iona's closed-offness. Lying alone in her room after the move, she would imagine Iona and Karen whispering into the night, sharing secrets that Libby would never be privy to. Michaela and Sophie might well have done the same too, but she never thought about that; theirs was not the club to which she wanted to belong. It was Iona she idolised: she thought her beautiful, poised, calm, capable. All the things Libby was not, feared she would never be. Teach me to be you, she would often long to say but instead she would stand in the distance and watch as Iona baked scones or applied her make-up or put the finishing touches on the watercolour for her A Level art portfolio. You're hovering, Iona would say. She'd say it with a smile, often. But still it meant, back off. Give me space.

Given Iona's introversion, it would have made much more sense for her to have had her own room after the move, but putting Karen and Libby together would have meant more fights than their parents had the energy to referee. They were too similar, the two of them; Libby had once heard her mother describe her as like Karen, only ten times more so – more so in every way – and Libby liked to imagine that without Karen, she would be the confidante; she would be the one sharing a bedroom and night-time secrets with Iona. Her mother had presented the idea of a bedroom of Libby's own as a favour, and maybe she really did believe it was a treat for Libby to have space. I know the move is tough for you, she'd said. But that was to misunderstand Libby so profoundly that it had only made her feel lonelier. Teenagers, her dad would sigh, and it would make her want to scream. Her unhappiness was in no way hormone-related, the way the enormous monthly zits on her chin were. She felt lost, forgotten, among this mass of dark-haired, brown-eyed girls, this family which outsiders looked at and envied and her sisters seemed to revel in. She sees it on their Facebook walls still, read it in the birthday cards she sneaked looks at back then, and she wondered how family could look so different from different angles.

She had been glad to leave all that behind when it was time for Cambridge, gladder still to have so effortlessly become part of this group of friends that evolved because of who sat next to whom in various lectures, who lived on the same floor of Market Hostel, who walked to ten o'clocks on the Sidgwick Site together. It was organic, unforced, and she was – is – every bit as much a part of everything as everyone else. She isn't the girl in the middle, swinging her legs and drinking in silence, hoping to be noticed. Mostly.

Ebba

'This isn't weird at all.' Ebba is babbling, and she isn't even sure if she means it. 'I was worried that it would be, but it isn't.'

Thom looks back at her across the tealight and the crisp white tablecloth.

'It's maybe weird that it's not weird,' he says. 'But mostly, nice is what it is.'

She cannot disagree. It is perhaps the wine, but she senses herself relaxing already. She could always be herself around Thom, let any pretence or performance slip away, and she is beginning to remember what that felt like; it is almost back in her conscious memory, like the face of a first-grade teacher you didn't imagine you'd ever forget yet here you are, one day, squeezing your eyes shut and trying to bring to mind her features. She had blond hair, and—

'We should have done this sooner,' he says. 'Spent time together.'

'I think that would have been dangerous.' She can't quite meet his eyes as she says it. She is all too aware of what she is admitting.

'Because I was married?'

'What happened with you two?'

'Oh, you know. Life. Nothing *happened* happened. No juicy gossip for the media. They tried so hard to find some, but nothing.'

'But the two of you always seemed so happy.'

'We were,' he said. 'And then we weren't.'

She senses irritation in his voice. She will wait until later to press him on this. She doesn't even know why the answer should matter to her; she cannot yet untangle the knot of emotions that took up residence in her stomach when she got Thom's Facebook message: *Those were some nice things you said about me in your book.*

She went back to her journal after she got this message, read again the parts about him, parts she had only skimmed over when she had been researching her memoir. (The thought of having to research her own life had made her smile.) She found quotes from him, snatches of conversation that she'd written down verbatim so that she'd always be able to hear him saying them. She had been in love, most of all, with his voice. She would close her eyes and relive their conversations, hear him again and again on her rare nights without him. He should do books on CD, she would tell him, but that was mostly for her own benefit, so she would be able to fall asleep listening to him.

'Maybe when I retire,' he'd said. 'Once, you know, I have no control over my own body to do the actual acting thing.'

They were walking hand in hand through Central Park that night early in the third year of his Juilliard MFA, and it seemed like the perfect time to ask him. 'What is it you want to be known for?'

'Shakespeare,' he said. 'The great stuff. I want to do great work with the work of great writers.'

There was an intensity, a focus in him, in his whole body, when he talked about acting, that made her fall in love with him a little more each time. But he saw it in himself sometimes, too, and he would pull back from those moments a little, as though he were afraid that his passion would cause Ebba to back off, to believe she was secondary to his happiness.

'I'll tell you what I don't want to do,' he said, kicking at a pile of yellowed leaves at the foot of their favourite tree. 'I don't want to be the brilliant villain that barely redeems otherwise unpalatable movies. You know, the kind of movie the fans will sit through because of me and then resent me because they've wasted two hours of their lives on crap.'

'Fans, huh?' She liked to tease him, gently.

'I didn't say there'd be a lot of them. Or that they'd have discerning taste.'

Sitting in this restaurant in Santa Monica now, she feels the sudden urge to say she has become one of those fangirls. That she has sat through all of those movies and never once resented him for it, though she has resented the studios for not recognising his talent, not giving him roles that were worthy of him. For often giving them, instead, to the men with the more conventional good looks, when the combination of Thom's acting skill and freckled charm made him head and shoulders more attractive than they were.

'I loved *The Classroom*,' she says instead.

'Everybody loved *The Classroom*.'

'I loved *you*.'

He is silent until she looks up at him.

'Yeah,' he says.

The server brings the entrées and the moment is lost, consigned with so many others to the box under Ebba's bed marked 'I'm not sure what that was about'. And they get talking as they eat, this talk becoming the easy chatting of old friends with so much to catch up on because they haven't seen each other in two weeks. Only in their case it's not two weeks; in their case it's eighteen years. Oh, they've seen each other: caught glimpses and exchanged awkward greetings and head–nods at movie premières, noticed one another attending their respective plays. But they haven't *seen* each other. Not like this. Not just the two of them. Because of Ethan, at first, but then also because of Jenny.

Thom tells Ebba about his life with Jenny. About the three daughters they had while both of them were at the peak of their acting careers, because that is the kind of curveball life likes to throw you sometimes: Jenny's nausea on the morning of the audition for that pilot wasn't just nerves after all. The exhaustion, the craziness, the diapers, the noise. So much noise. Happy noise, often. But incessant. They had three because Jenny knew that Thom wanted a son, ached for a son, wasn't even sure why, couldn't work it out by self-analysis and certainly didn't have time or inclination for therapy. He'd had a good relationship with his father, had nothing to make up for in that sense. They'd agreed that Juliette was the last, that they might have been crazy even to have three, but when Juliette was two and a half and finally out of daytime diapers Jenny broached it again. It could be another girl, Thom said. It could be, she said, but if it is you will love her, too. Thom thought about the days – too few, too far between, and all the more precious for their rarity – that he spent curled up watching *The Little Mermaid* yet again, one daughter cuddled on his lap, one squished against his side, one sprawled across the other couch, closing her eyes as she sang 'Under the Sea' as though oblivious to the world around her. Except she wasn't, quite, because when she was done she opened one eye to check he was smiling.

Yes, he would love another daughter. But as it turned out, the fourth was a boy, and Thom knows he isn't allowed to have favourites, but if he were, it would be Harry. It was a difficult pregnancy, an even more difficult birth; he'd always assumed that it got easier the more you did it, but evidently that was not how it worked. And the boy would not sleep. As he got older it became apparent that the only place he would reliably sleep was his parents' bed. They hadn't been having all that much sex anyway, so it didn't seem like a big deal, and in any case exhaustion drives you to irrational decisions and ridiculous trade-offs: anything, *anything* for six hours of uninterrupted slumber. This was the most basic of needs, more basic, perhaps, even than food, and certainly more basic than sex. But at Thom and Jenny's anniversary dinner just after Harry's third birthday, when talk of the children was forbidden, it turned out they had nothing to say to each other any more. His soulmate, the love of his life, and suddenly: nothing. The marriage had died like a thirsty plant, and they had been so busy trying to get Harry to sleep that they hadn't even noticed.

'That's sad,' Ebba says, and she means it. 'I thought you guys were going to be for ever.'

'I thought so too. Turns out I tend to get these things very wrong.'

Ebba reaches across the table and takes his hand. It's definitely the wine, and also it's not the wine, also it's because her heart is full of all the ways she wants to make it up to him.

'I'm sorry,' she says. 'He dazzled me, you know?'

'I know,' he says. 'And I'm not going to pretend it didn't break me. But you know, if you hadn't dumped me—'

She cringes.

'If you hadn't broken up with me, I wouldn't have these four amazing kids.'

She tries not to wince again, but he sees it, and catches himself.

'I'm sure you and I would have had amazing kids too. But I love the ones I've got. I can't love the hypothetical ones.'

Ebba nods, without meaning to. She has often thought about these hypothetical children, what they would be like. Her eyes fill, and she is mortified at this. She is not ready yet to be so vulnerable. Somehow he must know this, because he continues to speak. He does not ask her if she is okay. But he does thread his fingers through hers.

'I can't regret the fourteen years I had with Jenny, either. I can't. I don't want to. And it all gets a little existential when you start messing with what ifs.' He tops off her glass, an unspoken message: it is your turn to be honest. 'How about you? Regrets?'

'I've had a few,' she says, doing her best to lighten the mood so she can speak without her voice breaking. 'He made me who I am, Thom. I wouldn't be the writer I am without him. Or the person I am, either. I can't regret that any more than you can regret having your four kids. But I do regret causing you pain. It was inevitable, but I regret that it was inevitable. I wish – I don't know what I wish. But I'm sorry.'

A picture catches in her mind: she is in a lilac dress, the one she was wearing when Thom introduced her to Ethan – when he thought, at any rate, that he was introducing them. We actually know each other already, Ethan said, and Ebba wished he wouldn't grin that way. Russian Lit, sophomore year at NYU, she said, omitting the rest of the story and knowing as she did so that this incomplete truth would be the grey cloud over their relationship always. Would also give her an out, should she ever need one. O-kay, Thom said, the pause between the syllables pregnant with uncertainty. The grey cloud, already.

'Okay,' he says now, a very different okay, an okay she can't read, an okay that could be dangerous after three glasses of wine, but she will check herself, she will not act on impulse, she will not, she will not allow these muddied waters to be further muddled.

Libby

Reality, much as Libby hates to admit it, is not all that much like TV. Her students, bright and alert girls as they are, don't walk around the school with a permanent twinkle of inspiration in their eyes, as though poised at any moment to break into a song about the importance of perseverance in achieving one's goals. Mostly, like the girls – and the boys – down the road at Pimlico Academy, they slouch around the corridor, shuffle up and down staircases, avoid looking too directly at the younger teachers whom they not-so-secretly fancy. There are, of course, moments – today is such a moment; right now might be such a moment. Moments when she feels she was born to do this, that the TV programme she likes to say changed her life actually only nudged her slightly towards what was always going to be her destiny. But it's the beginning of the school year: it's always like this at the beginning of the school year. There is something satisfying about the first day, something inspiring even.

She delivers her pep talk to the eager year sevens, their uniforms still bright, or as bright as grey ever gets (the girls who go to this school do not, for the most part, have to suffer the indignities of hand-me-downs): I do not want to hear the word *boring*, and I do not want to hear the word *nice*. It still makes her smile, that she gets to say this, to quote so directly from *The Classroom*, though it saddens her to think that unlike in the series it will not be followed by Thom, or Thom as Callum, knocking sheepishly on the door to ask if he can see her for a minute. It's her own private joke, this line – the girls are too young to have watched *The Classroom*, too young to know Thom, if at all, other than through a comedy series that he grew a moustache for, and she does not like to bring up this element of his filmography. True, *The Classroom* is considerably grittier than Libby's daily reality. When she meets Thom, she intends to play down the comparative ease of her chosen career. Your character taught me to love Shakespeare, she will say, and to see the potential in the quiet kids. Though even this is not quite true: she was a quiet one herself, always knew their potential.

She won't mention to Thom that all the girls in her school have passed a test proving they are clever enough to be there, that their primary school teachers have all written letters guaranteeing they are diligent enough to be there, that many of them endure the crush and sweat of rush-hour Underground travel across London for the privilege of being there.

Teaching here is less heroic than it might be elsewhere, perhaps, but is it any less valuable? Is helping an intelligent, upper-middle-class eleven-year-old to reach her potential as a brilliant writer or an inspirational teacher herself somehow worth less than crossing the class divide? Libby does not believe it is, though she is impressed by and grateful for her colleagues at Pimlico Academy and schools like it. There may be no guns in these London schools, but there are plenty of drugs and there is plenty of violence, and goodness knows that in a civilised society it is vital that teachers gather the courage to rescue those children from the lives for which they seem destined. Libby, however, does not believe that is her strength. Let's face it, she would get eaten alive. And that? That would not help society in any way. It would not help the kids. And it would not help her.

Teaching is not fun every day. But first days come close. In year nine, she gets them reading out loud from *The Glass Menagerie*, discovers some latent acting talent in the class. In year eleven, she talks them through the trials to come and then relaxes them with a quiz. Not a test given a more palatable name, but an actual quiz, with lollies as prizes. And over lunch, something happens that makes Libby's heart jumpy with pride. Gemma Taylor knocks on her classroom door. Gemma, the frizzy-haired, bespectacled genius in her A Level class. She doesn't often put her hand up, but when she does, she always has a good answer, a profound answer, often an answer that sparks discussion and infuses new energy into the class. She is clever, conscientious, every teacher's dream of a student, every teacher vying for her to study their subject at university. She is taking English, French and Geography for A Levels, having – of course – aced her AS exams in Psychology and History.

Mrs Delacourt often speaks of Gemma with slightly teary eyes. 'I keep telling her,' she'll say, 'if she does French she'll get to spend a year there. It will be so good for her, and who wouldn't want to spend a year in Languedoc Roussillon? Eating freshly baked bread and drinking local wine under an unrelentingly shining sun?'

'Or Calais,' Greg Wilkinson chimes in. 'Where it will constantly rain and she'll never meet any French people because everyone will be huddling indoors all year round. Not everyone gets to go to Languedoc Roussillon.'

'Don't be ridiculous,' Aurore Delacourt always replies, crossly. Or not so crossly: Libby can never work out if this rivalry is a form of flirtation, if he has learned to pronounce *Languedoc Roussillon*, the 'R' deep in his throat, in order to impress her. There are rumours, of course, but there are rumours about everyone all the time; that is what staffrooms were made for.

And yet here Gemma is, telling Libby she won't be living in Languedoc Roussillon and she won't be studying geography either, because she wants to do English and she wants to go to Cambridge, and does Miss Bolton think she has a chance? This is not, of course, about Libby, but it is a little about Libby and she wants to hug Gemma. She imagines dropping it into casual conversation after tomorrow morning's staff briefing, at the coffee urn as mugs are being refilled, just loudly enough for Aurore and Greg to hear and yet not suspect that the news was in any way directed at them. It is not bad for Libby's hopes of promotion that she has been inspirational enough that Gemma would pick her subject over goat's cheese and olives (though these things are also available in Sainsbury's in Cambridge, should her budget stretch further than Libby's had). Later, when she tells this story with damp eyes – and she can't wait to tell Vicky; she can't wait to tell Dan – she will omit these unpretty, self-centred thoughts and tell them only of the others, which, to be fair, are just as real: pride and excitement. For her favourite student to study *her* subject at her old university is a particular kind of joy; Gemma's uncertainty as to whether she is Cambridge-worthy is endearing and genuine, endearing because of its very genuineness. She has every right and reason to be proud, this student whose parents have never seemed very interested in her education. This student who treks across London from Willesden Green to Pimlico on the Bakerloo and Victoria lines every day, leaving far earlier than even Libby, committed as she is, can imagine having the stamina for. Libby, who, when it comes to work mornings, rolls out of bed and turns a couple of corners and still only just makes it in time for staff briefing every day.

'Of course,' Libby says to Gemma. 'They'd be crazy not to take you.'

The reality, of course, is that Cambridge may very well not take her, not out of craziness or wilful ignorance but because there is an abundance of Gemmas, of perfectly qualified and worthy candidates that there just isn't room for, but Gemma doesn't need to hear this. If Gemma were one of the overly confident ones, then Libby might have played up the harshness of the system, the seemingly random cruelty of it, but this is not a girl who needs to hear this. This is a girl who needs to walk a little taller, to gain enough assertiveness to claim the place in the world that can rightfully be hers.

'I'll help you, of course,' Libby says. 'With your application and your interview technique and all that. The technicalities. But you'll be fine.'

Dan

Dan can't bear to see Libby sad. Dejected. Disappointed. Disillusioned. He can't bear it when it's something he can't fix, like her youngest sister's unexplained seizures back in the second year or her first (and, as it turned out, only ever) 2.2 on an essay. He wants to make the world right for her, and so when he can, when there is any hope at all that he can, he does. When she saw his room on the first day of their final year and looked at him the way she did and said, oh, Dan, this is such an amazing view, you can see the chapel *and* the river, he didn't say, actually, you can only see the river if you lean slightly too far out of the window. Instead, he said, we can swap, if you want? After she'd checked he was serious, she hugged him tightly enough for him to be far too aware of all her curves and said, okay, but you'll have to hang out in my room a lot, and he never regretted it thereafter. Today in the Caffè Nero near her flat she sits scooping up latte froth and looking sad and he wishes it were as easy to fix as the room thing.

'I put my book up on *Authonomy*,' she says.

He tries not to panic. 'The peer critique review site?' The people on these sites can be brutal in their honesty, and he wants to shield her from such brutality. For the rest of her life, if she would only let him. 'What kind of feedback have you had?' It doesn't take rocket science or even a Cambridge degree to get at the answer. He knows she is sad. He knows her book is still in the rough draft stage, still very much a work in progress. He knows what she is going to say.

'They've slammed it.'

'I'm sorry,' he says. Sorry for not being more honest? He doesn't know. What on earth was he supposed to do? She had him cornered.

'I need you to be honest with me, Dan.'

Uh oh.

'When you said it was very good—'

'For a first draft,' he says. He can't look at her. 'I meant for a first draft.'

'Then why didn't you say so?'

Because you looked at me the way you're looking at me now, is what he wants to say.

'I know how fragile an author's heart is,' he says. He thinks, not to mention mine.

'That's very sweet,' she says.

She does not seem to be angry. He is surprised and confused by this and also greatly relieved. He tells himself, as he always does when she says this, that she means 'sweet' as a compliment. He would rather be strong and sexy and heroic and irresistible, but he'll take what he can get.

'I need it to be good, though,' she says. 'I need it to actually be very good.'

'Why?'

He knows why. He also knows that the reason is not sufficient if she is going to put in the hard work, sacrifice evenings at the pub and Saturday picnics in Green Park, work as hard as she needs to in order to make this book as good as it can be. And it can be. He believes in her. She can do it. You don't get to Cambridge from a mediocre comprehensive school unless you have backbone and determination. You don't make it through Cambridge either. Come to that, you also probably don't make it to the end of the first draft of a novel.

'You've got to want it,' he says into her eyes. Her deep brown eyes. Borrowing a trick from Thom-as-Callum. 'You've got to really want it, for its own sake. Maybe it'll get published, maybe it won't. Maybe it'll get made into a film, maybe it won't. Maybe' – it pains him to play her ridiculous game but he knows he has to, for this to get through to her – 'maybe you'll get it to Thomas Cassidy somehow and maybe you won't, and maybe he'll read it and maybe he won't, and maybe he'll love it and maybe he won't. But you can't write for any of those reasons. You've got to write because you want to write. All the rest is a bonus. You can't rely on it to get you through. So go and think about it. If you really want this, I'll help you. I'll give you better edits. Style pointers. Help you rethink the structure.'

'That sounds like a lot of hard work for you too.' She touches his forearm, waits for his response, his okay, his reassurance.

'I'm happy to do it,' he says. Here is, after all, an excuse to spend a lot of time with her. A reason, if she makes it, and even if she doesn't, for her to be grateful to him. 'Plus,' he says, 'we get bonus points in my business for discovering new talent.'

'Talent.' She is grinning. He has fixed her. 'Is that true?'

'That you're talented?' He wants to keep saying it because he likes what it does to her. The way her face opens up, brightens.

'I mean about the bonus points.'

'Yes.' Finding a Hot New Author (particularly a young one, and particularly one who is actually hot) is every agent's dream. And he needs to find a way to get moving up this ladder before he has to start saying no to group holidays with the King's gang, the ever more luxurious holidays worthy of upwardly mobile management consultants and bankers.

'So I'd be helping you out, too,' she says.

'Yes,' he says. 'But that shouldn't be what motivates you either.'

'Not even a little bit?'

'All right,' he says. 'Maybe a little bit.'

He has never really blamed her for thinking about herself so much: after all, he spends a lot of time thinking about her too. But this is new, this looking out for him, and he likes it. He stands up for her when her selfishness is brought up on the pub nights when she doesn't make it.

'Yeah, but no one else paid attention to her when she was growing up,' he always says. 'So she had to do it herself. It's a difficult habit to break.'

The rest of them shake their heads, believing him a lost cause. They mutter things about love and blindness. And just as predictable is Nicola's response.

'Yeah, well,' she says. 'I'd give anything to have four sisters. She should think about that.'

'That's like saying, finish your vegetables, think about all the starving children in Africa,' Dan says. 'If I eat my vegetables, how is that going to help them?'

'Well, anyway,' Charlotte says, because she likes to have the last word. 'She should be here. We all have busy lives. We make time to meet up. But whatever. Who wants another drink?'

So he will be teaching her to write, and he will be teaching her to be a better person. To do something, at least a little bit, for someone else. The world will be a better place as a result. Spending time with her will be a public service, really. He heads home from coffee with her with a lighter step and a smile that does not fade even when he misses the train and has to wait for eight minutes.

Libby

Libby screams when she sees the email. Actually screams.

The door to Vicky's room squeaks open.

'I'm guessing you've just read the email from the Cambridge Union?'

'This is huge,' Libby says from her own room, the door so close to Vicky's there is no need for either of them to move.

'Mmm hmm.'

Later, it will occur to Libby that Vicky could have shown more enthusiasm in this moment. But for now, she is busy trying to regain enough composure to formulate the sentence she has always hoped but never been sure she would have reason to pronounce.

'I'm going to meet him!'

'Yes.'

They'd both joined the Union at the Freshers' Fair. The lifetime membership had seemed a little steep at over a hundred pounds, but they'd been dazed by the multitudes of flyers thrust into their hands as they made their way around the crowded sports centre, and starstruck by names of previous speakers at the debating society: Germaine Greer! Winston Churchill! The Dalai Lama! They'd kept quiet about their new membership in the face of Nicola's loud and frequent assertions about the right-wing over-privileged twerps who joined that kind of exclusive club and that this epitomised everything she hated already about Cambridge. A hundred pounds seemed like nothing now; she'd pay double that, ten times that – heck, if she had it, a hundred times that, for this, her chance, this, the beginning of the Rest of Her Life, this, the opening page of the fairy tale, where everything that has gone before has just been one overly long prologue.

'He's coming! To England! To my university! To an event you can only go to if you went to that university!'

'It's a sign, yes.'

Later, Libby will also be unimpressed by the sarcasm in Vicky's tone. For now, she chooses not to notice.

'It *is* a sign!'

Click, click, booked, ticket reserved. It's on a school night but that's okay. She'll pull a sickie the next day if he whisks her off to – where? Paris? A hotel room at the Cambridge Arms? She has a ten per cent discount card for that hotel, as a lifetime member of the university. Not that he will care about a ten per cent discount. Nor, come to that, will she, ever again.

How many days away? October to May: seven months. She gets out her calendar, counts the days, her index finger moving along each numbered square. She writes the number of days in marker pen on flipchart paper and Blu-Tacks it to her wall. Every night, she will cross off the number and write a smaller one below it, like she used to before holidays and birthday parties. But this is so much better than camping in France or playing Pass the Parcel. Indescribably better. This is an evening with Thom Cassidy, listening to that mellifluous voice advocating the importance of literacy and libraries and talking about his role on the TV series that changed Libby's life. She will be mere metres away from him. She will be breathing the same air.

The Classroom came to British television when Libby was thirteen, but at first she didn't watch it. When you're at school every day, when you get home and around the dinner table your parents are talking about school, and not just any school but the one that's the reason for this stupid move out to the middle of nowhere, the last thing you want to do is watch something on telly about a school.

'But it's different,' Iona insisted. 'The writing is really amazing.'

'Yeah,' Karen added, 'and there are some really gorgeous blokes on it too.'

'It's a bandwagon,' Libby said. 'I don't *do* bandwagons.' But she caught the 'flu that winter and there were only so many repeats of *Friends* she could watch in a row.

'Here,' Iona said to her, handing her the DVD of *The Classroom*. 'Try it. Just try it. I guarantee you'll love it.'

'Guarantee?' Libby arched her eyebrows as best she could, given her headache.

'I know you,' Iona said. 'And I don't know why you're being so stubborn.'

It hurt to read and she was bored of dozing, so Libby heaved the family laptop onto her bed and clicked through to play the DVD. The opening music was a little pompous. It announced itself. She would have rolled her eyes if she could have kept them more than half open. But despite herself, something like excitement fluttered in her stomach.

It washed over her at first. She was too tired, her brain too addled by her high temperature, the American-accented words spoken too fast for her to keep up, but there was a rhythm to it, almost a melody. And then, a slower scene. A young teacher sits in a room, looking into her coffee, despondent. You think I'm going to be fired? she asks, and the camera pans to a character called Callum. I won't allow it, he says, and a part of Libby knew she should at least be wanting to roll her eyes, but she couldn't, and this time it wasn't because of her temperature. It was because of this man. The authority in his voice. The affection in his eyes. The heroism of the promise. She wanted him to be her hero too.

And now, now she is going to get to meet him. And somehow between now and then, she has to finish the novel. And it has to be good. It has to be more than good. That means early mornings. It means more coffees with Dan. He's been weird with her lately, not quite meeting her eyes, sometimes not as keen to meet up as he has been in the past, but never mind. The time has come to push. To lean on his friendship. This is it, her moment: surely he will understand that. Because this is the dream! Even if – and this is a painful possibility, but it is a possibility nonetheless, and Libby must face facts – even if it is not the beginning of anything more than a beautiful friendship, maybe even not a friendship at all (she should probably be prepared for all eventualities), if Thom loves her book, it could change her life. If he champions it. If he introduces her to people who could make it a success. Not that her life really *needs* changing, as such, though it might be nice to be able to pay her rent every month without digging deeper into her overdraft. These are not big ambitions. They are not unreasonable ambitions. They are the ambitions she will admit. To Dan, if he asks. To Vicky. The other stuff, she will tell herself she has grown out of it. But the big red numbers Blu-Tacked to her wall will tell a different story.

Ebba

Ebba's path crosses the mailman's as she leaves for her daily walk on the beach on this October morning, and he hands her a blue airmail envelope. Yes, a letter: an actual, handwritten letter, all the way from England. No one writes these any more; even the handful of devoted fans of her theatre work mostly tweet now, to tell her they hope to see her at the stage door or that they enjoyed her guest role on *Castle* or *NCIS*. The novelty pleases her, even more than letters did in the days when they were more common. Simpler times, people sometimes wistfully sigh when they talk about the early 1990s, but to Ebba they had felt anything but simple.

Her crush on the unattainable Ethan Cohen certainly wasn't simple; she stared at the back of his handsome head in Russian Lit class, thinking of a hundred ways to get his attention, a thousand ways to start a conversation, but never quite dared to attempt any of them. Her broken heart when he dropped out of NYU and moved to Los Angeles: nothing simple about that, either.

Simpler, perhaps, was the ease with which Thom Cassidy walked into the video store on the Upper West Side where she worked, and thus into her life. It might have been simpler still if crucial moments came with crescendos and soft focus, the way they did in movies; she might have been less distracted by how much she missed Ethan. Or by watching the girl in the romantic comedy section of the store who always waited until Ebba was serving a customer to slip out unnoticed with a couple of videos under her coat. Or by endless adding and subtracting, multiplying and dividing: how many extra shifts did she need to do in order to afford the adorable red shoes she had seen earlier in the day? Ebba had always wanted red shoes, like Dorothy's, red shoes to run away in, if only to discover there was no place like home, like New York City. It would be nice to know for sure. Crucial moments, though, were barely noticeable in real life, given all of the noise in Ebba's thoughts. So she hadn't known, when the door to the video store had sung out the annoying half-tune that she'd almost learned to block out, on that particular time, on that particular spring Saturday, that nothing would be the same afterward. How could she be expected to know?

'Hi,' said the guy, walking straight up to the counter. Blondish hair, maybe slightly red, or was that just the way the light fell on it? Freckles. Cute. Not as cute as Ethan from Russian Lit, but then who was? This guy here had a nice smile. *Thomas Cassidy*, his membership card read. She thought Thom was a sexy name. Sexiest of all if you kept the 'h'.

'I need a recommendation,' he said. 'Surprise me.'

'That's a lot of responsibility.'

'I trust you.' He looked into her eyes as he said this and something turned gooey inside her.

'You just met me.'

'I come in here every Saturday night and you're always here. And I hear people thank you for your recommendations.'

How could she not have noticed him before? 'Okay,' she said. 'Tell me what you like.'

He walked out with an armful of movies but not her phone number. That summer, when he went home to Michigan for all of June and all of July and almost all of August, he occasionally wrote to her via the video store. He asked if she'd been to see a Shakespeare play yet because he still could not believe that someone who was planning to major in English didn't 'get' Shakespeare, whatever that even meant. He promised or teasingly threatened that when he came back for his second year at Juilliard he would drag her to one, kicking and screaming if necessary. Ebba looked forward to his intermittent letters – witty, well written, grammatically and orthographically impeccable – with a level of enthusiasm that surprised even her.

Letters: always positive, when they were handwritten. When Ethan's brother wrote to her after reading her memoir it wasn't a handwritten letter. It was, instead, an email, leaping off the screen and assaulting her. He didn't appreciate, he said, the way she had 'taken credit' for one of Ethan's most famous screenplays, though she had been holding him together with both hands as he wrote it, hiding the pills, making sure he ate. Though she had, in fact, written a substantial amount of it with him, had never asked for recognition, had barely hinted at this in her memoir. Besides, the brother added, you have him to thank for your acting career, and I don't see that in here. And yes, sure, Ethan had introduced her to the right person at the right time. But it was Thom who had encouraged her into acting at all. Thom who, after he'd taken her to *Swan Lake* one night, had held her as she told him of her once promising dancing career, of the heartbreak of injury when she was seventeen, the sound of her Achilles tendon snapping like something between a wet rubber band and a watermelon being cracked open. The end of everything. Who, after he made her hot cocoa and she dried her eyes and he knew that she was ready, made her laugh again.

'So I guess without ballet, life seems kind of pointless?'

'Pointe-less?'

He grinned. 'No pun intended.'

'Your puns are always intended.'

'Just trying to keep you on your toes.'

'Stop,' she said, 'stop.' Laughing at the lameness, delighted at his efforts. His clowning, she knew already, an act of love.

'You laugh too easily. You have to set the barre higher, Ebba.'

'Seriously, stop.'

'My position is clear.'

She kissed him. A keeper, she knew then.

It was Thom, also, who two days later, when she was reading through a script with him, suggested she take acting lessons. 'I think you could be good at this,' he said. 'I think that a lot of what you loved about ballet you might be able to find in drama.'

The letter she holds in her hand now as she digs her feet into the warm sand of Santa Monica beach has come via her publisher. The original address has been written neatly, as if with great care, though the person who forwarded it has taken no such care, has crossed out the details with a heavy black marker and scrawled Ebba's actual address in its place across the front. She is lucky the letter got to her at all. She suspects that many don't, and it makes her sad, these wasted words, these people waiting for a response, perhaps imagining she doesn't care, and disappointed because that seems to be at odds with the person they have gotten to know in her book.

Dear Ebba, the letter says. *Can I call you Ebba? After you've shared such an intimate part of yourself with me through your writing, I feel like we're on first name terms. I wanted to tell you that I am in love with your book. Your writing is so elegant – I could have underlined almost every sentence.*

I didn't expect to even like it. I don't think I've ever read a celebrity memoir, because I always thought they were bound to be terrible. I'm so happy to have been proved wrong.

I write too, by the way. You might be interested in the novel I'm working on; the main character is maybe a little bit inspired by Thomas Cassidy. I know you probably don't have much time, and for all you know I'm a terrible writer, so no pressure – no expectations at all, really – but I'm just letting you know in case you want to read it, because I would really love that.

In the meantime, I'm looking forward to your next book. There will be a next book, won't there? I hope so.

Ebba finds herself wiping her eyes, which is plainly ridiculous. Get it together, she tells herself. But it touches her, this letter. It touches her that someone has made the effort. That someone who knows good writing (though admittedly Ebba has no way of verifying this) would have nice things to say about hers. The name at the bottom of the letter seems familiar in some way. Hmm. Is it the girl who tweeted her? It might be the girl who tweeted her. Ebba doesn't usually bring her phone to the beach – the beach is for thinking, for allowing her mind to wander, which technology invariably impedes – but she is glad she has made an exception this time. In a few clicks, she finds Libby, finds also a review she has written of *Not Meant To Be*. A review that is thoughtful and well-crafted and very complimentary. Is she over-compensating for the tweet condemning Ebba's life choices? Maybe. But if she's honest, if the tweet hadn't been about her, she would have loved the refreshing honesty of it. And she likes the unassuming, undemanding tone of the letter. She'll write back later – a letter is so much nicer than a tweet. *Find me on Facebook*, she will tell her. *I've set my profile to invisible, but here's the link.*

Libby

When Libby is called to the headmaster's office, her first instinct is to assume she is in trouble. An old instinct, from childhood, persistent, like a sniffly nose that won't go away for weeks after a cold. Her stomach knits itself into a knot and a single drop of sweat trickles down her back under her blouse. She thinks back to the seven weeks since the beginning of this autumn term, to last year: what has she done that is questionable? Plenty, certainly – it's only her third year teaching; she is very much still finding her feet – but questionable enough to be called into the head's office? Maybe she is sillier with her students than she should be sometimes. Maybe she can't always justify the clips of *The Classroom* that she shows them to illustrate this or that point she is trying to make. And, on reflection, maybe using Thomas Cassidy as one of the false answers on a multiple choice test about the men in Jane Austen novels was a mistake. But none of these, surely, is enough to warrant her firing, her demotion, or even a verbal warning. Surely the headmaster has other things to do, better things, things more worthy of his time. But she can hardly tell Eric Flint, thanks, but no thanks. So she stands, and she knocks, and after Mr Flint says come in and she sees him smile, she realises she has little to worry about. Or does she? Maybe he will tell her off with a smile on his face so that it will seem like he is the good guy even as he snaps her in half. True, this theory doesn't seem to be in line with the personality he is rumoured to have, or what she has observed of him herself. He is tough, of course – you don't get to be head of a school like Greycoat without being tough and serious, and Greycoat wouldn't be Greycoat without someone tough and serious in charge. But he is also fair, and wryly funny, and deeply compassionate. He seeks to understand his staff, and encourages his staff to seek to understand their students.

'I know there's not much time,' he will often say at staff meetings, especially on the first day back after Christmas or Easter or half term, 'and I know there's all this pressure, and I know you are all very dedicated and always wish you could do more but there just aren't enough hours in the day, and you don't have the energy, but if there's one thing I want to encourage you to excel at, to push yourselves at, it's empathy. See the potential of these girls, and encourage them to develop their strengths, to work on their weaknesses, and above all to believe in themselves. Of course we want all As and A stars, of course we want to keep climbing those league tables, of course we want to keep attracting the best and the brightest, but we must always remember they are people and not grade machines. I want these girls to leave this school equipped for a successful life, a fulfilled life. Not just with a pocket full of exam certificates.'

And to his credit, Mr Flint doesn't treat the staff as grade machines either. He wants them to develop; he believes that a school can't fail to be enriched when all staff members play to their strengths, dig into their own individuality – like, Libby has always thought, her 'obsession' with *The Classroom*. It is, after all, a part of who she is; it is what makes Libby Libby. An individual. Different. In a good way. She hopes it is in a good way.

She smiles back at Mr Flint as she walks in, hoping to telegraph whatever it is he wants to hear from her: thank you for seeing me, I can do better, I am not nervous, I have nothing to be nervous about.

'I wanted to speak to you personally,' he begins. Libby holds her breath. 'I've heard good things about you lately. Gemma Taylor told me you're going to help her with her Cambridge application.'

'Yes.'

'Splendid, splendid. She speaks very highly of you. She says your enthusiasm is infectious.'

'Well.' Libby is still wondering where this is going. If it is going anywhere at all. 'Thank you.'

'It's not the first time I've heard this kind of thing said about you. I wanted to congratulate you. And I also wanted to let you know that if you keep this up, I see good things in your future.' He has put on a mock-spooky voice for the last part, caresses an invisible crystal ball, and Libby laughs, a half-laugh, an unsure laugh. 'A promotion. Next year, maybe.'

This is certainly clearer. And encouraging. And also helpful. Because, truth be told, Libby could do with a little extra money.

Lately, letters have been arriving from the bank at a much faster rate than just the monthly statements. She doesn't open the letters. They can only be portenders of doom, and who needs that? She doesn't want to be reminded that she is approaching – yet again – her overdraft limit, or that she is being charged twenty-five pounds because a cheque has bounced, or that her credit card limit is being reduced again. I'm doing my best, she wants to tell Barclays. What do you want from me? But here at least, in this office, someone is recognising that she is, in fact, doing her best. Being enthusiastic is getting harder, when she gets up an hour earlier than she needs to now to work on this novel so it can be ready to give to Thom next May. It's hard for your enthusiasm to be infectious when what you are most enthusiastic about is a full eight hours' sleep waiting for you on Friday. But the promise of a promotion, the promise of recognition, could help with all of that.

'Thank you,' she says to Mr Flint. 'That's very kind of you. I'll definitely bear it in mind.'

'I know you will. You were right when you said we would find you to be one of the school's greatest assets.' This was a line she quoted verbatim from *The Classroom* at her interview. Mr Flint smiled back then. 'That's a great TV programme,' he said, and she wondered if that was enough to sway his decision in her favour. She had felt as if she should acknowledge, ever so subtly, the source of her inspiration in seeking this job. It seemed, somehow, as if it might help. Like a talisman. There was, she knew, nothing rational about this. But rational things were overrated anyway.

'Thank you,' she says again to Mr Flint now. She leaves his office with a steelier gut, a fresh determination to be the teacher Callum McKenna would be proud of. To be a woman worthy of the actor who played him.

Dan

Dan is waiting for a train into work when he hears the song. A small girl holds her father's hand, swinging it as she sings. *Messing about on the river,* over and over. It is the only line she knows, but this line is enough, this line and the unseasonable November sunshine on the platform at Putney station, to make him miss Cambridge, post-exam Cambridge, the best time and place of all for messing about on the river.

He and Libby had finished prelims at the same time that first year, with a compulsory paper, and sat overlooking the Cam at a wooden table outside the Granta pub with the first Pimm's of the season, chewing over what they'd written. Libby, at least, chewed it over. For Dan, what was done was done, and no good could come out of this kind of post-mortem. He would never convince Libby of this, though: she needed to process, needed to get it out of her system before she could transition into post-exam mode.

'Why do they call it May Week when it's in June?' she asked him, switching – finally – to the topic of balls and garden parties.

'We missed out on May because we spent it revising and stressing out. So we get a week of fun in June to make up for it.'

Libby considered this. 'Okay. I don't think that's why, but it works.'

This amused him. There was so much about Libby that amused him. Not in a nasty way or a mocking way; rather, he enjoyed her uniqueness, her eccentricities. He had enjoyed getting to know them this last year, like an unravelling mystery. He had told her one Sunday night, after too many cocktails in the Vac Bar on A Staircase, *you're an enigma, Lib, I can't figure you out,* and she had laughed at him. *I'm the least enigmatic person I know,* she had said, and of course this was true. But it was also not true. Yes, her emotions were plainly stated across her face at all times – though he had yet to distinguish between the crinkled brow that meant confusion and the one that meant disagreement – and yes, there was never any doubt as to what she wanted, or what she was thinking about, because she just went ahead and told you, sometimes repeatedly until she felt she had been really, truly heard. Understood. But her mind: he couldn't quite figure it out. The way logic seemed to have no part in driving her, but if you asked why she thought something, it usually had an internal logic of its own.

A prime example being the next afternoon, when they lay on her fuschia duvet discussing the episode of *The Classroom* they'd just watched on Libby's computer.

'They missed a semester,' he said.

'What do you mean?' Her furrowed brow.

'In the last episode it was fall, and now it's spring break. Unless seasons work differently in America...'

'They're just jumping forward, that's all. It's perfectly legitimate.'

'Yeah, but they're still reading the same Shakespeare play? Come on. Six months of Macbeth? You'd want to kill yourself.'

'Well, whatever,' she said, and there was irritation in her voice.

'Doesn't it bother you? When they make mistakes like that?'

'I'm sure there's a good reason. Like maybe they read another play in the meantime and they're coming back to Macbeth for comparison.'

'Or maybe the screenwriters got a little bit drunk and lost track of where they were in the school year.'

She didn't say anything. This was a bad sign. Silence was always a bad sign where Libby was concerned. In groups, he'd learned, she went quiet when conversations upset her. No one else seemed to pick up on it – their gang, Silent Ollie notwithstanding, was full of noisy, opinionated people, people who often did not so much talk to each other as at each other or over each other, so that if one person stopped contributing, gaps were easily filled and rarely even noticed. But Dan noticed and if he was sitting next to her he would nudge her – or, after wine, maybe squeeze her knee – and whisper, you okay? She would smile and nod, and it was possible that the fact someone had noticed she'd gone quiet was, actually, enough to make her okay.

But now she had gone quiet on him, and he wasn't sure how to deal with this.

'I have to explain within the world of the story,' she said. 'Because—' She looked at him, uncertain of something.

'Because what?'

'You're going to think I'm crazy.'

Oh, Lib, he wanted to say. I already do think you're crazy, and that's part of why I love you.

Hang on a minute. Why I *what?*

At some level he had known this since freshers' week, of course. Since that furtive kiss he had hoped would be the start of something, before they had by silent mutual agreement decided it would be too dangerous for the dynamics of the developing friendship group they both already cherished, both desperately needed. But it was the first time he had used that word, even in his own thoughts. I like her. I am intrigued by her. I really, really fancy her. But he had never allowed himself to think about love. And now they were lying on her bed and he was having this realisation and it was all very inconvenient.

'I don't think you're crazy,' he said, which was both untrue and vastly inferior to the other version playing in his head, the version in which he had blurted out the thing that his over-cautious mind had filtered out. They could be kissing by now. He could be undressing her. Instead he stayed very still, grateful for his loose t-shirt and the partial darkness from the closed curtains. He counted backwards from 126 in sevens.

'I like to think,' she said, oblivious, 'that it's really real, you know? That it's really happening in some parallel universe. That's why I don't like to deconstruct it.'

This was a prime example of Libby Logic. Irrational but somehow coherent. He didn't quite have a handle on it; there was so much to discover. He was glad he had another two years in which to do so.

'You know,' he said. 'That actually does make sense.'

She smiled. They had to get off this bed before he lost it.

'It's sunny out there,' he said. 'We should go outside and enjoy it.'

'Let's go punting,' she said.

By which she meant, she wanted to sit in the punt and let him do all the hard work, pushing them along the River Cam with the aluminium pole from the precarious platform at the back, past the ancient colleges and the willow trees and the less-than-accurate tour guides on the other punts. Not because she was lazy, but because –

by her own admission – she was scared. He'd been there the first and only time she'd tried it. 'I really am very close to the water,' she kept repeating, her voice rising in both pitch and volume, and even though Charlotte pointed out that water was just water, that did not seem like a persuasive argument. The potential embarrassment was a worse threat to Libby than the river itself, polluted and disease-ridden though it was sometimes said to be.

'Good plan,' he said now. They had a couple of hours before Nicola and Vicky were due to finish their Use of French exam and begin their own celebrations with the champagne Dan and Libby would deliver outside the lecture block on the Sidgwick Site.

And that was how he found himself trapped; trapped on the end of a punt while Libby, seated on the squishy green cushions and facing him, interrogated him and offered unsolicited, contradictory advice.

'How's Chloë?' she asked.

Chloë the clarinettist from the chamber orchestra where he played the 'cello. Chloë the clarinettist, on whom he had had a crush since their very first rehearsal up at Churchill College. Chloë the clarinettist: entirely fictional. A useful stand-in to take the blame on the days he was even quieter than normal, a Valentine's Day perhaps. She had a boyfriend back home, he'd explained. So there was nothing he could do. Only admire her from afar. It wasn't a lie, exactly. He preferred to think of it as code. The guys all knew about Libby anyway – they had never discussed it, but it was hardly a mystery – and so they used Chloë, playing along. She got talked about at dinner; they asked when they could meet her. It was a shame her sister was getting married during May Week and she wouldn't be at the end-of-year concert.

'You know what it's like,' he said.

'I don't,' Libby said. 'She does know you like her, doesn't she?'

'She's got a boyfriend.'

'Everyone comes to uni with a boyfriend back home. They've usually chucked them by this point. Do you even know if she's still going out with him?'

It was unfair of her, cornering him like this. Short of jumping off the punt and leaving her to fend for herself, he had no choice but to stay and answer. To stay and listen. Because this was the start of a lecture. He could tell.

'Look, Dan. It's not complicated. Ask her out. Then you'll know if she likes you.'

'It *is* complicated though. Because we're friends, and I don't want to mess that up.'

'Risk,' Libby said, 'is what makes life worth living.'

A grand pronouncement of the type she liked to make. Some of them she only half believed and many of them she completely failed to live by. This was the girl who refused to stand on the end of a punt in case she got a little wet. And when was the last time she'd asked someone out? Never, that was when. And when she drank a little too much at Formal Hall and afterwards the gang crowded into a booth in the bar with the leftover wine from their table and a bottle or two extra just for good measure, sometimes she even admitted there were some risks not worth taking. Love messes you up, she would say. It's not worth it. It was always terrible timing, because those inebriated nights were when he fancied her most, in her pretty dresses, her hair done differently and a little extra make-up, some lip gloss, and they were when his guard was let down just enough to maybe attempt to ask her out. Or take her hand. Or, you know, *something*. Anything.

'Don't be such a Clarissa Dalloway,' she said now. 'Always choosing what she fears least. Choosing Richard because he's safe instead of risking it with Peter, who is clearly the love of her life.'

'Fine,' he said. 'I'll do you a deal. You risk some punting and I'll risk asking her out.'

'You want me to catch some horrible waterborne disease in exchange for losing one of my best friends to some girl I've never met? That doesn't seem like a very good deal to me.'

He was taken aback. He focused for a moment on digging the pole into the gravelly river bed, on keeping the punt straight, on avoiding the group of tourists who'd given up on the proper way to do it and were rowing – splashing about, really, not going anywhere – with their tiny emergency paddles.

'Why would you think you were going to lose me?'

She shrugged. 'It's just what happens. *I've got a girlfriend now, see you when we break up.*'

'That's never going to happen to us. I won't allow it.' The thought of him and Libby drifting from each other's lives turned his stomach the same way the colour puce did.

'What if it was you?' he asked. Not looking at her. 'You and Clive the clarinettist. Would you ask him out?'

'No. I want the guy to do the asking.'

'That's not very enlightened of you, Lib.'

'I'm an old-fashioned kind of girl. If the guy can't take that, we're probably not meant to be together anyway. If he falls at the first hurdle.' She paused, as if for effect. As if, he would later think, to underline her point. 'I want to be wooed.'

'Wooed,' he repeated. He saw the many vowels in the word as he said it, lengthened the sound of it accordingly.

'Yes. Wooed.'

It sounded like a challenge. And not the good kind. The death-defying kind.

'What happened to love not being worth it? That's what you always say.'

'That's what the wooing is for. To make me forget I think that long enough that I fall for you and then it's too late.'

She was being, even by her standards, unusually honest for the middle of the day. For broad, sober daylight. Maybe it helped that he wasn't looking at her. Or maybe it was post-exam insouciance. Maybe he should keep punting as far as he could, take her far, far away, or at least the two miles to Grantchester, where he would buy her lunch in the pub that Rupert Brooke had frequented. He would read her Brooke's poems – they were bound to have copies of them there. Did that count as wooing? Surely poetry counted as wooing.

'Obviously,' she said. 'I don't mean *you*, you. I mean in a general way. Hypothetically.'

'Oh,' he said, and this time he made deliberate and direct eye contact with her. 'Obviously.'

Libby

Libby stayed up later than usual last night, not marking essays, not reading, but writing, under the light of her too-bright desk lamp. She usually doesn't have the energy in the evenings, but she felt inspired: something someone said in the staffroom sparked a scene in her mind, a scene that is key to reaching the novel's climax. She has never known the words to flow so easily: could this be it, the moment when she is truly born as a writer? Has she made it now? Does she get it, know how it's done? She is almost as excited by this prospect as she is by the scene itself. Thom will love it. He will look at her in wonderment, if that is even a word, and say, you're a beautiful writer, and then he will kiss her.

None of these thoughts is conducive to sleep.

She is, however, exhausted. She drinks more coffee now, has to pop to the loo sometimes during lessons, often doesn't feel as if she was ever fully present in the classroom anyway. She is getting through her expensive Benefit under-eye concealer at an alarming rate, and even so, Vicky often tells her she looks tired, pointing at the bags under her own eyes to give her argument greater weight. But it helps her fall asleep at night, this constant tiredness. Without it, she is certain she would be incapable of it, would be buzzing instead with thoughts of meeting Thom, of showing him her novel, of The Plan coming together, of their wedding, maybe on a Hawaiian beach, invitations distributed and flights fully paid for those of her friends who have always supported her. Who have believed. Sometimes, more often than she'd like, she wakes up at 2 or 3 or 4am, after dreaming of missing a flight or forgetting her passport or losing her suitcase; other times, it is as if her subconscious wants to give her the opportunity to think happy thoughts. Sometimes there just isn't enough time in the day for this: life gets in the way. Teaching and marking and staff meetings and lesson planning. Though sometimes when she is standing by the photocopier waiting for it to spit out twenty-eight warm copies of a ten-page summary of *Wuthering Heights* she allows herself a little time to daydream. To plan.

She wakes up this morning with the panicked feeling, the missing-the-flight-to-Los-Angeles feeling, but when she looks at the clock expecting 3am she finds she has neither missed a flight nor woken in the middle of the night: it's time to get up; it's morning. All is well. The front door shuts behind Vicky: Libby's cue to get up, shower, flick on the coffee maker, which she has, as usual, diligently prepared the night before: see how organised she is capable of being?

It's only when she is lugging her bag full of marked exercise books to Greycoat that she remembers: crap. It was today. Today, Gemma is going to Cambridge for her interview, and they were supposed to meet at 7.30, for a final run-through, a final calming of Gemma's nerves before the train ride up. Libby imagines Gemma leaving home at 6am, darkness shrouding north west London, her breath a few centimetres ahead of her in the December air, dragging herself to Pimlico on two Tube lines as she does every morning, sweating through the layers of clothing essential for bracing against the cold outside but unnecessary and cumbersome on the overheated trains. Today, Gemma would have done it with her heart in her throat, her nervous leg likely twitching incessantly for the entire hour, even when impatient passengers tried to get her to stop with a pointed look, the way Libby does in class. Gemma will have been counting on Libby to help her find the confidence she needs to ace the interview. She has the skills, the knowledge, the predicted grades. She and Libby have talked about body language. She knows how to sit – forwards, but not too far forwards, and to make eye contact, but not too much. But none of that will matter if she lacks the confidence that Libby has striven to build in her these last few months. Her shoulders will slump; she will make herself small in her chair. It is her natural tendency. And this last meeting: it was supposed to be the antidote to all of that, to these destructive natural tendencies of Gemma's. And now what? She is probably on the way to King's Cross, feeling defeated already. Hopeless, when Libby had intended to send her on her way full of hope. Angry, instead of calm.

And they would all know, at school: Gemma would have been

looking for her. So much for Mr Flint's grand expectations, for her potential promotion. All of it gone, poof. A scene from *The Classroom* comes unbidden into her mind: Callum McKenna is standing at the front of the class. Crossing his arms. 'I'm very disappointed in you,' he says, and this reverberates in Libby's ears and echoes in her bones.

***

'How's the novel going, Lib?' Nicola asks at the first Chandos gathering of the New Year.

Libby leans against the dark wood panelling, sips her tepid rosé, and considers how to answer this without sounding arrogant. The fact is – yes, the fact: she is almost sure it is not just her opinion – it is going well. Really well. When she compares this draft to the first one, she can't believe she was ever anything close to happy about the original version of it. At first she didn't want to hear Dan's comments. She wanted to do it her way. She used words like *artistic integrity* and *authentic voice*. But she also wanted him to take her seriously. She wanted fellow writers on Autonomy to say nice things, but the only people who had said nice things were those who messaged her begging that she would also read their books, clearly desperate for their own positive reviews. And she also, of course, wanted Thom to be wowed when she gave him her novel at Cambridge in May.

So she listened to Dan. She restructured. Over the course of the autumn term and the Christmas holidays, and into this new year, she has read books and writing magazines and blogs; has taken online classes. She has thought deeply about her characters, their motivations, their desires. The moments in their backstories that have defined them the way Jeremy's death seems to have defined Iona. Or the way that Dan's father hit him when his grandmother died. Stop that, he shouted at the five-year-old. Stop crying. The first time he raised his hand to his son; only his wife had borne the brunt of his violent tantrums until that point. A week later, they left him. And now Dan never names emotions, only the colours that represent them.

Libby has found herself increasingly itchy to get to her writing. She has found herself daydreaming about her characters, wondering what they are doing right now. She has experienced the kind of exhilaration, sometimes, that feels like the runner's high some of her friends talk about: a sense of profound well-being, of floating, almost. She has experienced afresh the single-mindedness of the Cambridge student, singularly focused on their chosen academic subject. At Cambridge, it was acceptable, expected, almost cool, to be nerdy, and for this, for being among her kind, Libby was grateful. But there was passion, too, for the extra-curricular. There were, for example, the Christians, full of zeal and a deep-seated conviction that college was their mission field; there were the politicians; there were the musicians; and maybe they *were* studying politics or music, or maybe they somehow squeezed JCR meetings and orchestra rehearsals between essay crises and Saturday morning chemistry lectures, though for them it was the extra-curriculars which became the defining feature of their Cambridge experience. For Libby, Cambridge meant falling asleep to the closing notes of *The Classroom*'s theme tune, the music pumping her with inspiration, enthusiasm, renewed hope, mingling with and becoming indistinguishable from her innate passion for literature, strengthening it, renewing it.

And Libby, with this novel, is experiencing this all over again. She has got up an hour early and sat in coffee shops at weekends and spent all two weeks of the Christmas holidays at her desk and learned what *show don't tell*, *point of view violation*, and *authorial intrusion* mean. She has phrased and rephrased awkward-sounding sentences until some of them are, she thinks, rather beautiful. She has cut back on the schmaltz. And now she thinks maybe it's ready.

'It's going well, I think.'

She looks at Dan. He nods, smiles, and it's a real smile: he means it. He has promised to be brutally honest, or, okay, not exactly brutally, more like gently and sensitively, but honest, that is the key thing here.

'It's coming together really nicely,' he says.

This pleases her more than anything she can imagine. The only thing better than a genuine compliment from Dan would be a genuine compliment from Thom, but one thing at a time. Publication, first: over the last few months this is what she has begun to yearn for. Her name on the cover of a book on the tables at Waterstones where the three-for-two deals used to be. Facebook messages from secondary school friends, and those who now would pretend they had been friends despite their previous belief that she was a little stuck up, a little pretentious with her Cambridge aspirations, her near perfect grades, and her snobby accent. *The name on the cover, is that you, Libby?*

'So you going to get it published?' Nicola asks.

'That's the plan.'

'Hey, Dan,' Charlotte says. Libby cringes. She knows what is coming, and she knows you aren't supposed to ask. She tries to silence Charlotte with round eyes and an almost imperceptible shake of the head, as if that has ever worked before and stands any chance of working now. 'Sounds like what she needs is a good literary agent.'

'She won't have any trouble getting one,' he says. 'It's a good book. Tons of potential.'

Is this code? Is he saying, of course I'll take it on? He did say, that time, that he needs to discover new talent, that she could be his way up the career ladder, and that is why he has spent so much time with her, expended so much energy on this project. He has never, it's true, said out loud that he would be her agent, but she has assumed, and surely she has no reason not to assume…

'I say we toast you, Lib,' Dan says. 'You and your imminent success.'

'Remember us when you're rich and famous,' they say.

'We all get copies, don't we?' they say.

'You're the next Zadie Smith,' they say.

'Zadie Smith lived on S Staircase, you know,' Libby says. 'In Dan's room, actually.'

'The room you picked originally? Is that why you picked it?'

'No,' she says, unsure now. But it seems as if knowingly rejecting Zadie Smith's old room for the sake of such a trivial thing as a view of an immaculate lawn (and, okay, also of King's College Chapel) has to be bad luck for a writer. She tries to shake free of this thought.

'So what's it about?' they ask her, and she is surprised by how much pleasure she takes in talking about it, after all these months of only talking about it with Dan, the way you talk about the baby only with your husband in very early pregnancy.

'It's about an English teacher, who's really great at his job. But really all he wants is to be an actor. So this colleague of his who has been in love with him for, like, ever, encourages him to go and study acting, even though he'll have to go far away and she knows he's going to meet all these glamorous actress types and she's going to lose him.'

'Heartbreaking,' Nicola says. 'I love it.'

'And not at all based on your crush on Callum McKenna from *The Classroom*,' Matthew says.

'Well.' She pretends to consider this. 'Maybe a little.'

'You don't say. Where's the acting school?'

'New York. Juilliard.'

Matt rolls his eyes. 'Let me guess. That's where Thomas Cassidy went.'

'No,' Libby says. 'I mean, yes. It is where he went. But I needed somewhere prestigious and far away from London.'

'Yes, because there are no prestigious acting schools anywhere else in the world, I suppose.'

Libby clenches her jaw. She won't mention that it has to be New York, because in the movie she wants the romanticism of autumn in Central Park. She wants the Macy's Thanksgiving Parade and she wants, for some reason, the yellow cabs. She wants those red Juilliard stairs, for the grandeur, the glamour, the metaphor of climbing to greatness. She wants that extra, silent I, like a secret password into an exclusive club.

'They get together in the end, though, don't they?' Nicola seems genuinely excited, and Libby is glad about the shift in subject away from the inspiration behind the novel, which she is vaguely embarrassed about though she can't pinpoint why exactly. *The Classroom* is legitimate, intelligent television; Thom is a critically acclaimed actor. It isn't as if she was inspired by *Twilight*, or fan fiction for *Home and Away*.

'You'll have to read it and see,' she says.

'I'm not reading it if it doesn't have a happy ending.'

'Don't be silly,' Charlotte says. 'Of course you'll read it. We'll all read it. Won't we?' She makes eye contact with each of them in turn. Matthew. Nicola. Silent Ollie. Liam. Back to Nicola.

'And,' she adds, 'of course we'll all come to your book signings. We'll be rent-a-crowd.'

'You're jumping the gun a little,' Matthew says. He is being Vicky tonight, a stand-in for the Voice of Reason when she has to work late. 'She has to get it published first.'

'Which is where Dan comes in,' Charlotte says. 'Easy peasy.'

Dan takes a sip of his beer and says nothing, and Libby does not like this. She does not like it at all.

Dan

'Dan,' Libby says, catching up with him on the Tube platform. 'Listen—'

He looks up at the countdown to the next train. This is a longer conversation than they have time for.

'I just want you to know that I really appreciate everything you've done to help me with the book.'

It's sweet of her to say so, and he knows she means it, but he also knows that isn't what she has rushed after him to say. She wants to know the thing he has been avoiding telling her for months because he really hoped she would be able to work it out for herself and they would not have to have this conversation ever, let alone on a damp January evening after sprinting through the drizzle to catch one of the last trains.

'Thank you,' he says, pretending. He takes his eyes off the countdown board just long enough to look straight at her and smile. If she is going to say it, then let her say it. He knows she hates conflict and difficult conversations of any kind and it will take a superhuman effort for her to bring it up and so maybe he still stands a chance of escaping, and, damn it, why does it still say three minutes up there? It has said three minutes for hours.

'Listen,' she says again. Tucking a phantom strand of hair behind her ear over and over again: psyching herself up. Will it work?

'I'm listening,' he says, buying a few extra seconds, but simultaneously showing interest and eagerness, which may have been a mistake.

'The agent thing.'

'Yes.' She is going to have to spell it out. He knows this is mean of him. But honestly, he can't do it. He can't stand there, in this overheated station, on this slippery Piccadilly Line platform, and tell her no. He is stalling for time so that he won't have to, not tonight. He can't put it off for the rest of their lives, he knows this, but he can put it off for tonight.

'I'm going to need one,' she says.

'You'll get one. I'll help you with your query letter. I'll introduce you to some people.' You can't say fairer than that, can you? You really can't.

'I was hoping,' she says. Waits.

I was hoping we'd be together by now, he wants to say. You don't always get what you are hoping for.

'I can't be your agent, Lib.'

'Oh,' she says. He can't look at her. He absolutely can't look at her. If he looks at her, it will be just like all the other times when he says no to something and then looks at her.

'This is the longest minute of my life,' he says. One minute, still. Come *on*.

'It's a London Underground minute.' He smiles despite himself: he knows what she is referring to. The two of them, last summer, waiting for ever for a train, rewriting the words to Don Henley's New York Minute, even though it didn't quite scan, detailing all the things that you can do in a London Underground minute. Paint your nails. Eat a sandwich. Make a friend. Make a baby. It had got more and more ridiculous until they got to 'give birth' and people started looking at them oddly and it was a relief when the Tube came and they stopped because their stomachs were hurting with so much laughter.

Meanwhile it still says one minute up there on the board. Has he got away with it? Is this the extent of this conversation? Maybe if the train comes now... Now, he wills it, *now*. Now. He has done this a thousand times, eight hundred of them on this very platform, and he knows it doesn't work, or hasn't worked until now, but still, maybe today will be the day it finally does. Sooner or later things have to start going his way, don't they?

'Why?' she asks. 'The dad teaching you to drive thing again?'

'Kind of,' he says. 'Yeah.'

'It's not because you secretly think it's a terrible book?'

No. No, no. It is absolutely not this. She has worked damn hard at this book, and he has been impressed by her. Awed by her all over again. She is not, admittedly, Zadie Smith. She is probably not even Sophie Kinsella. (Her ending would need to be more upbeat, for a start.) She won't ever win the Costa, let alone the Man Booker. The novel needs more work, more tweaking, a revision or two; it is not as ready as she thinks. Fundamentally, though, it is publishable; it is, in fact, deserving of being published, though those are two very different things.

It is important that she know this. But it is starting to be breezy on the platform, the kind of breeze that feels refreshing in the stuffy, overheated station where they stand in their coats but is in fact a carrier of city filth and quite possibly carcinogens of various kinds. The breeze, though, that announces that the train is imminent, that their interminable wait is almost over. Dan looks at Libby. It is important that she hear him. Really hear him.

'It's a good book, Lib. I'm not just saying that.'

'Then—'

'Conflict of interest.' The rumble of the train gets louder; its front lights are visible now along the tracks. The wind intensifies and the train rushes in.

'Conflict of interest how?' she shouts over the noise. 'Because we're friends?'

The train is level with them now, has slowed, is stopping. People around them rush forward to crowd around the train doors as if determined to stop anybody from getting off. Dan and Libby will get on this train and they will be confined in a tiny space and surrounded by strangers, some of them drunk, some of them irritated by the various annoyances of London life, some of them humming along to the music in their earphones, some of them brazenly, plainly eavesdropping, and this is not how he wants to have this conversation.

The doors open. Mind the gap, mind the gap. This is a Piccadilly Line train to Heathrow terminals one, two, three and five. The next train is one minute behind this one. There is no need to push.

He could pretend not to have heard her. But he knows she will not let him.

'Is it because we're friends? Is that it?' She has walked onto the train as she says this, turning her head, assuming he is going to follow her, because of course why would she not assume that, when they've been waiting together for this train for three long minutes? But he can't.

He can't bring himself to watch her reaction when he says what he is going to say. She teases him for not being able to watch the gory bits on *Casualty* and this is the same kind of thing, only a million times worse. He will deal with the aftermath, but he cannot deal with the moment of impact.

'It's because I'm in love with you,' he says as he watches the doors closing on her and the train taking her away, and thinks, how apt a metaphor.

Libby

Is it Libby's imagination, or are they looking at her oddly on the Tube? Pity, maybe? Is it pity? Her skirt is probably on backwards. Or her mascara is running. But Dan would have told her, wouldn't he? He wouldn't have let her make a fool of herself. Then why are people looking at her? She'll be glad when she changes trains in a few minutes at Green Park. People aren't supposed to look at each other on the Tube. At least, not like this. So openly. It can't just be because the doors closed before Dan got on, can it? That happens all the time on the Underground. Do they think she is evil for having got on without him? It's not like she planned it. They were halfway through an important conversation. She still doesn't know why he won't be her agent. He was telling her, when the doors closed. She doesn't know if she'll ever be able to work up the courage to ask him again. She has used up her moments of bravery these last few months.

Writing to Ebba, for example. She doesn't know why it felt as brave as it did. Maybe because she was allowing herself to be vulnerable. Her friends, whom she has known all her adult life, know all about her, including the fact that this so-called crush on an actor she has never met is a tiny facet of her otherwise complex, interesting and (mostly) balanced personality. But why would you tell someone's long-ago ex-girlfriend that you have written a novel in which he is basically the hero? Why would you openly admit to being a fangirl, even though you are well past fifteen years old, and desperate to be taken seriously by someone important, as a writer or just as a human being? And yet Ebba has been extraordinarily gracious. She has not told her to get a grip. Instead, she has said, *I'm sorry, things are a little busy right now so I don't have time to read your novel. But I have something better for you. My editor saw your review of my book and she likes the way you write. Do you want to send it to her instead?*

Does she ever! She was going to mention this to Dan tonight; she wanted to tell him first, without the others, to tell him properly, not by text but face to face, but there just wasn't the opportunity and then he was being weird with her and now she isn't sure she really wants to. She can do this without him. She really can. She wishes she could be angry towards him. That she could say, fine, be like that, I don't need you anyway! But her book wouldn't be her book without him so it wouldn't be true, it wouldn't be fair, and most importantly of all, because of those things, it wouldn't be satisfying.

Still, she can barely believe it. Wouldn't it be perfect if a book she wrote about Thom got published because of a book she read about Thom? Not as perfect as The Original Plan, but perfect enough. She thanked Ebba profusely and is mentally working on the email to the editor in her head when her Tube arrives at Pimlico station, where it is, of course, still raining, because it is January and that is just life. Vicky is drinking hot chocolate and watching the news when Libby opens the door.

'You look wet,' Vicky says.

'Wet and cold,' Libby says.

'Yeah. How was the gang?'

'They're all fine. Missed you, though. More and more of these late nights, aren't there?'

Vicky makes a noise somewhere between a groan and a sigh. Libby bites her lip and doesn't say anything about promotions or money. This is not out of kindness or decency; it is mostly because she suspects that when Vicky gets her much-deserved pay rise, she will Re-Assess Things. Things like sharing a small and slightly damp flat with her melodramatic and rather messy best friend. So Libby steers clear of these topics.

'Dan was a little weird,' she says instead.

'Oh?' Vicky mutes the television and pats the space next to her on the sofa.

'He says he can't be my literary agent,' Libby says, sinking into the sofa. 'He won't tell me why.'

'You don't have any inkling at all as to why that might be?'

Libby shrugs. 'Conflict of interest.'

'Well, yeah.'

'What, so just because we're friends we can't help each other out? That seems backwards.'

'I don't think *friends* is the issue here,' Vicky says.

'Well, it can't be because we kissed once in a sweaty bar approximately—' She pauses to do a quick calculation, as quick as her calculations ever are. 'Six and a half years ago.' It has never been discussed, this kiss. She isn't sure anyone else knew about it. And yet Vicky does not appear shocked, or even remotely surprised. And then she says what she has said many times.

'It could be,' Vicky says, 'because he's been in love with you for those six and a half years.'

'Don't be ridiculous,' Libby says, as she always does. 'He's not in love with me any more than he's in love with you or Charlotte or Nicola. We're just all friends, that's all. Fond of each other.'

'Okay,' Vicky says, in the tone of voice that riles Libby most. The tone that says, I'm right, I know I'm right, and I know you know I'm right, and I am too secure in that rightness to have this argument with you.

But Vicky is not always right, despite what she might think. What she obviously does think. And she is definitely not right this time. Libby would know about it if Dan liked her. He has never asked her out. He has given her Valentine's Day gifts, of course, but they all did that for each other back at King's, went across the road to the fudge shop, to the market for tulips, to the Lion Yard shopping centre for a box of Millie's Cookies, and then bumped into each other in the mailroom when they were (supposedly surreptitiously) distributing the goodies in the various pigeonholes. They all loved each other, in a way. They were like family. More than family, Libby thinks sometimes. They put up with Charlotte's bossiness, with Matthew's terrible taste in women, with Ollie's silence and Liam's political rants, because that is what you do with family. You're stuck together and you don't really have a choice. Disowning each other is not an option for them any more than it is for a family. And, of course, because they are in their mid-twenties and because they met in their late teens, and because unlike an actual family, they are not related by blood, because there have been parties and balls and pretty dresses and moments of euphoria after exam results, over the years there have been celebratory kisses, hugs that lasted a little too long, ill-advised trysts of various kinds. But none of that has lasted. None of it is meant to. It's part of being friends with people who know what you look like in pyjamas. Who have held your hair back as you've been sick after mixing too many drinks. It's not romance. It's not being swept off your feet. It's not what Libby sees on telly or reads in Ebba's memoir and it's not what she wants. She wants passion. Excitement. Drawn-out sexual tension with a satisfying resolution. Not the relational equivalent of a fluffy pair of slippers. Anybody in their right mind wants the same thing she does. And Dan has always seemed to her to be in his right mind. He must, therefore, want this too.

Vicky is wrong, sometimes, and this is one of those times.

Ebba

Ebba has told Libby she doesn't have time to read her book, and it's true. But she has the link to the website where it is posted for feedback from other authors, the blind leading the blind, the unpublished advising the unpublished. You're better than this, she wants to say to Libby, but of course how could she know if that is even true? She hasn't read the novel. She clicks on page one and begins, not expecting much. Oh, but that isn't it exactly either: it is more that she doesn't know *what* to expect.

She is relieved that the writing is good. It draws her in. It is mostly error-free and correct in its use of punctuation: the little things which show that a writer is serious about her craft. And it is clear from the first page that the author herself is in love with this character she has created, this Thom who isn't Thom yet at the same time is totally Thom. It moves her, this devotion. It seems like more than just regular fangirling. It prods at something inside her, something long dormant that was stirred by that dinner with him last summer, those eight months ago. At the part of her that fell in love with him even before she really knew him. In Libby's book, he will not – she is fairly certain – forget to empty the dishwasher or use up the last of the toilet paper and neglect to replace it. These are the things of reality and reality does not cohabit in easy harmony with novelistic daydreams, or with the early days of a crush – celebrity or otherwise – those blissful days of being in love with the idea of a person rather than the person himself. Still, two years she and Thom had been together: plenty enough for her to be familiar with his faults and foibles, and if Ethan hadn't waltzed back into her life to claim a prize he did not deserve but that he (and she) believed was rightfully his, the decision would have been made: Thom was a keeper. Unequivocally, unmistakeably a keeper. For all Thom's need for attention, his insecurity sometimes, his competitiveness, his desperation to be right, and yes, the dishwasher and toilet paper issues, if you put that on one side of the scales they would barely register when weighed against the joy he brought her, the way he listened attentively to her even when he had heard it a hundred times and never said enough already about these finals. His acting talent. His passion and earnestness when he talked about his future career. The way she felt when he kissed her.

But then there had been Ethan, who rendered all weighing systems obsolete. Ethan, who in the end brought her infinitely more pain than happiness, though he kept promising otherwise. She was foolish; she was young. She is neither of those things now, and so although her fingers hover over Thom's name on her phone, she does not call him. She does not say, listen, I missed you, and I know this is crazy and it's been twenty years but can we maybe start over? She does not email him to tell him about Libby's book, though she knows that Libby would like nothing more: there is no way she is getting in the middle of that.

Maybe once the divorce has been finalised she will reach out to Thom again. Ask him if he has gone to therapy. She spent years caring for a damaged man and she is not sure she has it in her to do that again. She closes her laptop before she changes her mind.

Libby

The day, the day. Months of waiting, and finally it's May; finally the day is here. Libby makes it through the teaching, somehow, in a caffeine-fuelled fog as befits the day after a night during which she slept for three hours. Vicky tried so hard to calm her down. Even tried to make her drink chamomile tea. (Yuck. Libby took one sip, and no. Just no.) She tried to lower Libby's expectations. That has, in fact, seemingly been Vicky's mission for longer than Libby can remember. Vicky does not believe in The Plan. Vicky says things like, he's a Hollywood actor, Lib! He's almost twice your age. Which, on a surface level, Libby cannot dispute. But, come on. What was it Eleanor Roosevelt said, the quote that Callum McKenna wrote on the board at the start of every school year in *The Classroom*? The future belongs to those who believe in the beauty of their dreams. She believes. The future is hers.

And in Vicky's defence, she is at least coming to Cambridge with Libby. To try to stop her making a fool of herself, whatever that is supposed to mean.

'Hey, look,' Vicky says at King's Cross station. 'Platform nine and three-quarters. While we're here maybe we could try and see if we can get to Hogwarts.'

Whatever. Vicky will be sorry when she doesn't get the all-expenses-paid invitation to the wedding on a Hawaiian beach. Except that she needs to be a bridesmaid. Okay, fine. But first Libby will make sure Vicky does some serious grovelling.

A train, a taxi through the narrow streets and past the ancient stone colleges to the Cambridge Union, and by the time they get there the queue will stretch all the way around the corner. Except, no. It doesn't. No queue! How could there be no queue? Don't these people know who Thom Cassidy is?

'It's coming up to exam season,' Vicky says, to explain the absence of the expected crowd, and she and Libby pause for a moment of silence, of reverence for the memory of their days by the river, pretending to revise, absorbing – they fervently hoped – academic vibes by osmosis. In memory too of the oppressive atmosphere in the dining hall each night, when hundreds of stressed, single-minded high-achievers congregated with nothing to talk or think about other than their impending doom. Three-hour-long silences, aching wrists, the pressure of proving one's acceptable levels of knowledge and intelligence by regurgitating enough facts and coating them with a veneer of something resembling independent thought but not straying too far from the received wisdom. A delicate balancing act. This, needless to say, they did not miss, though they often reminisced wistfully about the celebrations that followed. The balls, especially… all the champagne you could drink all night, the posh-accented boys from other colleges, frightfully handsome in their dinner jackets, the *a cappella* close harmony groups and the jazz bands and the string quartets, the dodgems, the bucks fizz and *pains au chocolat* and bacon butties at an early breakfast, the survivors' photo at dawn.

And survive they had, not just the balls and not just the hangovers, not just the exams, but the whole Cambridge experience, and now here they are, claiming their prize. The degree certificate, framed in what was once her bedroom at her parents' house, is nothing compared to this, the chance to engage with – to perhaps even meet – Thomas Cassidy.

They creak open the oak door to the Union bar, through which they will later gain access to the hallowed debating chamber where Thom will speak.

'Since there's no queue…' Vicky hazards. Libby raises her eyebrows. 'Maybe we could go and get something to eat?'

How anybody could think about food at such a moment is way beyond Libby's comprehension. '*You* can,' she says. 'I've got work to do.' She takes out her make-up from her bag and heads to the loo.

'It's okay,' Vicky mumbles. 'I have energy bars.'

'If a queue starts to form while I'm in there—'

'Yeah, yeah. I know.'

Mascara, Libby knows, is a risk when her hands are shaking the way they are. Still, after two attempts she is done. She brushes and rebrushes her hair, practises tossing it to one side, playfully, sexily, and then after an hour of fidgeting next to Vicky and trying not to drum her fingers on the table or crack her knuckles because Vicky has already had to ask her to stop tapping her foot, finally Libby can take it no more.

'I'm getting in the queue,' she says.

Vicky makes a show of spinning round to look. 'What queue?' she says.

'The queue I'm about to start,' Libby says. 'You coming, or what?'

'What,' Vicky says, shaking her head, but coming too nonetheless. Sure enough, the queue starts to form behind them: nervous excitement runs through the assembling crowd, though how much of that is simply a result of leaving the library during exam season Libby cannot be sure. They seem excruciatingly young, these undergrads – excruciatingly young and so painfully keen – and she wants very much to stand apart from them, to be the sophisticated grown-up, the equal of Thom and not of them.

And then it is time to go in, to have the inevitable, interminable debate about where to sit for the best combination of proximity and visibility. Which chair will be his, and which will be the interviewer's? Where will his line of sight be? Why are there all these reserved seats in the front row with nobody in them? Libby checks in her pocket mirror: her mascara has not smudged. Her hair looks more than passable. Her handbag, where to rest her handbag? Is it okay just under her chair? Chill, Vicky says, as if such a thing were possible. Libby has never in her life been chilled; now seems an unlikely moment to try out this new stance towards events of supreme importance. For her manicure, she has chosen a red called 'Bastille My Heart', an attempt at sending herself soothing vibes. She sees now how futile this was, though she is pleased with the colour, a deep merlot. Sexy and sophisticated.

She sits. She waits. And then, finally, finally, there he is: Libby sees him standing the other side of the door, a blurry figure through the misty glass of the window. Until this moment, all of her life has been nothing but blurry figures. The door is pushed open and Thomas Cassidy strides in, all confidence, dark jeans, a green blazer, his winsome smile, mere metres away. The air he is walking through is the same air that envelops her. Hence, goosebumps. Hence, a slight shiver. Related? Perhaps. Chemistry. There is so much chemistry. She knew there would be.

'Thank you,' he says in response to the applause, elongating his 'a' American-style, Callum McKenna-style, bringing to mind a thousand scenes from *The Classroom*. The moment before Callum finally kisses Sarah, for example. The moment she has watched a hundred times.

Thom does not look at Libby as he walks past her. Their eyes do not lock. That's okay, she tells herself. Not yet. It isn't yet. When he does, there will be electricity. Possibly the room will spontaneously combust.

Libby leans forward, rests her chin on her fist. I am listening to you, she communicates with every fibre of her being. Watch me listening to you. No one has ever listened to you the way that I am listening to you right now.

It isn't long before her cheeks ache from smiling. It is a little longer before she is able to concentrate on what it is he is actually saying. There in front of her. Mere metres away.

In answer to the Union chairman's questions, he speaks about literacy. He speaks about the actress who played his love interest in *The Classroom*. He speaks about the importance of quality education for all children, for their own good and the good of their nation. He speaks – carefully, diplomatically, though after chortling a little – about the 'special relationship' that Brits try so hard to cling to and Americans occasionally remember. Then he takes questions, and Libby's hand shoots up. And again after the first question. And again after the second. She will be patient. She has nothing to prove.

Although, by the fourth question, Libby is starting to bounce in her seat, to pump her arm up and down as she used to at primary school when she knew, she knew, she just *knew* the answer. 'Oh come on,' she stage-whispers, when yet again someone else is handed the microphone for their chance to speak to Thom. He catches her eye and chuckles, and her insides turn to goo. Okay, she thinks. It was worth it. For that moment of eye contact alone it was worth it.

Which does not stop her bouncing in her chair and pumping her arm more violently still on the fifth attempt. And then, a miracle: Thom turns to the moderator.

'I think,' he says, 'I mean would it be okay if I took a question from the girl in purple?'

Vicky squeezes her hand. Keep calm, says the hand. Remember to breathe. It is a timely reminder. Libby exhales deeply as she takes the microphone. This is your moment, she tells herself. Do not blow it. Be normal.

'Hi,' she says. So far, so good.

'Hi,' he says back, and a tiny part of her brain thinks: I could give the microphone back now. Mission accomplished. He has spoken to me. He knows I exist.

'Your show changed my life,' she says instead. She is sure the microphone must be picking up the thumping of her heart. 'I said I'd never go into teaching because my parents are teachers and that just seemed a bit lacking in originality, but your character inspired me. And now I'm writing a novel, just like Callum told his favourite student to.'

'That's great,' he says, and oh, that smile. 'What's it about?'

'It's about—' Libby pauses, but really at this point what choice does she have? 'It's about an English teacher who really just wants to be an actor.'

'Sounds great,' he says. 'Should we get some wine later, talk about it some more?'

The audience laughs. Vicky squeezes her hand again: breathe, remember to breathe. Libby knows he doesn't mean it, that it is in keeping with his playful spirit to say something like this, but still, all she wants to do is get on Twitter and tell the world, you guys, Thomas Cassidy just asked me out on a date.

Instead, somehow she composes herself. She hopes Vicky is proud.

'I know that you wrote a couple of the episodes of *The Classroom*, and they were some of the best.'

'Thank you,' he says, graciously.

'So I was wondering if you still write, if that's something that's still on your radar.'

She will have to listen to the answer later, when the video of the event goes up on YouTube. Because for now, all she is capable of processing is that Thomas Cassidy is looking at her, he is talking to her, and he does not seem to think she is crazy, and oh my gosh, he is utterly charming.

Thom

They are really milking him for all he is worth, before he gets back in the car and is driven to Oxford for the next stop on this tour of elite British universities. After the Q & A, there is an interview with the student newspaper, and after the interview when the door is opened he comes face to face with the mob he heard from inside, that he (inexplicably) hoped would have dissipated by the time he was done in there. It's a small mob, a calm and patient mob – these are, after all, not just Brits, but comfortable, highly educated Brits, and thus ridiculously polite – but a mob nonetheless.

Still, he wants to say, there's a bar, guys, and comfy chairs, leather sofas, just right over there, a few feet away, and the jet lag is making me dizzy. Maybe we could sit? But of course sitting would not lend itself to the system they have going, an orderly 'queue' of sorts – Brits! – as people line up for photos, for autographs, or to tell him, I'm going into teaching because of you. He wants to say, you know I hear this every day, right? But he remembers, as he always remembers in these moments, a stage door, himself as a sixteen-year-old, a letter thanking an actor for inspiring his own professional ambitions. He remembers the letter being passed from the sixteen-year-old to the woman with the actor. The actor looking at it, dismissing it, mouthing something, *later,* maybe. The woman scrunching up the envelope and dropping it in a trash can.

The girl who asked him about his writing, the girl with the novel, she is there too, twirling a strand of hair between two fingers, hanging back a little, as if wanting to signal, it's okay, I know I've had more than my fair share of your time already. I don't want to be unreasonable. He finds himself wishing she would step forward in the line. He wants to enjoy her enjoyment of him. It is not, by any definition, reasonable or normal that simply meeting him could bring anyone so much pleasure, but he loves to bring pleasure, even unreasonable pleasure. That was in part why he played along with her during the Q & A, turning to make eye contact for fact-checking purposes when he referenced episodes of *The Classroom*, sometimes deliberately planting the tiniest of mistakes in his statements so she could have the joy of correcting him, of being the expert in the room: yes, that was a Christmas episode, but it was season six, not five. She is not creepy, though, or crazy. True, she exhibits some of the behaviour he recognises from the creepies, from the crazies, but he knows in his gut that she is okay, and her hanging back, letting people talk to him while she jokes with others, this seems to corroborate his theory. She is fun, he can tell: he wishes there were time for that glass of wine he jokingly suggested. So when she hands him a brown envelope, says, it's my novel, in case you're interested, he takes it. He is surprised to hear himself say, I'll read it. And he means it, and he loves the joy this brings her too: she is biting her lip to keep from grinning too much, too unbefittingly.

***

He really does mean to read it, but the pace of life is picking up. For the first time in a few years, the first time really since the end of the show that made him famous, he finds himself busy, good busy, borderline crazy-busy. It stops him thinking about how lonely he feels in his still-newfound singleness. It stops him thinking how empty his new house is, how quiet without the laughter of his children. In Cambridge that time, as he leaned against the wall sipping mediocre wine and making small talk with strangers after a night of interrupted airbound naps, his publicist checked up on him: you okay? Well, he joked, I'm a little sad sometimes. She laughed; he laughed too, but it was true. It was, if anything, understated. He was more than a little sad, more than sometimes.

So he is glad, enormously glad, that the movie he was in last Christmas, an unlikely hybrid of horror and comedy, has put him back on the radar of casting directors. This fall he has another movie out, and a half-decent sitcom that might even survive for more than a season. And then just before Christmas: the prize. The film he is proudest of, perhaps in his entire career, finally coming out, a film that could be nominated for Oscars for the prominent lead actors. A film at whose name he won't cringe when he sees it listed on IMDb, one which the fangirls will not have to drag themselves through, martyr-like, for his sake, one to which they could proudly invite friends without having to admit they only wanted to see it because of him.

Busy, busy, busy and all the schedule gaps his work leaves him are filled by his kids. Daddy dates with his eldest sipping watermelon lemonades. Rides to piano and ballet and viola lessons and play dates, normal moments of fatherhood that bring him this new combination of joy and sadness which he does not quite know what to do with and which exhaust him almost as much as his job does. His children and his work, his two greatest achievements, his two reasons for living: exhausting. So Libby's novel sits untouched among a pile of books and screenplays to be read when, if, life calms down a little. In his defence, though: he does not throw it away. It does not even cross his mind to do so.

***

After that first meal in the restaurant on the Third Street Promenade in Santa Monica, Thom and Ebba have met from time to time for coffee. They talk books, movies, life: these coffees are a refuge in what sometimes feels like the intellectual wasteland of Los Angeles. In June, Thom tells Ebba about his trip to England, that he'd had no idea *The Classroom* was so popular over there.

'Cambridge is kinda idyllic,' he says. 'Beautiful.' And then the words are out of his mouth before he can apply any kind of filter to them. 'We should go some day.'

'You and me?'

'Sure. You'd love it. It's quaint and just so very – English, you know? I've never seen anything like King's College Chapel. It has an amazing ceiling.' Fan vaulting, the guide had said. 'I kept walking into things because I was looking at the ceiling.'

'That ought to be fun to watch.'

'See, that's what I'm telling you. So many reasons to go.'

He is aware that he is not being entirely fair to either of them. Dangling romance in front of her – in front of himself – when he isn't sure he has anything of that to give, when he isn't sure, even, how these things work when you have kids already, when you work as hard as he periodically does these days. Sex, one-night-stands, sure: not a problem (he has tested this theory out already, several times), but Ebba deserves better than that. His career, he is almost certain, the crazy hours, were in part responsible for the break-up of his marriage, and how does he know it won't happen again? He cannot bear the thought of losing Ebba a second time. *Losing Ebba*, he thinks; if I write a memoir of my own one day that could be a good title.

Ebba, perhaps sensing some of this, changes the subject. Lets him off the hook. She has always been far kinder to him than he deserves. 'So you've got British fans, huh?'

'Lots of them, apparently.'

'British fans with cute accents.'

'Yes. And, get this, one of them gave me a book she wrote. Basically I'm the hero, as far as I can tell. Or, you know, someone who looks a lot like me. And has my name.'

'Ha,' Ebba says. 'You and your fangirls. What do they see in you?' She brushes his arm as she says this, and the feel of her skin against his awakes something in him. A flash of a memory: dancing together at his sister's wedding, mentally formulating his own proposal.

'I dunno. Boyish charm, I guess.'

'Wait,' Ebba says. 'What was her name? The girl who gave you the book? It wasn't Libby, was it?'

'Libby.' He turns the name over in his mind and tries to conjure a mental image of the girl in the purple top. 'Libby. Yes. Maybe. Why? You know her?'

'She tweeted her disapproval of my having broken up with you.'

This pleases him greatly. 'Wise girl,' he says.

Ebba punches his arm, playfully. 'Did you read her novel?'

'No. I mean, I said I would, but you know how it is.'

'You shouldn't have promised.'

'I know.'

'But you did promise.'

'Yes.'

'So now you have to read it. It's an honour thing.'

'Okay,' he says.

'I mean it.'

'Okay. I will.'

And so he does. Waiting around on the set of his sitcom, which is where he always gets most of his reading done. The Steve Jobs biography can probably wait. Her book is really not that bad. It is a little girly – she gave it to him printed and bound, and he is glad the cover was not pink and glittery, as it surely would be if it were ever published. The main character is a little too much like him, or a younger and idealised version of him, the same number of kids, a Juilliard degree, and of course the freckles. (Who knows why women love his freckles so much?) It's uncomfortable, but it's something else too: flattering, maybe. He sees in his character an echo of his younger self, of the person he wishes he could be, of the man he desperately wants others to think he is.

The story is a melancholic one, of love lost, of longing, of regret, of being unable to shake a first love. He can certainly identify with that. There are some beautiful phrases, but it is not Great Literature, not by a long shot – and yet it does something to him, twists his insides somehow. He has long since lost the Post-It note Libby had stuck to the front, but he remembers, roughly, what it said: that she can see it as a film, that she wants to write the screenplay with him. And, you know, maybe it isn't a terrible idea. Maybe it could work. Later in the summer, maybe, when there's a break in filming for his new show? He mentions this to Ebba: does she think it is crazy? She does not. She is, however, less sure about another part of his idea: Libby's living in the annex above the garage. In the line to buy coffee, she stands very straight, as she always does, a throwback to her ballet days, and crosses her arms.

'It's a completely separate apartment, Ebba.'

'You think that's going to matter to the press?'

But he knows, and he knows that Ebba knows, that the press, even the crappier branches of the entertainment press, have bigger fish to fry than him, and certainly bigger fish to fry than who it is that he houses in the apartment above his garage. He suspects that Ebba's objections have more to do with something he's said, something about how, now that he thought about it, Libby looks a little like Ebba. A newer model, she said. I guess I'm in trouble. She grinned, and he didn't want to spoil the moment with over-analysis: it's okay, you're actually way better looking. She's a little overweight and her teeth could use whitening, and she doesn't have those killer blue eyes of yours, and that beautifully straight posture, and the graceful way you bend at the hips with one leg straight out behind you, and you're you and she's not, and anyway, what do you think I am? I'm old enough to be her father.

'Do you have her contact details?' he asks Ebba, and she locks eyes with him. It feels as if she is taking an X-ray of his soul, deciding if he can be trusted with Libby's email address.

'Sure,' she says.

He is, after all, a grown man. Responsible for his own decisions.

Libby

'Where are my shoes?' Libby asks. 'Has anyone seen my shoes?'

Karen is getting ready with their mother in her room, last minute adjustments to her veil, that kind of thing – and so it falls to Sophie to patronise Libby. She shakes her head. 'Didn't you keep them in a safe place?'

This question seems unnecessary. Pointless, even. If Libby had kept them in a safe place, would she be looking for them now? But Sophie has always been the queen of such pointless questions, such disdainful remarks. Or perhaps not the queen: princess, rather. She has learned from Karen. In family lore, Iona and Karen each have a mini-me in Michaela and Sophie, respectively. Michaela has been designated sensible, quiet, poised, discreet. Like Iona. Libby has never bought into the received family wisdom: Michaela and Sophie have always seemed equally silly to her, and now when one of them phones she needs caller ID to tell them apart, so similar are their voices, their turns of phrase. University – Exeter for Michaela, Edinburgh for Sophie – really ought to have differentiated them, given them some semblance of a distinctive personality or at least an accent, but no.

'They're in our wardrobe,' Michaela says. 'We kept them all together, remember?'

'Thanks,' Libby mutters, and as she squeezes her too-wide feet into them, she remembers. Losing the shoes was probably a deliberate act of her subconscious. They hurt, and they don't fit, and this is the perfect metaphor for this family, for this day. Iona should be the one getting married first, to this tall, blue-eyed junior doctor who for reasons unknown has chosen Karen.

Libby has made an effort in the last few weeks, has attempted to allow herself to be submerged by the family excitement the way you pinch your nose and dive under the froth of a wave. Maybe, if she had been an actual bridesmaid, she would have managed it. 'I can't,' Karen said. 'There are four of you, and I want all three of my housemates, and that makes seven. Which is just ridiculous. We aren't Americans.'

This seemed to Libby an unnecessary dig, a grenade lobbed at her under the guise of innocence. She thinks she knows the real reason for Karen's decision: she didn't want *her*, Libby, as a bridesmaid. Libby has always been like an irrelevant irritation to Karen, a piece of lint you pick off your jumper. But their mother, or perhaps Iona, had put her foot down and said, you can't do that, it's all of them or none of them.

They have, to soften the blow, all been given plus-ones, but this only helps Michaela and Sophie. Libby, of course, assumed Dan would come with her: he is such a great dancer, and always in favour of free food, but he made up some excuse. Do you really hate weddings that much? she asked him, and he nodded yes. I'm not getting married, he would often say in post-Formal-Hall inebriation back at King's, until in their final year she could take it no more: enough, Dan. Enough. You are going to make someone very happy one day. When he looked at her sceptically she named the previously unnamed. You are not your father, Dan. He jerked back, as if jolted out of a nightmare, and later that night as they fiddled with the locks to their bedrooms on opposite sides of the corridor she wondered if he was working up the courage to come up behind her and kiss her. But he didn't, and he hasn't come to Karen's wedding, and Iona has not brought anyone either. I'll be your plus-one, Libby said to her, and Iona laughed. You're a sweetheart, she said, but Libby wondered if what she was really thinking was, we are not married, Libby, let me breathe. And now, after the vows and the hymns and the confetti, after the endless family photographs and speeches, she watches Iona dance with the best-looking usher and she feels angry. It is all she has ever wanted for Iona, happiness in a man's arms, and the moment might finally be here and instead of being happy she is angry. She doesn't want to think about why: each of the reasons seems unbearably ugly. She is angry that he isn't Jeremy. Angry that Iona isn't playing along with the narrative she has imagined for her. Angry that she, Libby, is left on the sidelines with no dancing partner. This is what her friends have warned her about. Live a little, Vicky has said to her countless times. Don't decide in advance what happiness should look like. Let yourself be surprised. But this is the price she has to pay for holding out for the best, this moment when the evening inevitably ends with a slow dance, Iona blushing a little as she leans in closer to her new friend, everyone partnered up except Libby.

Dan

Often, when Dan skips the Chandos nights, he doesn't have a valid excuse. Not one that would be considered valid by his friends, anyway. They might be sympathetic to the actual reason if he were to tell them, but he is embarrassed and a little ashamed at his increasing reluctance to be around Libby, the slight tear in his heart each time she laughs. She is his friend and he should get over it, is what they might say, and they would be right. He is not unsympathetic to this argument: it is one he has made to himself many times down the years. It is one of the many reasons – reasons? Excuses? – why he has been so reluctant to act on his feelings. To ruin the dynamics of the group they both so love, have come to need so deeply, would be unthinkable. To lose Libby's friendship would be unbearable.

Tonight, though, and increasingly, Dan finds he does have an excuse, one that is wholly acceptable to his socially mobile group of high-achieving friends: work. His agency's recent mention in *Writing Magazine* has resulted in a predictable glut of submissions, an overflowing slush pile that threatens to swamp all of them; among them, he is sure, a gem or two waits to be discovered, polished, shined. He sits tonight, feet up on a chair, green-inked pen in his hand, and makes his way through the first of the manuscripts he has requested. On the stereo, his iPod shuffles through the classical music playlist. It is, by now, a well-honed routine, the music somehow sharpening his senses, making him more alert.

He misses playing the 'cello: there isn't much time for it in his life now, and after university there isn't much opportunity for music if you're just an amateur, if it's all just for fun. He wasn't bad at music, though, once upon a time; he might even still not be bad. It had been touch and go as to whether he would study music or English at Cambridge, and after the first few weeks, he began to suspect that he had made the wrong decision. When he walked into the orange-hued, musty library at King's, his stomach would begin to cramp, and he'd picture himself as a cartoon character flattened by a giant pile of books, the sheer volume of them squelching him, his life, and what had been a very real love of the written word. Fifth week blues, he would later learn it was called, though to him it was a darkish grey. It strikes most acutely of all in the first term of the first year, among people from state schools who find themselves relegated from easily head and shoulders above everyone else in every subject to, at best, average, in the one subject they are most passionate about.

'You're quiet today,' Libby said to him, on the way back across King's bridge from the Twentieth-Century Lit supervision during which she'd had to do most of the talking, to rescue his awkward silences and stilted sentences.

'Yeah.' He hadn't yet learned that this was her way of asking him to talk. Of saying, I care about you, I want to make whatever is hurting you not hurt you any more.

'I've got a pack of those caramel digestives you like in my room. Come up for a cup of tea?'

He knew then that she was going to make him Talk About It, and he didn't want to talk about it, but he was rather keen on those biscuits, and rather keen on being in Libby's room, though it drove him a little crazy to look too directly at her bed.

'I think, maybe,' he said when she handed him the tea, 'I made the wrong decision about doing English.'

Someone else might have taken the reasonable approach. Might have pointed out that it may not be too late to switch subjects, or maybe, if he still felt this way at the end of Part I in the second year, he could switch to a Part II in music? Someone else might have looked at the issue from every possible angle. But he already knew back then in the fifth week of the first year, had already known for five weeks, that Libby was not like everyone else. That reason was not her strongest suit, but that what she lacked in analytical thinking she more than made up for with passion.

'Oh, but Dan! There's so much beauty in the English language. There's so much truth and history in those books. And when else in life are you going to have the chance to spend all this time with them? It'll be worth it. It'll be worth it, I promise!'

He left her room an hour later, high on the sugar in the caramel digestives, but high on something else too. It was as if he had been given a transfusion of Libby's enthusiasm, of Libby's energy. And how glad he is now! He loves his job. He thinks about how close he came to going in a completely different direction, and it makes him shudder. He can't imagine another life, a life surrounded by anything other than books, than discussions about plot and motivation and word choice, than the excitement of bringing a new voice onto the literary scene, than the joy in writers' responses when he tells them his agency wants to sign them. They try so hard, some of them, to be calm, to sound professional, but others don't bother to mask it: this is, after all, for some of them, the culmination of years or even decades of hard work and hopes endlessly deferred. In their passion, too, he hears Libby. Everything circles back to her, so that he is always thinking about her, even when he isn't. To shake himself free of her would be no more possible than it is possible to remove ink from water: she has infused every aspect of him. His everyday activities, and a good portion of evenings and weekends, too: books, the things she loves most in the world aside from that TV programme and that actor. His pleasure in language, his increasing intolerance of bad grammar: he will never see a missing or misplaced apostrophe and not think of her. And then the butterflies, the high, of falling in love with a new author as he reads, of seeing possibility and potential in words on his computer screen: they remind him of freshers' week, of discovering her, of thinking, wow, I didn't know what I was looking for but I know that this is it. If you drew a mind map of his life, his career, his loves, she would be there, at the centre, connected to every one of them. So you see, he would tell his friends if he ever had the guts for this conversation, getting over her isn't really an option. She is woven into my DNA.

Thom

Thom is thinking about Libby and her book as he works through the grocery list at Whole Foods, the cart's handle cool against his hands. The list has always been necessary to keep his mind from wandering, but this has never been truer than today. He is thinking about Ebba, too, her reservations about Libby, her warnings. Weighing them up against other arguments, other feelings, other core values of his.

Whenever he can, he advocates for big ambitions. He quotes Thoreau: Go confidently in the direction of your dreams! He quotes Lincoln: Whatever you are, be a good one. Chase the impossible, he says, for what you catch when you are pursuing it will surprise and delight you. This final line is one of his own, one that has been printed on mugs and postcards and approximated on Target posters. He has preached these things for years, at college graduations, at award ceremonies, in fatherly lectures to his kids. Libby is doing exactly what he has always told her, told people like her, to do. Chasing her dreams, striving to be a good writer, believing in what must seem to her to be impossible. Thom holds in his hands the key that will unlock everything she barely dares to hope for. Doesn't he, in some way, have a responsibility to the people who take his advice and follow it to its logical extreme?

His character on *The Classroom*, Callum McKenna, would certainly have argued this. Callum didn't advise his students to write if he had no intention of mentoring, encouraging, advising them through the process. Thom was always so proud of Callum in those moments, this fictional and idealised version of him that had, from the start, been written with him in mind. He wanted to see himself reflected in Callum, and he did, often, but through a glass darkly, an imperfect reflection. The imperfections all Thom's, of course: reality leaves apparent and glaring the bumps and scars that fiction so often glosses over.

Thom is more than imperfect: sure, he has inspired countless people; sure, rumours echo back to him that he is a 'nice guy', whatever that means. But though he pushes to the back of his mind all that he has ever read and heard about the children of divorced parents, these things resurface in his nightmares. He has to swallow the urge sometimes, often, daily, if he's honest, to take each of his kids in his arms and apologise for messing them up, for the therapy bills that will plague their adulthoods. To emphasise all the good things about this relatively new life of theirs: two houses! Two bedrooms! Two swimming pools! Never getting bored of either parent, their rules, their food, because they only have to put up with each of them for a week at a time! It works, sometimes; he gets them to laugh, sometimes; but not nearly as often as he would like. When he tucks them in at night, reads them stories, such tenderness for them pinches his heart, but not only tenderness, not only love: also guilt; also sorrow. He would have given each of these children the moon if he could, and yet he has failed to give them the family they deserve, the family they need.

And here he is, metaphorically faced with Libby, with a chance to make a dream come true instead of crushing a life: why would he not do this? Probably it would not redeem him in his own eyes, or the eyes of whatever higher power calculates these things, but it would make him feel like himself again. Those things he preaches, about being brave, about striving for the best, about dream-chasing: they are things he deeply believes, whose magic he has experienced himself, a Midwestern kid growing up with stars in his eyes and an all-consuming love for the theatre. He hardly ever feels like himself these days.

He is thinking about these things as he pushes the cart around Whole Foods, concentrating on too many things at once already, and so he almost walks into Jenny without noticing her. Jenny, but not just Jenny: Jenny and a man whom Thom doesn't know, has never seen before.

'Well,' Thom says, reaching for a joke, failing to find one. 'Look who it is.'

'Hi,' Jenny says back, the picture of composure, and for the briefest of moments Thom hates her for this. 'We're just getting some burgers to throw on the grill for Rosie's school friends.'

We.

'I don't think we've met,' Thom says, extending his hand, proud of himself for being the bigger person in this hateful moment. 'I'm Thom.'

'Steven,' says the man – taller than him. Younger than him? Steven shakes the hand Thom has extended. A firm handshake. A kind voice. Of course: his wife – ex-wife – has good taste. Damn it. She's moving on. How can she be moving on so soon, when it is taking Thom so long to get his act together? They exchange pleasantries and platitudes, only half Thom's mind on the actual words. By the time he is home, his anger has deepened and a thought has formed, a thought he will later recognise as ugly, but by then the die will have been cast: see how easily I can make a new friend too. No, Ebba will say of the email, you probably shouldn't have done it, but you did do it, so now you have to follow through.

Dear Libby, he types.

Libby

When the email comes, at first she doesn't believe it. I mean, would you? All your life (more or less) you have been waiting to meet the man who inspired you to go into the career you love. Who, the camera zooming in on his green eyes, once spoke through the screen and directly into your heart: I believe in you. You can do this. For whom you have consequently been doing everything that you do – the novel, the teaching, everything. Who also happens to be very handsome and newly single. You meet him, and it's magical; it's everything you dreamed of. Your perspective is slightly warped by this: what is and what isn't possible? And how can you even know? Your understanding of these things is shaken, and your grip on reality was never that firm in the first place.

But weeks have passed, six of them. Your second eldest sister has got married. Your friends have acquired and unacquired boyfriends and girlfriends. Ofsted has been and gone and declared your school outstanding and you have all survived. And then you sleepily reach for your iPhone one Saturday morning in mid-June and there is an email from Thomas Cassidy. Or purporting to be. Or whatever. Who knows. But it says exactly what you want it to say. It says, *I'm sorry it took me so long, but I've read your novel, and I like it a lot, and if you're still up for writing the screenplay with me, then let's do it.* (You rub your eyes, look around your room: everything is exactly where it was when you went to sleep. The empty ice cream tub with the spoon sticking out of it is on your bedside table. The book you are halfway through is under your pillow. The group photo taken at the John's May Ball in your final year is tilting at exactly the angle it always does on your wall.) It says, *If you have time this summer, you could come to LA, and we could make a start on the screenplay. I have an annex above the garage where you could stay if you wanted, or otherwise we can come up with another plan. Think about it. Let me know. T.*

T. Just the initial.

I mean, think about it. You wouldn't believe it either, would you?

Dan

Why? Why must she persist in tormenting him like this? Dan catches himself: he is being overly dramatic; her love of melodrama is obviously contagious. She has forwarded the email to him not to hurt or torment him, not to thumb her nose up at him – *told you so!* – but because he is her friend and she wants him to share her excitement, or because she needs him to confirm that she isn't dreaming, or losing it. He chuckles to himself: she lost it a long time ago, she might not even have ever had it, and this is part of what he loves about her, her passion and devotion that verge on craziness. Does he wish they weren't directed at a man a hundred times more attractive and a million times richer than him? Of course, but you can't have it all.

It looks real, he writes back. *And wow, Lib! Are you going to go?*

But of course he knows the answer. He knows that first there will be unnecessary soul-searching. There will be hours of wine-fuelled conferences with various members of the King's gang. (He thinks about texting Vicky: *You coping okay?*) There will be fiery arguments with her mother, who will say things like, he just wants to sleep with you, and then you'll get pregnant, and then what? Not realising that is exactly the plan, and Libby will roll her eyes and text Dan, saying something about how her whole childhood all she wanted was for her parents to notice her, and now, now that she was hoping to slide away under the radar, *now* they decide to pay attention? And she will agonise about her school: does she resign? A six-week summer might not be long enough; will they let her hand in her notice for the autumn term, now that the May half-term has come and gone? But of course, of *course* she'll go. This is her dream. This has always been her dream. For as long as Dan has known Libby, there have been Post-Its on her wall: Shoot for the moon. Even if you miss, you'll land among the stars. All the cheesy stuff. Cheesy, but sort of endearing. It might be easier to get over her if she didn't persist in being so endearing. It might also be easier to get over her if their names weren't so perfectly matched: he saw *Libby* as a royal blue colour, *Dan* as a cherry red,

Primary colours, meant to go together, to partner in creativity. He wishes he weren't given to that kind of sentimental thinking – it is unbecoming of a sensible person – but this is what she does to him.

She's left Thom's email address in the body of the forwarded message. She might kill him for doing this, but he does it anyway. Not immediately. He thinks about it first, of course, draws up a mental pros and cons list, though he finds it is not a long one. He attempts to sleep on it, but after he has closed his eyes for a minute he realises that sleep is not an option until this email is sent.

Dear Mr Cassidy, he writes. *You don't know me, but I'm a friend of Libby's. She's rather excited about your invitation, as you can imagine, and as her friend I am too, so I just wanted to check a couple of things. Namely (1) that you really are who you say are, and (2) that it's a serious offer. Would you be able to confirm both of those things? I hope you don't mind me writing this – I'm just looking out for her. Oh, and if you even think about breaking her heart, I will personally come over and kick your good-looking American 'ass' until you wish you had never been born.*

He deletes the last sentence, though the sentiment behind it stands; he signs off and presses send. And then he panics. He is, as established, not given to melodrama, so it is low-grade panic. A slight quickening of his heart. But though his email to Thom seemed the right thing to do, now he worries: what if he has ruined everything? He waits a day, usually, before he sends messages of this importance. He is not impulsive; he must have been caught up in Libby's excitement. She does this to him, makes him less cautious, more spontaneous, and the slightly dangerous feeling of this is part of why he loves her, why he thinks she would be good for him, and though it scares him to think that she has the power to alter such a fundamental part of him, it is intoxicating. But what if Libby was trying (failing, of course, but trying) to be cool and collected, in an attempt not to scare Thom away? What if Dan's email, too quick, too eager, too earnest, *does* scare him away? It would mean, of course, that Thom was unworthy of her – falling at the first hurdle as she called it that time they went punting – but Dan is sure the rules would not apply when it came to Thom. The unworthy one, to her, would be Dan. She would never forgive him.

But there is nothing to do but wait now, wait and hope, and he is well-practised at those. And thankfully he doesn't have to wait long: when he wakes up the next morning he has his answer.

Dan,

Of course I understand your concern! I really am Thom Cassidy – I realize this email is no proof of that, so you (or she) can call my assistant on the number below to double-check. And yes, it is a serious offer. I can't promise we'll sell the screenplay, or that if we do it will be made into a movie, let alone a successful one. But it would be fun to give it a try. If you have any other concerns, feel free to write again.

Thomas Cassidy.

He likes the full stop after the name; he doesn't know why. Maybe it signals decisiveness, trustworthiness, or something. He texts Libby.

I think it's legit.

How do you know?

He knows there and then that he is never going to tell her. He is never going to tell her that he risked her dreams for the sake of her emotional safety. It is not a choice she would make herself. She would be furious that someone else, well-intentioned as he may be, had made it on her behalf. It turned out okay, but it might not have, and then what?

I just know. Call it gut instinct. You should go. Just, promise me you'll come back?

No promises, she says, and she follows it with a winking face, but still, he feels punched in the stomach. This is exactly what he feared.

Thom

'This is a really bad idea,' Thom's assistant says when he phones to tell her about his plans for the summer. He arches an eyebrow. Andi doesn't normally speak to him with so much vehemence. She doesn't normally even give her opinion unless he asks for it, which admittedly he has done more and more since the divorce. Little things, usually: this shirt for the first interview, that shirt for the second? Which one looks better on TV? Maybe I should just wear the same for both? And it is, to some extent, her job to be sure of herself, unequivocal. Still, the force of her verdict sort of shocks him.

'Which part is a bad idea?'

'All of it.'

'You think I should spend the summer differently?'

He knows that she does. Raising his profile. Building his brand. But he is exhausted. He wants a break. He wants to get off the rollercoaster for just a few weeks. Will his pilot be picked up or won't it? Will the network order nine more episodes or won't it? Will they ever start actually promoting it, or is he going to have to get himself a Twitter account? Every Thursday morning, constant refreshing of the website that carries the ratings. Disappointing news most weeks. And through all of that, keep filming the show, keep being enthusiastic, ignore the discouraging signs. Keep putting everything he has into what he knows is failing, though it is not his fault it is failing and there is nothing he can do to stop it.

Exhausting.

Exhausting, too, the dating: feeling the women grade his successes out of ten, ascertain how talented he is, where on the Hollywood totem pole he stands. He aches to be appreciated for who he is, independently of his career, of the awards, of the characters he has brought to life. Ebba knew him before all that, championed his successes but loved him apart from them. He misses her; he misses those simpler times. And then, of course, the challenge of co-parenting after the divorce. Of putting on his reasonable face when he deals with Jenny. Of fighting the bitterness he sometimes – too often – feels rising in his throat: his anger at her, his disappointment at himself for having failed at the most important thing in his life.

He does not think it is unreasonable to take the summer off.

'A change is as good as a rest,' he says.

'Writing instead of acting. Yes. Writing is a great idea. But don't do it with some unknown twenty-five-year-old who's probably just a crazy, obsessive, untalented fangirl. And certainly don't do it in your house.'

'Okay. First of all—' But Thom doesn't know what to say first of all. Almost every word of her tirade can be, needs to be, rebutted. Libby *can* write. The book is good. He likes it. He has already visualised some of the scenes: the parts in New York City are his favourites. He can even hear the soundtrack. 'She's actually a really good writer. I'd give her an eight out of ten, easily. Maybe even an 8.5.'

'Fine,' Andi says. 'So she stays in a hotel. I'll book a conference room and you can meet her there every day.'

Thom doesn't want to write in a conference room. He wants to sit in his garden, in the shade of the Pasadena oaks. This isn't a business meeting. It's a creative process. He wants the two of them to be relaxed. He wants them to build a rapport. He has never co-written anything with anyone but it seems to him that rapport must be important. Like between a president and his speechwriter. That kind of thing.

And, also. Also.

He doesn't hate the idea of company. Company with boundaries: he explains about the apartment. They will write; they will then go their separate ways. He has this big house. The hot tub. The swimming pool. The garden. And every second week it's empty. The silence, the freedom, the space: they remind him of his failure as a husband. As a father. They depress him. He doesn't want to spend the summer depressed. He wants the summer off from all of that, too. He wants to spend the summer feeling like a normal person, doing something he enjoys, with a new friend. It may come to something: they might sell the screenplay. They might not. But it sounds like fun. A different kind of fun from acting. A different kind of fun from weekends at the beach house in Coronado with the kids.

'But she might be crazy,' Andi persists, as though he didn't hear the first time. Or the second.

'So if the worst comes to the worst I put her on the next plane home.'

Andi laughs. 'Come on, Thom. You and I both know you would never have the heart to do that.'

'I would,' he says, and he hears a foot-stamping, petulant child's voice in his own.

'Can I ask you something?'

Oh, so *now* she switches to politeness, to checking if he wants her input.

'Sure.'

'Would you have invited her over if she were a guy?'

'Of course,' he says. Reflexive. Defensive. It will be Andi's turn to arch an eyebrow. He thinks about the question later; it niggles at him like an aching tooth. And in the end he has to admit it, if only to himself: what he really misses is not just company of any kind. It is, specifically, female company. The company of a woman who looks at him like he is everything. That won't last, he knows – she will discover he is human – but it will be pleasant while it does. Besides, the email from Dan: she has a boyfriend. It will all be fine. Fine, and fun. That is not, of course, what Andi thinks. She sends him an email later: *It's going to end in tears.* This seems histrionic. Ridiculous. Wrong.

Libby

When Libby reads, she usually hides her phone in a drawer, so that she is not distracted, not tempted, by the lighting up of the screen every time something happens on Twitter or Facebook. A new comment on a photo, a new reply to her latest deep insight on whichever episode of *The Classroom* she has just rewatched. She silences the phone, hides it, and gets on with the book, though for the first few minutes her fingers are almost itchy. Her phone is rarely used as nature intended phones to be used, as a method by which one person speaks to someone not normally within the range of their voice. The closest she comes to this is usually an exchange of texts arranging coffee so that the speaking can happen face to face. And she certainly never picks up her phone when the number is unknown. She does not like the uncertainty, the lack of control. *Email me*, she thinks. *So I can have time to think and respond and I don't feel trapped by whatever demand you are about to make of me.*

This Saturday morning, however, things are different. She has slept badly – for good reasons, because of excitement, because of waking up every few hours to check things like how engagement visas work – and as a result she feels discombobulated. So her phone is still out and she is about to tap the Facebook icon when the screen lights up with the words 'private number'. She is going to press reject when the thought occurs to her: it could be Thom. It could be Thom's assistant. Maybe she should break her rule. She presses the green button.

'Hello?'

'Could I speak to Miss Elizabeth Bolton, please?'

Nothing about this pleases her. Not the formal British accent, which dispenses immediately with the Thom theory. Not the sound of her own full name, and certainly not its connotations. When someone calls her Elizabeth, it means she is in trouble. For a second she is tempted to say, wrong number.

'Miss Bolton?' says the voice again.

'Yes,' Libby says. 'Yes. That's me.'

'This is Chanelle Johnson, from Barclays Bank.'

This is not good news. It doesn't put Libby's mind at rest.

'Yes,' she says. 'Hello.'

'Before we go any further,' says the voice. 'I want to confirm your identity. Could you tell me your postcode please?'

Is this some kind of joke? Maybe it's some kind of joke. The stupid security stuff is bad enough when *you* call *them*. But when *they* call *you*, interrupting what has been a perfectly pleasant lie-in, yank you out of your daydreams, on a number you yourself have given them?

'SW1P 4AS,' she says, mechanically. She is asked about her direct debits, and her latest purchase, and she answers those mechanically too, her stomach tightening, her limbs tingling with fight-or-flight adrenaline.

'I'm calling about your overdraft,' the voice says at last.

'Okay?' Feign surprise, Libby tells herself. In this kind of situation, always feign surprise.

'As you know, you are well past the post-graduation two-year grace period. And you're still £2,279 and 56 pence overdrawn.'

'I'm a teacher. Teachers don't—'

'I understand that.' There is no hint of saccharine in this voice. 'But we're going to need you to pay us back so that we can close your account.'

'So that you can – what?'

'Close your account. We're reviewing our customer database and you are no longer eligible to maintain an account with us.'

The room is starting to spin slightly. 'I don't—'

'You have fourteen days to clear the debt,' the voice says. Snaps. As though Libby were a toddler refusing to do something that was well within her ability to do. 'I will be sending you a letter to that effect. Otherwise, I'm afraid we must initiate legal proceedings.'

'Okay. Thanks.'

Thanks? Why on earth did she say thanks? She sits on her bed, her legs suddenly immobile. Her screen lights up with a comment on a Facebook photo but she doesn't tap it. Every month, her salary brings her closer to the magic nought in her account, but by the end of that month she is back at the same negative figure where she started. It's how she lives; it's how she has always lived. It's how she pays for the ridiculous rent of half of this tiny flat in Pimlico. It's how she goes skiing and sunbathing with her increasingly affluent friends, who are kind enough to plan their weeks away around the school term even though it puts the price up for them. It's how she pays for the flights—

Flights.

How is she going to get to California without an overdraft facility? How is she going to get to California without a bank account? How is she going to find two grand in the next two weeks to avoid – what, exactly? Prison? How do these things even work?

She sits, and sits, and ponders this. No, ponder is the wrong word. Ponder implies calm, and order, and remembering to breathe. Panic is more accurate. She sits, and panics. Waits for the buzzing in her ears to die down. Then, exhausted from the panic, she gets under her duvet and goes to sleep.

Dan

Libby is unimpressed that dinner at Pizza Express is happening without her. *You knew it was parents' evening*, the subtext reads in her reply to the group email. *You knew I couldn't make it.* Yes, my darling, Dan thinks. I know, and that's exactly why I planned it for tonight. This is not just dinner. This is an emergency summit.

Two days ago when he'd met Libby for lunch, he'd asked her if she'd booked her flight yet. He asked it encouragingly, with warmth and a smile and as much enthusiasm as he could muster. All the trademarks of a supportive friend. He expected her to provide him with date, time, flight number and the number of hours from now until take-off. Libby is not the most organised of people, but when it comes to important things – to the things, that is, which are important to her – she switches into OCD mode. In this, as in so many other things, she is all-or-nothing. One of the many things about her that had intrigued him, taken him a while to work out in the first year. I'm having no children, or four children, she said once. It makes perfect sense to him now – though it terrifies him: *four?* – but at the time it was one more facet of the contradictory enigma that was Libby, one more reason for him to think about her more than was justified, to try to work her out. But he has long since cracked the code, even if the habit of thinking about her far too much is a tough one to break. Impossible, maybe. It's ingrained now. It's in his bones. His muscle memory. The muscle memory of his memory. Which probably doesn't even make any sense. But then, very little of this does.

So Dan was surprised that Libby hadn't bought the ticket yet, if nothing else so she could start counting down the days.

'I'm still thinking about my options,' she said. Deliberately vague, it seemed.

'You know the prices go up the longer you leave it.'

'I know.'

This was a new enigma. It should have been an easy one, now that he had cracked the Libby code. He looked at her and she held his gaze for long enough that if the secret were somehow written in her eyes he would have been able to decipher it.

'The price is rather high already,' she said into her coffee. She must have known he wouldn't let that go.

'But if you marry him and he buys you a house?'

He played the game in order to get her to smile, and it worked.

'Absolutely,' she said. 'I'm not saying it isn't a wise investment. But you have to have the money in order to invest it, you know?'

'So you're waiting for your salary to come in at the end of the month?'

Libby brightened. 'Yes.'

But when the waiter came over with the card machine, he saw it was something else. Her card had been declined.

'I must have put the PIN number in wrong,' she said. This was how he knew how flustered she was. She doesn't say 'PIN number'. The N stands for number and so the word number is redundant, and he always thinks about Libby when he sees the word PIN because she has been repeating this for as long as he's known her. Still, he let her try and key it in again before he stepped in.

'I'll pay,' he said. 'It's just easier. There's obviously something wrong with your card.'

'Thank you,' Libby said, and he saw that there were tears pooling in her eyes. These, he knew, would be his undoing. He couldn't pretend he hadn't seen them. He couldn't pretend she didn't need a hug. She had always been terrible with money. He remembered standing next to her at the cashpoint on Market Street in Cambridge, hearing her mutter please please please to the machine as though the inanimate object could possibly care that she really did desperately want to go to St John's May Ball. Her parents had been of the school of thought that they would provide their daughters with the necessities; there was no need for pocket money – no means for it, either – beyond a few pounds here and there in exchange for the odd chore that wasn't considered part of the general life of a family of seven. So the student loans had made Libby giddy. She had never seen so much money, let alone in her own bank account. And when you added it to the student Barclaycard and the three-thousand-pound overdraft facility that would remain interest-free for two years after graduation – practically for ever – she'd been sure it would last as long as she needed it to. But it didn't. Which didn't stop her wanting nice things, like the way-beyond-her-budget flat in Pimlico she shared with Vicky. And it's not as if she doesn't work hard for the money she has. She puts everything into teaching, or at least she did before this whole Thom-and-the-novel thing.

He squeezed Libby's hand under the table. 'How bad is it?' he asked.
'It's bad,' she said.

Outside the café, he hugged her. He had warned himself not to indulge this kind of impulse, but this was an emergency. She needed him. This was, after all, what friends were for, wasn't it? And she fit so snugly in his arms. She needed to cry. He was performing a valuable service, he and his t-shirt, and the t-shirt probably needed a wash anyway. There were so many things he couldn't do for her – he couldn't, for example, write her a cheque for ten thousand pounds – but he could hug her. So he hugged her until she pulled away, wiped her eyes, thanked him, said she was being silly and she was sure it would all be fine.

How? He wanted to ask. How would it all be fine? If her card wouldn't allow £8.26 through, how was she paying her rent?

'It *will* be fine,' he said. 'We're not going to let you starve.'

He'd used the *we* as protection – we your good friends, not just pathetically devoted little me – but as he said it, it gave him an idea. Hence the hastily convened dinner.

***

'So that's the issue,' Dan says, downing the last of his wine as they wait for the next bottle and the starter.

'It's always been the issue,' Liam says. 'She's always been terrible with money.'

Nicola shoots him a disgusted look. 'It's not easy being skint all the time.'

'Nobody forced her to go into teaching,' Liam says.

Dan pours more wine. 'She's a great teacher.'

'Speaking purely objectively, of course,' Charlotte says.

Dan feels his cheeks reddening. He is more embarrassed by the blushing than by the implication of his unrequited and by now slightly pitiful crush.

'In fairness,' Nicola says. 'I think she probably is quite good at it.'

'Still,' Liam says. 'If she doesn't want to be skint…'

'Okay. I'll pitch the career change as an option. But right now she needs to pay her rent, and she needs a plane ticket to Los Angeles.'

Liam snorts. 'Needs,' he repeats.

'Yes,' Dan says. 'Needs.'

He is surprised at himself, and a little proud. Charlotte is the assertive one. And Nicola. Vicky, sometimes. Even Liam. Dan is the peacemaker, the reliable one, the go-along-with-it one. He wonders if convening everyone together like this is a moment of personal growth of some sort. He sees, nevertheless, looks being exchanged, and this does not please him.

'It will crush her if she doesn't get to go,' he says. 'So yes. Needs. She needs to go.'

'It will crush her more in the end if she doesn't learn to be responsible with her money,' Charlotte says. They have guessed the purpose of the meeting. They are trying to wear him down before he gets to the Big Ask. 'Come on. You really think this is going to be good for her? This American thing?'

'She'll come back insufferable,' Nicola says. '*SoCal* this and *Cali* that and *Lahs Angelesse* the other and *oh, my gahsh, you guys, America is so ahhhhsome.*' She says this last part through her nose and her accent is terrible, yet she has somehow captured everything that Dan finds profoundly irritating about Libby's obsession with America. He can't help but smile. Take that, Thom, he thinks. Or Tahm or whatever your name is. But he feels instantly guilty about these thoughts and about laughing along with the rest of them. These are Libby's dreams they are trampling on. 'She also might come back with an offer on her screenplay.'

'Might,' Nicola says.

'So anyway,' he says. 'I was thinking maybe we could help her out.'

The waiter saves them from the awkwardness of the moment.

Dough balls are shared, slathered in garlic butter, scrutinised and savoured. Wine glasses are drained and refilled. Throats are cleared.

'How about,' Charlotte says eventually, 'we all have a think and drop you an email?' She makes it sound like a question, but it's an order. Case closed. On with the night. Partial success, at best. Dan is less proud of himself than he hoped to be.

Libby

Parents' evening, interminable though it seemed, is over, and for the eighty-sixth time this week, Libby opens the Expedia website, plays with dates and times and airline combinations until she gets the cheapest price she can imagine for a summertime London to Los Angeles flight. Cheapest is not exactly the word. Least expensive. Least extortionate.

Still, she argues to herself and to everyone who will indulge her long enough to listen, if I marry him, it will seem a tiny, well-spent, wise investment. She feels dirty even thinking like this. Truthfully – at least she thinks, she hopes, it is truthful – only a tiny percentage of her attraction to Thom has to do with his money. The glamour of a Hollywood life is not entirely without appeal – lacks for nothing in the appeal department – but that is not what attracts her to him.

What attracts her to him is first and foremost his personality; she has long since learned to put it into words, an answer to the bewildered not-exactly-critics-but-critics-nonetheless in her friendship circle and beyond. The warmth that comes across in interviews and that she has now witnessed in person. His humour, his kindness: on the many message boards and Facebook groups she frequents – *occasionally* frequents, you understand – everyone speaks of his generosity when they've bumped into him at airports or waited for him at stage doors. He has never been anything but kind to his fans in those moments. Of course, it's two minutes, five minutes, ten minutes tops: of course, she acknowledges to the not-exactly-critics, it's easy to keep up a pretence for that amount of time, anybody can do it, but the point is that not everybody does.

She always suspected this to be the case, but when she went to see Sandra Connolly in *Who's Afraid of Virginia Woolf?* last spring her suspicions were confirmed. Fine, fine: it was cold and raining, but Libby had stood in that cold and that rain waiting for Thom's co-star, the one who had got to kiss him despite not being the blonde he was destined for. She had stood outside the theatre shivering and being splashed by passing taxis for a good forty minutes while other, less devoted fans of *The Classroom* came and went and successive waves of curious tourists swelled and receded. And when Sandra emerged, met at the door by her driver with a large umbrella that was more than sufficient to keep her perfect hair intact, she barely scribbled her name on a few programmes, making as little eye contact as possible. She posed for a photo or two but her body language made it clear that she was doing it begrudgingly. Of course, maybe she was tired, or coming down with a cold, or had to get back to her children – these people are human, Libby, Vicky reminds her, takes pleasure in reminding her – but the point is: there are no stories of Thom being this way. He jokes, flirts a little, puts his arms around shoulders as pictures are taken. It says something about him, Libby insists. It says that he is humble enough to remember that he's got to where he's got to because his fans have put him there. It shows that he has not forgotten what it is to be a normal human being, to have hopes and dreams, even supposedly silly ones like a few minutes of conversation with the actor whose character inspired your career. She saw on Twitter once that after one of his plays, with dozens of people waiting for an autograph, he stopped to talk to one aspiring actor. Maybe we'll get to work together one day, he was heard to say, and those in earshot felt their hearts melt a little. See, Libby says when she tells this story, he is kind. He makes time for people. And he is articulate and intelligent, too. He's written thoughtful essays in online publications, made brilliant speeches at graduation ceremonies and at educational events and at charity fundraisers promoting literacy. Literacy! How can you not love a man who champions literacy? Who makes YouTube videos of himself reading to his children to encourage other parents to do the same?

The point is, money is low down the list of what makes Thom Cassidy attractive. Libby is no gold digger. Her love for him is pure and real and for all she cares they could live in a grass hut. But in justifying what has sometimes been vast Thom-related expenditure, it is good to have the logic of investment and potential return on that investment. It all makes perfect, logical sense if people would just follow her logic. The only problem with the investment theory, though, as she told Dan the other day, is that you need to have the money to invest in the first place. She can click on Expedia all she likes, but Barclays have put a stop on her debit card, and her credit card has long since been revoked. Of all the things to get in the way of Libby's dream coming true, is it really going to be something as mundane as money? As if she needs the reminder that she doesn't live in a Hollywood film? She will not allow this. There has to be a way, and she will find it.

Dan

By the time Dan gets home, he is downright angry. The wine relaxed him at dinner but he is sobering up now, too much to send the email he really wants to write. Look, he wants to say. When one of us hurts, all of us hurt. She'd do it for any of you. You know she would.

He can't prove this, of course. Not with logic, or facts, or her past record. It is a conviction in his gut – the same part of his gut that tells him when he has found a manuscript worthy of publication – but a conviction in your gut is not contagious in the way that a solid argument might be. Like Liam's: she needs some tough love from us. She needs to learn her lesson. She'll learn it far better if it really costs her something. Still, Dan wants to say: don't you remember? Don't you remember how she organised us to buy a toastie maker for Charlotte's birthday? Don't you remember the tulips she picked out to brighten up Nicola's room after she broke up with Jonathan? Don't you remember the Little Miss Wise book she bought for Vicky, with added personalised details? Don't you remember what a good friend she's always been to us? Okay, fine: she could have bought more rounds in the college bar. And these days at the Chandos she could buy some rounds sometimes. But you can't put a price on friendships like theirs. You don't ostracise Charlotte for being bossy or Nicola for her lectures on the word bossy. It's not how it works with them. They are practically family. They are a more meaningful family unit, Dan often thinks, than his own blood relatives are to him. And of course – of course – they are not ostracising her. But they could go this extra mile. She'd do it for them: not a financial extra mile, though if she could, she would: he remains convinced of this. But an extra friendship mile.

Like that time in Nicola's room halfway through the first term. Fifth week blues: Dan had been subject to a virulent strain of it, and now it was Nicola's turn. Buckling under the weight of her Sartre essay, Nicola was losing it. Cross-legged on the worn-out brown carpet in her bedroom in Garden Hostel, passing around Haribo and leaving the fried-egg shapes for Nicola because they were her favourites, the girls took turns convincing her to stay. They talked into the night, way past the point where the Haribo had all been consumed, fried eggs and all, and the one who stayed latest was Libby, even though she had an essay of her own due the next day. And after they hugged and Nicola promised to at least think about staying at Cambridge, Libby went back to her room and wrote her a list of reasons why she appreciated her, why King's was lucky to have her, and slipped it under Nicola's door. The letter got her through the next day, and the next week, and into week six, and the home stretch. Nicola got herself through Cambridge – she had been capable of that all along; nobody but she had doubted it – but the point was that didn't it show Libby cared? Would do anything for any of them if she could? Don't they, in some sense, owe her? 'Owe' was the wrong word. He knows this. But still, he is angry. Dan the peacemaker. The hater of conflict. The steadier of rocked boats. Angry. But too sober now to send the email he wants to send.

He opens his computer nonetheless, because an idea has begun to form. He'll set up a GoFundMe page, send the link to everyone he knows, to all his and Libby's Facebook friends. A few pounds here and there; it's bound to add up eventually. A message from Nicola pops up in his GChat: *I think it's really sweet of you, Dan. You know I'd give if I could.* He does know this. Nicola has been temping as a medical secretary for longer than even she cares to remember and has her own debts to consider. He also knows that Liam, the hot-shot management consultant, could single-handedly wipe out Libby's debt and barely notice the dent in his savings account. And that is what riles him.

Look, says Liam's email, as if Dan has conjured him up with his frustration. *I'm not going to give her the money. I know you know I have it, but I'm saving up for a flat, and I worked damn hard for that money. I refuse to feel guilty for keeping it rather than funding Libby's ridiculous fantasy. But if you want to borrow it – you, not her – I'd be open to that. £8,000 tops? Let me know what you think.*

It is not a difficult decision, though it is also not one Dan takes lightly. He will sleep on it, though he already knows what his answer will be. He doesn't want to seem too eager, too obsessive: he has a reputation for reasonableness to maintain.

Libby

You busy? Dan has asked Libby, by text. *This weekend?*

No busier than normal. A bit of lesson planning, some marking, you know. But otherwise, no.

Let me take you out for lunch.

This whole money thing, it is so depressing. Her dream within reach and yet so far out of reach. The lead weight in her stomach a constant reminder of the conversation she must have with Vicky: listen, I'm not sure how I'm going to pay next month's rent. Vicky will make her phone her parents; if Libby is lucky, she will be able to avoid telling them about the horrible call from the bank. Play instead the dutiful public servant: well, maybe I should move to a private school, I'd get paid more there... But her streak of luck – fabulous though it has been – has ended with Thom's email. One day, if her luck recovers just enough for her to have children and grandchildren, if she ever finds a man whom she loves as much as she could have loved Thom – as much as she does love him – she will tell these grandchildren what might have been. Who she almost was.

So no, she has no plans for this weekend. Other than wallowing. Other than avoiding Vicky and The Conversation. Being taken out for lunch sounds nice. Spending time with Dan sounds nice; maybe he is feeling guilty for arranging the Pizza Express dinner without her. And this 'I have something for you' sounds nice, too. Positive. Intriguing. She wonders, of course, what it is. He knows this about her: her overactive imagination, her endless what ifs. He must be building the anticipation on purpose: it must be something good, something big, for him to raise her expectations this way.

'Hi,' she says, hugging him outside Pizza Express. He is smiling, lit up, animated. Animated for Dan, that is. But still. His eyes are dancing. It's all in the subtleties. They sit, order olives. Order wine this time, because it's Saturday and they can. And also because there is celebration in the air. Has he found her an agent? Has he, even better, despite telling her he couldn't be involved, secretly been sending out her novel to editors? Does he have a contract for a book deal in the folder he was carrying, that now sits on the table between them?

'Is that for me?'

Libby can only feign nonchalance for so long. Or, what is she thinking? She can't feign nonchalance at all. She has never been nonchalant about anything; she can't feign anything, ever. She likes this about herself; she knows that others do too, that they find it endearing. Nonetheless, at times it would be a useful skill to mask her emotions. Useful to learn how to sit still in a chair and not feel as though her heart might explode any minute.

'That? No. That's a client manuscript I need to read today.'

'Oh.' Other manuscripts. Other clients. Of course. She is not the only star in his universe. She is just one, amidst a constellation. But he opens the folder and takes out an envelope, slides it towards her. Libby looks at Dan, for permission to open. He nods.

'It's not my birthday,' she says, though of course he knows this.

'Am I only allowed to give you things on your birthday?'

'I encourage the giving of things as often as possible.'

He smiles. He knows. 'Open it, Lib, for crying out loud.' So Dan *has* been feigning nonchalance. He has been as impatient to give this, whatever it is, as she is to receive it.

Libby takes the knife from the table – still clean, still free of the garlic butter she is about to spread on warm dough balls – and slits open the top of the envelope. Inside, a cheque. She is briefly transported back to the Christmases of childhood, to money in birthday cards, back when ten pounds could buy two, maybe three, books, painstakingly chosen from a shortlist piled on the threadbare carpet in the local WHSmith. She takes it out of the envelope, blinks a couple of times. It's a cheque for eight thousand pounds. Eight thousand pounds! She has never had this much money in her possession at a time. The signature on the cheque is Dan's. How? What?

Before she is able to translate these jumbled thoughts into anything resembling a coherent sentence, he says, 'It's from all of us, Libby. Should be enough for your flight and some spending money? And pay your rent while you're out there so Vicky doesn't need to get a new flatmate?'

He is watching her intently and Libby sort of wishes he wouldn't, because she can feel her face crumple and this is surely most inelegant. Though quite why she cares about that in this moment, she is not even sure.

'Dan,' she says. Sniffing. 'This is the nicest thing anyone's ever done for me. This is incredible.'

He puts his hand on hers. His hand is warmer and softer than she expected. 'It's from all of us,' he says again. 'We love you. Now go and chase those dreams and all that. Just don't forget all about us, all right?'

Libby wants to hug him, but it's too awkward, this combination of being blocked in by other tables and being too British to make a fuss. She will hug him after lunch, hug him so tight. For now, she leans across the table and kisses his cheek.

'You are amazing,' she says. 'Thank you.'

'It's from all of us,' he says, and she wonders why he keeps repeating this. He, surely, has been the one to organise it all. It is just like him.

'Then you're all amazing,' Libby says. 'I have the best friends. The best friend, really.'

She is, in this moment, dazzled by him. If it is possible to be dazzled by kindness, by thoughtfulness, and not only by things that matter less than these: beauty, glamour, talent, fame. He has dazzled her before, in other ways. A 'cello recital in May Week of the first year: Elgar's concerto, Dan's solo soaring in the Provost's Garden.

'It was so great,' she told him afterwards. 'You were brilliant.'

He looked at her intently: 'Are you okay? You crying?'

'No,' she replied. 'It's just really embarrassing. When I'm moved by something, when I'm fascinated by something, it's like all my emotions leak out of my eyes. Like there are too many of them for my body to hold.'

'I love,' he said, and then he paused. 'I love that about you. That passion.' It was a moment, one of their many. He didn't lean in, exactly, but he didn't lean out. If she would just turn her head a little... But she didn't. She never did. She might be tempted now, if it weren't for the timing. Her dream is just around the corner, an eleven-hour flight away. She has never been one to settle for second best. And Dan: Dan deserves more than that too. Moments like these just go to prove it. There's no one like him, in the whole world.

Thom

When a call comes in the middle of the night, you are prepared. Or, as prepared as you can be in the time it takes you to realise that the phone is ringing, that you were asleep and now you are awake, and that the combination of those things means that the ensuing conversation is unlikely to be pleasant. You, therefore, assume your serious, sombre voice and brace yourself. But when the phone rings during the day, when you have just a towel around you and are dripping swimming pool water across the kitchen floor, when it's sunny outside (which, this being Southern California, is almost always), a crazy hot late-July day, sometimes you don't even check caller ID before you pick it up and breezily greet the person on the other end.

'Thom, it's Ebba.'

He recognises instantly in her voice that something is wrong. Very wrong. Middle-of-the-night-phone-call wrong. He grips the receiver a little tighter in response.

'Ebba, what's up?'

'I'm sorry to call. It's just—' She evidently can't bring herself to say it, whatever it might be, so he fills the silence with reassuring words, words he means with every part of himself.

'Don't ever be sorry for calling me, okay?'

'My dad died,' she says. Thom takes this in, or tries to. 'I thought that you would want to know.'

'Ebs. I'm so sorry.'

Back in the day, Marshall Brown and Thom played tennis together. They smoked cigars together. They sang Christmas songs together one year, around his piano, and while Ebba and her mom were in the kitchen mulling some wine he turned to Thom and said, 'Just so you know, if you wanted to marry my daughter, that would be okay with me.' And when Ebba came back into the room he had to come up with a ridiculous explanation for the grin he couldn't seem to take off his face. To be loved by Ebba was miracle enough; to be accepted and deemed worthy by her doting, talented father was better luck than he could ever have hoped for.

Holding the phone between his ear and his shoulder now, he doesn't know what else to say. How is it, he wonders, that we've all had those phone calls and yet for all our twenty-first-century knowledge, all our wizardry, all our supposed sophistication, we still have not figured out an appropriate response to this, the most certain of human facts: death? But even the shared silence is something. Ebba told him once, towards the beginning of their relationship when he was still constantly and desperately trying to impress her: you know, sometimes, it's okay to just enjoy being together. We don't always have to talk. So he is here, just being. Only the telephone doesn't quite feel right.

'Do you want me to come over?' he asks.

Another silence. He imagines her wiping her eyes with the heel of her hand, reaching for the Kleenex, and he is suddenly desperate to take her in his arms. To hold her. To squeeze the pain out of her, if that were only possible.

'Let me come over,' he says.

'Okay,' she says, and on the long drive across the city he reflects on how much quicker she was to say yes when he presented it as a favour to him rather than his fulfilling a need of hers. She has, he thinks, taught herself not to need, not to depend, because life has hardened her beautiful heart, her soft heart. She was always strong: that's what her name means, Ebba, named by her hippie parents with a kind of faith after she was born five weeks premature. Ebba, he said back in the early days, it's funny, I see that as a name full of grace and floatiness, not strength. And she had replied, yes, strength and grace, both those things – it would have been the perfect name for a ballet dancer. She was always strong, but she was not hard. Thom is not a violent man and yet he is overcome by a desire to find Ethan, to make him bleed, to break his jaw. To make him pay for taking this treasure from him and damaging her. But Ethan is dead and he will never pay, and it seems to Thom that this is profoundly, outrageously unfair. He'd thought that only threats to his children could make him feel this way. He had forgotten about Ebba, how it felt for his care for her to tug at his gut this way.

The traffic is unbearable – Saturday afternoon in LA – and he is beginning to imagine he will never get to Santa Monica, never get to Ebba's house, but then there he is, the GPS tells him so: you have arrived at your destination. If only life were like that, if only you could just follow a set of directions and when you veered off them the journey would correct itself and you would arrive right where you were meant to be all along. If only there weren't all these things, all these people, all these choices, that changed the course of everything, irrevocably, for ever. Ebba opens the door, and he can't wait one more second; he can't wait, even, for the door to close behind him. He wraps his arms around her and they stand, her shoulders shaking, his hands moving up and down her back in the way they did with Jenny during labour those four times; he is similarly powerless, similarly desperate to soothe an unsoothable pain.

'Did you eat today?' he asks her.

She shakes her head.

'Honey, you have to eat.'

'Honey' feels so natural in his mouth; it hangs in the air, settling around them and on them like fairy dust. He opens the fridge: tomatoes, not much else. But if there's pasta somewhere and some dried herbs he can at least make a sauce.

She watches him with something like amusement in her eyes. 'When did *you* learn to make a meal out of nothing?'

'Sometime between my mid-twenties and my mid-forties, I guess,' he says. 'I know it's hard to believe.'

For some reason, this makes her laugh. She laughs through her nose and snot comes out and it's gross but it's also endearing. It's real. They will not, after today, go back to being just polite over restaurant tables.

After he has cooked for her, he makes her coffee. He talks her through the logistics, and they make lists of what must be done. He sits beside her as she makes the endless stream of administrative phone calls, or stands behind her, massaging her shoulders. He sits with her, and listens to her silence. He will be there, too, he assures her, when she wants to talk. And then it's night time, and he realises he has not thought through the practicalities of that.

'Do you want me to stay?' he asks her. If she doesn't respond, if she seems unsure, he will ask it in a different way: please can I stay? But she nods, quickly.

'I don't want to be alone,' she says. 'Not tonight.'

Other days, or way back when, he might have been irked by this, by what sounds like an implication that anyone will do, that it just happens to be him tonight, but today he chooses not to hear it this way. Today he is glad, though his heart is breaking for her, that he is the one who is there, the one of whom she will later be able to say, I would have been alone if it wasn't for him.

'My dad was all the family I had left,' she says.

He remembers this from when Jenny's mom died, the way grief begets grief, feeds itself on pain, undealt-with pain, lingering pain. So he is not surprised when despite the lateness of the hour, despite the exhaustion he reads in every part of her face, she begins to tell him about Ethan, about the way the end came for them.

They had been together four years.

'I want a baby,' she'd said to Ethan.

'With me?'

'I wasn't planning on sleeping with anyone else.'

It was a joke – a lame one, admittedly – but Ethan responded with annoyance. 'You don't always *plan* these things, Ebba.' He said it lightly, and of course she should have known, right then. And she probably did, if she's honest, but she loved this man, or thought she loved him, which to all intents and purposes is the same thing. (It's not, Thom wants to say. It's really not.) She wanted to fill a house with laughing children: she had always planned this, throughout her lonely, too-quiet siblingless childhood and into her teens and twenties, and now it was time. So because Ethan hadn't explicitly said no, and because she didn't know, or pretended to herself that she didn't, about his unfaithfulness, and because her thirtieth birthday was coming up, she began to be a little less careful about taking her pill. On the day she told him she was pregnant, he disappeared, for two nights and a day. She never did find out exactly where he went, but she suspects it was on a bender, or at least that whisky and women were somehow involved, and again Thom feels rising in him this uncharacteristic temptation to inflict violence on the man.

'He pretended to be sorry when I had the miscarriage,' Ebba says. 'He did a great job of pretending. But I knew. He was on the set of some movie and I was kneeling in the bath, in so much agony I couldn't get to the phone. I was four months. I'd told people I was going to be a mom—'

Thom takes Ebba's hand. 'You would have made a wonderful mom.'

'Well, I guess we'll never know,' she says, her voice cloudy with tears, tears that mingle with his own now, his own mourning for the hypothetical children he hadn't thought he could love. They cry together and the crazy thought occurs to him that it's not too late, they could make a baby, right now, she is only forty-one, it is not at all impossible. He considers saying this, ostensibly to lighten the mood, but there are some moods, even dark ones, even heavy ones, that are best left as they are. And on the way over on that long drive from Pasadena to Santa Monica, he promised himself that no matter what, no matter how his body responded to her need of him, no matter how painfully his feelings for her were remembered and perhaps rekindled, today was about friendship, nothing more. Nothing less. He doesn't want either of them to look back and wonder if he'd taken just the tiniest advantage of her vulnerability, and he doesn't want Part II of their story to start with the words 'the day after my father died...' Nevertheless, he brings her cocoa in bed and allows himself to kiss her forehead before he goes into the guest bedroom.

'I'm right next door,' he says, though of course she knows this. 'If you need anything during the night.'

'Thank you,' she says, and he thinks he may have seen a smile, a real smile on her tear-stained, exhausted, beautiful face.

Libby

It's a long flight from London to Los Angeles, more than eleven hours, and then the craziness of this immigration line. And for all these many hours, impatience and excitement boiling in Libby's veins and jumping in her limbs, so that by the time she is fingerprinted, interrogated, she is close to tears. She wonders, does anyone really ever say, I'm here to get an illegal job? I'm here to assassinate the president? I'm here to reclaim the colonies for my homeland? I'm here to marry a movie star and have a child with him and then you'll never be able to kick me out, ha!

Vacation, she says, when she is asked for the purpose of her stay, using the right word and everything, but also milking the English accent while she can. The immigration officer looks at her, expressionless, failing completely to be charmed. He probably hears British people all the time. She will have to wait for the first gushing compliments about the way she speaks. She can't wait to feel exotic, special. At Cambridge she never felt as if she was as well-spoken as she should be; here, people will not be able to get enough of her. At least she hopes that's how it will work.

***

A thousand times Libby has pictured this moment, nine hundred of those since she got Thom's email seventeen weeks ago. (The other hundred of them in the old days, the days before she found herself living in a fairy tale, the days back when people kept telling her not to be ridiculous. Well, here she is, in America, and she will show them. She'll show them all.) A thousand times she has pictured it: Thom waiting for her at arrivals. In the fantasies even she recognises as a little extreme he is wearing a tux, and in the more extreme versions still he runs towards her and people around them mutter, isn't that Thomas Cassidy? I guess that must be his girlfriend. But being more realistic about it (yes, she does understand the meaning of the word realistic, so shut up), he will probably be wearing a baseball cap and sunglasses so as not to attract too much attention, too many requests for photos and autographs. Or, if she is really going to push the realism thing, he will have sent a driver, who will be standing expectantly with her name on a piece of cardboard. Sort of silly but also sort of cool. She has never been important enough to warrant her name on a piece of cardboard at an airport before, and this, she knows, is just one of the myriad ways in which her life is about to change.

But in no version of this much-daydreamed moment did she come through after customs and find nothing: no Thom, no driver, no cardboard. Her stomach sinks. How could she have been so stupid? If something seems too good to be true, her mother was fond of saying when Libby was growing up, that's usually because it is. And of course, if she was going to be right about anything, she was going to be right about this. This whole thing. Has it been someone's way of teaching her a lesson? Or, worse, someone's idea of a joke? Surely, if it had been, they would not have let her negotiate a sabbatical from work until October half-term? Surely they would not have let her get on the plane, would they? Or, if they had, they would have been right there with her? That is exactly what would happen in a romantic comedy. Someone, Dan, maybe, would pop up behind her – surprise! – and say, see, aren't I better than the fantasy? She would be unconvinced at first, but he would take her on a road trip and show her all the most romantic spots and at the Grand Canyon they would kiss and she would long since have forgotten about the silly actor guy who was too old and too famous for her anyway.

But there is nothing comedic about this moment, though she supposes whoever set up the joke is enjoying himself or herself. Himself, probably. Only a guy could be this unthinkingly cruel. There isn't much that is romantic, either. She's done her best with wet wipes, with re-applied make-up and deodorant, but she still feels sticky and smelly and exhausted and in desperate need of food that is not pre-packaged and not plastic. She doesn't feel like the glamorous future wife of a Hollywood star. She doesn't even feel like a charmingly down-to-earth-girl-next-door type trying her best to approximate one.

Thom asked for her flight details, and didn't he say someone would meet her? Or maybe he didn't, explicitly, and she just assumed… She shouldn't have assumed. That much is glaringly apparent now. Her phone doesn't work here. She doesn't have his address. He must know she doesn't have his address. What is she meant to do – get in a cab and ask to be taken to Thomas Cassidy's house? No, no, don't worry, I'm not a stalker, he invited me here? Yeah, that didn't sound cracked at all.

Oh, gosh. She actually *is* crazy, isn't she? There is no way the email was from him. Anyone can set up an email address pretending to be anyone. She can't bear to think about how smug Vicky will be. Maybe it'll be good for you, going, she had said, when it had become obvious that Libby could not be talked out of this ludicrous venture. Get him out of your system. You'll find out that he's not perfect after all, that he's just a man, and it will break your heart, but it will be good for you because, oh my goodness, Libby, you have got to get over this ridiculous obsession!

Okay, she needs a plan. Think, she tells herself. Think. She finds a seat and watches people hug each other. Airports are the worst places on earth to be alone. And the prospect of having to be practical when her head is throbbing, her eyes are aching, the voice over the tannoy is breaking into her thoughts every few seconds and she is gasping for fresh air after fourteen hours of airports and aeroplanes… the prospect is overwhelming and she collapses into tears.

She is blowing her nose with a dried wet wipe when someone taps her on the shoulder. It's mortifying enough to be crying in public; don't people know to leave her alone, to pretend they can't see her? In England they would have known. She wipes her eyes and turns to look at the person to whom the hand belongs.

'Libby,' he says. He. Capital H He. 'I'm so sorry. Something came up with a friend.'

And then, of course – of course! – she starts crying again, out of embarrassment and relief and because this was so not how her new Californian life was supposed to start out, how Thom was meant to see her before he'd even had a chance to fall in love with her, and she hates herself for crying and this makes her cry more. She is half-tempted to pretend she doesn't recognise him, and get straight back on a plane home. Everyone was right. This is a disaster, and she hasn't even left the airport.

She is on her feet now – she didn't even notice herself standing up – and Thom is shaking her hand, warmth travelling from him to her. All the anger she should feel dissipates in this warmth.

'I know long flights are pretty draining,' he says, touching her shoulder. 'I get emotional too.'

Libby is almost certain this is not true, but it is a kind thing to lie about.

'Yeah. I'm just tired, I think, and jet lagged,' because that is probably better than I thought you weren't coming and this was all a horrible mistake and everyone was right about you not being the great guy you always seem to be in interviews.

'Why don't you go freshen up,' he says. He brushes her shoulder again. 'I'll take care of the bags and get us some coffee.' Go freshen up: code for, oh my gosh, you look dreadful, go and pull yourself together and attempt to look normal at least. And in the mirror she sees that if that was his point, it was not an unreasonable one. She is grateful that he is giving her another chance to make a good impression with him.

'I went for latte,' he says when she comes back, her hair brushed, her eyeliner freshly applied. 'I figured that was the most inoffensive choice if I got it wrong. How was your flight?' She is grateful, too, more grateful than she imagined she would be, for the coffee he hands her.

'Long,' she says. She does not add that rewatching her favourite episodes of *The Classroom* made it feel considerably shorter. He passes her his coffee to hold so he can wheel her luggage out of the sliding airport doors and to the car.

'You planning on staying for good?' he asks, gesturing towards her enormous suitcase.

Yes, she thinks. That is exactly the plan. He is a fast learner.

'We'll see if California is all it's cracked up to be,' she says instead.

'Oh,' he says. 'It is. Tomorrow I'll show you. I figure you can unpack and rest today, and tomorrow I'll show you some of my favourite places.'

'Okay.'

'I really do apologise for not being there when you arrived. That was kinda crappy.'

'It's okay,' she says again, because even though it isn't, she is in California, in Thomas Cassidy's car, driving towards Thomas Cassidy's house, with Thomas Cassidy, so really, how long can she possibly stay upset?

***

The house, predictably, takes Libby's breath away. She has looked it up online, of course, so she knows the style is Italian Renaissance Revival. She knows about the pool and the spa and the library and the granite kitchen counters and the marble-surround fireplace and the leaded glass windows. She knows that the beautiful dark brown floor is burnished walnut hardwood. She knows about the palm trees in the front garden, and about this she allows herself to comment, because this, she feels, says California is so amazing rather than you are so rich and I am not used to this world. Otherwise, she plays it cool, or at least she tries to, using words like nice and lovely rather than amazing and impressive and expensive-looking. She has primed herself about this in advance, written herself notes in what she has called her Pasadena journal, where she will record every moment of this improbable adventure. She doesn't want to take a single moment of it for granted. And she needs notes for the memoir she will write about this one day, when she and Thom are married.

Thom carries her case up, effortlessly, to the self-contained apartment that will be her home for the next three months. There are fresh lilies on the coffee table and she has never much liked the scent of lilies but now they smell to her of dreams come true, and she intuits that this will be her Pavlovian response to them for the rest of her life, this silly teenage-girl-in-love grin.

She has her own lounge – complete with a television far bigger than she could ever need or justify – and her own bathroom and her own mini-kitchen. This apartment is easily the biggest space she has ever had to herself and she feels the tears welling up again, different tears this time, tears of gratitude and amazement, but she chews on her inside cheek until the threat passes.

'This is fab,' she says to Thom. To Thom! She was watching him on her iPad screen on the plane just a few hours ago and now here he is, in front of her, looking – well, truth be told, looking a little dishevelled, perhaps, in need of a shave and freshly ironed clothes, but she likes the day-old stubble on him; she likes the creases, the imperfections. The reminders that he is only human after all. Human like her.

'I'm glad you approve,' he says. Smiling. 'There's the bare essentials in the fridge – a couple of pizzas and some milk. Apparently you Brits need milk for your tea. Just let me know if you need anything else. I'll be right next door.'

'Thank you,' she says, and when he leaves her she stands for a few minutes. She looks at this new life of hers, the framed photo of the Juilliard staircase, the fluffy pillows beckoning her to rest. She wonders how much of this is real.

Dan

He thought it was just drinks, but it's an ambush.

'Daniel,' they say, using his full name as they haven't done since freshers' week. As nobody, in fact, has done since then. 'It's time.'

'Daniel,' they say, ripping open packets of crisps. 'We want you to be happy.'

'Daniel,' they say, making deliberate eye contact. 'You have to move on.'

See? he thinks. This. This is why I never come to the Chandos. He looks around at his friends crowded into the old wooden booth, makes eye contact with each of them in turn, and smiles. 'I'm fine,' he says.

'We do not believe that to be true,' Charlotte says.

'And even if it is,' Vicky adds, 'even if you are fine now, what about in five years' time? Ten years? Dan, what if you end up single for the rest of your life?'

This is a little melodramatic for Vicky. The Sensible One. She has clearly been prepped. It's a little melodramatic for anyone, truth be told. They are in their mid twenties, for heaven's sake, he points out. It's far too soon to be able to guess who's going to 'end up' anything. He, for one, is far too young to worry, or to think of singleness as a negative thing. Singleness means freedom! It means fun! It means, let's be honest, lots of sex with hot women who love the idea of a straight man who works with books. This is not such a terrible thing. But instead of simply thinking these thoughts, nodding, and buying the next round, he makes the mistake of voicing them.

'Mate,' Matthew says. 'Mate. If that was what you were actually doing, we would not be having this conversation.'

'We're worried about you,' Charlotte says, nodding in that earnest way of hers, with her wrinkled brow. 'It's been, what?' She looks at her watch, as if Dan's devotion to Libby could possibly be measured in minutes. Which, of course, it can: 2,491 days, one hour and ten minutes since she sat down opposite him in her asymmetrical purple dress at matriculation dinner. (Aubergine, she had corrected him.) Or 3,587,120 minutes.

'It's been nearly seven years,' Charlotte says, approximating. 'If it was going to happen, it would have happened by now.'

'Not necessarily,' he says. He is going to wise-ass this one, if that's what it takes. 'Ross and Rachel from *Friends*. Josh and Donna from *The West Wing*. Callum McKenna and Sarah Johnson from *The Classroom*.'

'Mate.' Matthew puts down his pint to free his hands, so he can grab Dan's shoulders. 'You know what all those people have in common?'

'Average guys who score amazing women after a long time of waiting?'

Liam and Ollie snort. He knew they would break first.

'No, mate, no. Fic. Tion. Fiction! They're not real!'

'Oh.' Dan puts a finger on his chin, in perfect imitation of his younger self piecing together the moving parts of a difficult strain of literary criticism. '*That's* what fiction means. This whole time, all the way through my English degree at one of the best universities in the world, I was wondering what fiction meant. Thank you so much for clarifying.'

'I don't like him like this,' Charlotte says to Vicky, but it is no more meant for Vicky than it is meant for God when a mother prays, Dear Lord, please help Daniel to learn to tie his shoelaces himself and be more patient with his sister.

'No,' Vicky says, joining in the game. 'Bitter. Sarcastic. Wry. He's better than this.'

'Which is why this needs to end.'

'Exactly.'

'Mate. Listen to the girls.'

Liam and Ollie exchange looks and sip their beers. They have obviously been instructed – by Charlotte, almost certainly – that if they don't agree with the tactics, they are to keep quiet. This is for the good of Daniel, and by extension for the good of the group. Charlotte is small and blonde and Dan has never understood how she wields such power over the rest of them. The guys, okay, maybe: the curls, the dimples, the smallness of her which seems to say, please look after me! I need a big strong man, and you, spindly nerdy Cambridge boy who has not yet grown into bigness or strength, you could be that man! But the girls, even the girls: if Charlotte said they were meeting for dinner at 6.15 instead of the customary 6.30, then they were meeting at 6.15, and even Liam made it on time.

'Look,' she is saying now, thrusting a piece of paper at him. 'This is a list.'

'A list.'

'Yes. A list.' She crosses her arms and waits.

'Names,' he says.

'Yes. Names. Phone numbers. Email addresses. We know you aren't going to do anything with them, so they're just for your reference. These are the girls to whom we shall endeavour to introduce you in the next months.'

'And talking like a Jane Austen novel is going to figure into this plan how, exactly?'

Charlotte is momentarily thrown. The way he knows this is that she does not immediately reply. There is a gap of one, maybe two seconds.

'That's how I always speak,' she says. He hears a quiver in her voice and thinks, oh crap. I didn't mean to actually upset her.

'I think it's endearing,' Ollie says. Ever the peacemaker, like Dan. Ever hopeful of repeating the long-forgotten dalliance with Charlotte, ill-advised and short-lived and May-Ball-champagne-fuelled though it had been.

'Thank you,' Charlotte says. 'Anyway. That will be all, Daniel. Resume your libations.'

Self-parody? He hopes so, but he dares not laugh, just in case.

Libby

Libby sleeps much better on that second night. Which is to say, she sleeps a little. And the third time she wakes up it is actually morning: sunlight creeps through the curtains and draws patterns on the ceiling. She stretches in her king-sized bed, her freshly shaved legs luxuriating in the still-crispness of the sheets. Her whole body is smiling. She has finally landed. This wasn't a dream. She'd better get moving: have a shower, dust on subtle make-up, throw on one of the summer dresses she's bought especially to wear for Thom, multi-coloured and knee length with a sweetheart neckline: not too short, not too cleavagey, not yet. When she goes downstairs and into the house, she finds Thom sitting at the dining room table, surrounded by index cards.

'Morning,' he says. 'Sleepy head.'

Something inside her stomach jumps. She will probably have to learn to control this if they are going to have any kind of normal relationship. Any kind of friendship which will lead to the other stuff. Which. Okay. This line of thinking is not actually helpful for the stomach. But come on. Thom is wearing a khaki t-shirt that brings out the green in his eyes and shows off his muscular, toned arms. And he is smiling at her as though there is no one he'd rather be spending his morning with.

'There's coffee and a muffin in the kitchen,' he says. She feels, nevertheless, like a thief as she walks through the house to pick up breakfast. Like an intruder. Like an imposter. She comes back and sits opposite Thom, picking at her muffin, ripping off tiny piece after tiny piece with her finger. This is not how she usually eats muffins: three or four bites and they're gone – that's how it usually goes. But she doesn't want to look uncouth. She savours the muffin – blueberry – bite by bite and it occurs to her that this is how she must savour the whole summer. Appreciate every moment. Take nothing for granted. Not that she can imagine taking any of this for granted, ever, but she reminds herself just in case. In the first year at King's, she would begin each morning walking through college to her pigeonhole in case there were any letters from home. She would make herself stop and notice the dusting of frost on the perfectly manicured lawn in winter, the crocuses along the path in spring (purple and white, the college colours). She would look at the chapel, imposing, secure in its knowledge that it dominated the landscape and the postcard market and she would think, I am so lucky. I can't believe how lucky I am. And now she looks at Thom and thinks the same.

'So,' he says. 'I made index cards of all the different scenes in the novel. The ones that are fleshed out already are on white. The flashbacks are on pink. The blue ones are the things that the narrator hints at but doesn't go into much detail on, which maybe could work as scenes in the movie.'

'Wow,' she says. He has already put in so much thought, so much work. He is taking this seriously. She wants to hug him, but it is probably too soon for random, spontaneous displays of affection.

'Does it feel weird, seeing your novel broken up like this?' He is, she realises, trying to interpret her 'wow'.

'A little, I suppose,' she says.

'Not too weird, I hope?'

He sounds sorry, and she almost laughs. There is no need to be sorry. He is doing her the greatest honour of her life. And anyway, she wouldn't have known where to start.

'No,' she says, as if considering this, deciding to forgive him and graciously move on. 'This is fine. This is all part of the process.'

'I wanted to make sure I actually got it. Understood the moving parts, the pivotal scenes. The scenes that start and end Acts One, Two and Three.'

Libby gets up from her side of the table and moves over to his. She stands next to him; she can hear him breathing. He has asterisked some of the index cards, laid them all out in order.

'This is just my take on it,' he says. 'I'm trying to wrap my head around the story. But it's your story. Why don't you tell it to me? Tell me what inspired you. Tell me the heart of the story.'

He nods towards the outside and leads her into the garden. All morning they talk, coffees in hand. No one, apart from Dan, has ever taken this much single-minded interest in this novel, her intentions for it, her inspiration for it, her love for it. Her arms and shoulders feel as if they might be burning in the sun, but Libby does not want to move from here, ever. Thom asks intelligent questions. He doesn't laugh when she says that she watched an interview of his and wished he would come and teach in her school for a week. She doesn't say that Thom the character is based on Thom the actor, or her perception of him, but she doesn't deny it either.

'Why don't they get together?' he asks. 'Thom and Lauren. She clearly loves him. Why does she push him away?'

'She knows he's in love with Zoe,' Libby says. 'She doesn't want to be second best. She thinks she deserves better than that. Or at least she hopes she does.'

Thom leans forward in his wicker chair. 'She doesn't want to try to win his heart?' Then he laughs at his own earnestness. 'I mean, not to speak in clichés.'

'She wants the best for him too. And she believes the best thing for him is being an actor. It's what he's good at. It's what makes him feel alive. And so she wants him to go and study at the best acting school.'

'That's very honourable,' he says. He says it with a smile, but still Libby isn't quite sure if he means it. If what he really means is, your character needs more fight. She can't read him yet. She thought she knew him; it is obvious to her now that she doesn't, not really. And this character of hers, this Lauren she has come to love, she feels protective of her. It is uncomfortable to have Lauren's motives questioned, her behaviour analysed. She understands intellectually that it is necessary, but it is also agonising in its own small way.

'The sun,' she says. 'It's making my eyes water.'

She doesn't even know herself if it's the sun, though she suspects not. You feel everything so deeply, Dan once said to her, which confused her. Is there any other way to feel? She is feeling all kinds of things right now, all of them deeply, and the only one she can name to herself with any certainty is vulnerability. She is so grateful to Thom for taking this time with her with her novel. But she is afraid, too. She wants him to love her characters as much as she does. She wants him to love the book, the story. To love her.

He takes his sunglasses off and gives them to her. 'I'm facing away from the glare,' he says. 'I don't need them.'

Libby thanks him, takes them, imagines that they tingle as she slides them onto her ears and down onto her nose, the way her fingers tingled when she first held Billy Jackson's hand in year seven. She could go and get her own sunglasses, take the opportunity to breathe deeply and compose herself, but that would break the moment. It is an uncomfortable moment but it feels like an important one. It feels like a moment that Thom would asterisk on one of his index cards. Don't look away at the points of tension, Dan said to her as they worked on this novel together. Stay in those scenes longer. It's where the story is. So she stays. She even stays when he asks about the ending, if there's no way they can make it happen for her characters, get them together.

'It'll just be easier to sell,' he says, and this crushes her. She thought Thom had more artistic integrity than this.

'It sort of undermines the whole point of the story,' she says. There is no 'sort of'. It is just something she says to make herself sound less obnoxious, less contrarian.

'How so?' Thom asks. Not aggressively. Now that his sunglasses are off she can see his eyes, the interest in them, the tenderness.

'He changes her for ever. She finds meaning in her work because of him. It's better to have loved and lost, you know?'

'Yes,' he says. 'It is.' He is silent for a while. Her forearms burn. She will have panda eyes with these glasses. Maybe that will make her somehow more endearing. She can't be the glamorous Hollywood type. She can only be her, and she hopes that is enough for him. Panda-eyed and sunburned feels like the real her. Feels like being vulnerable. It is also an opportunity for him to massage after-sun into her shoulders.

'Doesn't mean it isn't damn painful, though. Let's get lunch.' It was another asterisk moment, but he has missed it. Or pushed it away. He is not ready. Fine. She will wait for him. She has waited nine years. She can wait a little longer.

***

Libby is in love. With Thom, that much is obvious, and justified, and preordained. Not by Libby herself, but by fate or the universe or whatever it is out there that is making all of these impossible things happen to her. She is not, these days, above believing in some kind of a benevolent God. So she is in love with Thom, of course. But also with California, or at least the parts of it that Thom is showing her.

They work most days from around ten till around four, and for lunch he cooks or gets them takeaway. Someday, she will offer to make something for them: she is good at it, if she says so herself, but the thought of messing up someone else's kitchen – anyone else's, let alone Thom's, of accidentally scratching his non-stick frying pans – is a terrifying one. She loves the romance of his wining and dining her; she loves watching him bite his upper lip as he guestimates how much rosemary to add to the ham omelette, but she does not want him to think her selfish, or entitled. He needs to see that she is able to look after him too. To do the wifely things.

Weekends and evenings when he is busy or has his kids she sometimes explores Pasadena by herself. When Thom doesn't need the car, she drives to Santa Monica for a dip in the ocean or just to stand at the water's edge and let the waves break against her ankles. But often, Thom is her willing guide to the delights of Los Angeles. Delights: he says it with air quotes when he refers to Hollywood. A tacky tasteless tourist trap, Libs, but it has to be done. Nice alliteration, she says, and he laughs when she asks how come he doesn't have a star on the pavement.

He takes her to a baseball match, which he calls a Dodger game without the 's', the way he says goat cheese and doll house and game room, and even there Libby thinks she might be enjoying herself. To be fair, though, and as objective as she can be, perhaps that is mostly because of the company, or the occasional interruption – 'Aren't you Callum McKenna from *The Classroom*?' It makes her feel important by association, will lead later to her checking Twitter for speculation about the brunette he was spotted with. (Nothing. This is a little depressing. But she has the reality; who cares about perceptions?) Baseball is not too hard to follow (glorified rounders, basically, but she keeps this observation to herself) and, perhaps because of this, people don't seem to be glued to the action, leaning forward, focused entirely on the field, cheering on their team and taunting the opposition with chants as people do at football matches. (You mean soccer? Thom asks, but no, she means football, football is what it's called, but she smiles and indulges him and says, soccer, yes.) Instead, they share popcorn, take turns getting up to choose from the many kinds of different food that are available. She chooses the traditional Dodger Dog, forgetting the practical difficulties of eating a hot dog with anything resembling elegance or grace. Leaning over, Thom wipes a trickle of ketchup from her chin before it continues its downward trajectory onto her dress, and she thinks maybe elegance and grace are overrated after all.

Speaking of elegance, Libby does not think anything will top the Huntington Gardens. Thom took her there the day after she arrived and despite the jet lag and the resulting broken night's sleep she was enchanted. There really was no other word for it: she felt as if she had stepped into the illustrated pages of her fairy tale. Her favourite part, though she suspects this is not original, was the Chinese Garden, with its peaceful lake, its bridges with hand-carved symbols, its poetic name: the Garden of Flowing Fragrance. Close to the tearooms there was a courtyard that appeared to be set up for a wedding, and she mentally added it to the list of possibilities. Perhaps more practical than a beach. Certainly classier, more exclusive. It is possible that she started to say, we could— But Thom saved them both from embarrassment by completing the sentence: we could work here sometimes, yes. Beauty like this can't fail to stir creativity, right?

You sound like your character in the show, she wanted to say. She wanted to tease him, to be able to playfully punch him, but she didn't know him well enough yet. It was only their first full day together. She wanted, too, to be able to hug him. It is a well-known fact that he is a hugger. But at least they banter now, and he wipes sauce from her chin, so that's a start. Plus, they're making progress on the screenplay. Almost too much progress for one week. Too fast. So much still needs to happen between them before they finish.

Ebba

Why do people have the hold on us that they do? Ebba wonders about this sometimes. Chemistry is far too scientific a term, as if these things could be predicted and predicated, charted and graphed. As if each person could be reduced, Myers Briggs style, to a set of letters and simply paired with their ideal match, determined by a quasi-mathematical formula. And maybe, she thinks, those formulae do help explain why some relationships work and some don't. Fine: she is willing to concede that point. But they do not, they cannot, explain that initial, visceral pull towards a person. Like when you walk past someone in the street and you turn round moments later to catch another glimpse of them, only to find that they have done the same. That was how it was with her and Ethan: visceral. Unexplainable. Irresistible. Ever since they'd been paired up to present on *Anna Karenina* and she'd felt a dozen pairs of jealous, hate-filled eyes throwing daggers at her, ever since he had become more than just a theoretical person like the movie stars whose posters decorated her wall – had done since she was twelve and that was how she practised kissing, ever since he finally spoke to her, noticed her, flirted with her, her need for him had implanted itself deep in the pit of her stomach and refused to let her go. He wasn't just the handsome back of a head any more. He was real, and hot, and incredibly smart, and a talented writer, and he knew all of these things perfectly well and yet, improbably, his resulting arrogance seemed, if anything, to make him more attractive. And the only way she could explain it, had explained it in her memoir, was that he had somehow bewitched her.

And so on the Friday night, the last time they were due to meet before the class presentation on Monday, there was never any question that she would kiss him back when he leaned in and whispered, you're beautiful, Ebba. That when he unhooked her bra without her even noticing, when he ran his finger expertly up her thigh, she would let him do whatever he wanted, even though it hurt and he was not as gentle as she would ideally have liked, and when he saw the blood on the sheets he seemed panicked rather than moved and did not ask if she was okay. Nevertheless, she could not imagine anyone more worthy of this gift that she had been saving. I did not take your virginity, he would say later. You gave it to me. And she could not fault the logic. Would she have been less willing if she'd known that he would quit school two days later – leaving her to do the presentation alone – and move to California after it turned out that Hollywood wanted the script he'd worked on all summer? Possibly. She fancied herself the tragic heroine of a star-crossed lovers' story, though, so possibly not. Anyway, she foresaw a coda, an epilogue, where after school was done she would move out there with him and they would make many beautiful babies.

As it turned out, though, he was the one to move, two and a half years later, back to New York where he was directing his latest play, which had debuted in Los Angeles to – of course! – huge acclaim. A play in which Thom had been cast, his first off-Broadway production. Thom and Ebba had been together for two years by then, living together for five months, and never did she love him more than when he was on that stage, inhabiting the role that he had earned. Never, either, did he seem as happy, as buzzing, as when he came home from the preview performances. He had found his match, a writer–director as brilliant as the actor he was, if only it weren't for their history with the same woman. At the cast party on opening night, that awkward introduction as Ebba stood between the only two men she had ever loved, straight and still in her lilac dress, willing her voice to stay even, willing Ethan to have forgotten what he, of course, had not. We know each other from Russian Lit. Two weeks later, a call from Ethan: he hoped Thom would understand, but he'd found someone else for the role of Augustus, someone better suited.

'It's because of you, right?' Thom asked her.

Ebba thought that was spectacularly unfair. 'Of course not.'

'Don't think I don't know.'

'Know what?'

'That there's something between you.'

'Thom, that was years ago.'

In the heat of discussion she had briefly dropped her guard.

'So you didn't just know him from Russian Lit class?'

'We dated for a while.'

It sounded better, she thought, than he slept with me then left two days later to become the hot-shot writer everyone knows him as now. Still, she should probably not have bent the truth that way. Nor, probably, should she have omitted to mention that he had been calling her regularly since he got back to New York. We were kids, Ebba. I was a silly little boy.

'Well,' Thom said. 'It looks like he wants you back, doesn't it?'

'I'm with you,' she said, and then winced, because that should not have been her reaction. I love you, or don't be ridiculous, or he's the past, you're my future; any of those, cheesy and clichéd as they were, would have been preferable. Infinitely preferable.

'You're *with* me,' he repeated, his lip curling in disgust, or perhaps in pain. 'He didn't know that when he cast me. He knows that now.'

'He cast you because you're a fantastic actor.'

'And now that he knows who my girlfriend is, I'm suddenly a less fantastic actor?'

'Look,' she said, scrabbling for a way to end this argument, to quash the conflicting emotions swirling in the pit of her stomach. 'If you're right, and I'm not saying you are, but if you are, then what he wants is for us to fight. So let's not fight.'

'Yes. Let's sweep this under the carpet instead, and hope it goes away.' He smiled as he finished the sentence, and poured them both some wine, but she knew at the first sip that this was the beginning of the end.

Thom

On the third week, Thom makes another attempt at changing Libby's mind.

'You sure I can't convince you to change the ending? Make it happier?'

'No,' she says, shaking her head for emphasis. 'That's the whole point of the story, that life isn't like that.'

He looks at her, this young girl just twenty-five years old, and wonders where the maturity of such a statement comes from. He does not really know her yet, but he thinks he can hear sadness, regret, rather than bitterness, in her voice. She is a brunette – like all the women he has loved, with the exception of the blonde who broke his heart in the sixth grade – a girl-next-door type, the size and shape of someone who enjoys life and does not subject herself to a hundred diets and restrictions every year for the sake of the camera. She is pleasantly curvy, too – and he yanks his mind back to the task in hand. She is young enough to be his daughter, and she is living with him. And they have work to do.

'It may not be life,' he says. 'But this is Hollywood.'

He knows it won't sell without the happy ending. That this won't be the last time they have this conversation. Still, he has to admire her for sticking to her principles, to her creative integrity. There is something attractive about that, too, perhaps because he recognises it in himself. That's out of character for Callum, he would tell the screenwriters on *The Classroom*, and they would let him rephrase something, or they would rethink the arc of an episode. But thinking was as far as they ever got. It made him crazy when they didn't listen to him. He knew Callum McKenna, lived inside his skin, felt his emotions on a gut level. Allowing certain plot twists felt like betrayal. So he understood Libby, really he did. But, still. He wanted this screenplay to be a success; he wanted to see across the screen: Written by Thomas Cassidy. This kind of credit would be different. New.

And newness was exhilarating. Pushing boundaries was exhilarating. Exploring life beyond his comfort zone.

Of course, it wouldn't just be: Written by Thomas Cassidy. It would be: Written by Thomas Cassidy and Libby Bolton. The other fans on the sites she frequents (he has done his research) would congratulate and applaud her, while secretly wanting her to die an ugly death. He suspects this is exactly the reaction she is going for. People talk of fandoms as 'communities', as if it's all sweetness and light, as if there isn't resentment, competition, jealousy. He knows, though, that girls (inevitably girls) would gouge each other's eyes out if it meant getting closer to their idols. Not perhaps in the *Classroom* fandom. You saw that more with the super-famous, the Brad Pitts, the Tom Cruises, and (heaven help us) the Justin Biebers, and he was under no illusions with regard to his own pulling power compared to them. He'd met enough fans of *The Classroom*, though, to know that their smaller numbers did not mean they were any less rabid. Sometimes he wants to tell them, you know we're just people, right? We have mothers. We crap and we belch and we cry. We have sex (and hate to disappoint you, but usually not with fans). We have fragile egos and we get mad when we aren't nominated for awards.

Libby, he senses, is trying hard to be 'normal', whatever that means. She lets him make coffee and cook for her. She compliments his house but not over-effusively, as if she's been in a hundred houses like this one, which he is pretty sure she has not, unless schoolteachers in England are paid substantially more than in the US, and he doubts that. She interacts with his kids as if they were like any other kids, which of course they are, at least he thinks so. They seem to like her: Juliette and Rosie have told him that they do, in the unselfconscious way of seven- and nine-year-olds, though the jury is still out with Clara. He has asked her, on a scale of one to ten, how much does she like Libby, but she rolled her eyes and refused to answer the question: she says my name wrong. It's not Clah-ra. He explained it's her accent: it's sophisticated and cool, and she looked at him in that pre-teen way, Dad, what would *you* know about cool, and said, but it's my name, and it's pronounced the way I pronounce it. She gave him the same look that past weekend when they had all gone to the beach house in Coronado and Libby needed someone to put sunscreen on her pale English back.

'I'll get sunscreen greasiness on my book,' Clara said. 'You do it, Dad.'

So he reluctantly began to rub the lotion into Libby's shoulders. Reluctantly began but not – let's face it – reluctantly continued. Her skin was soft and warm and the smell of the sunscreen reminded him of his own youth, summer days on Lake Michigan, the delicate balance between being the first to offer to help the girls with their lotion and affecting nonchalance. All in all, he was grateful his kids were there with them, though he would have preferred it if Juliette hadn't asked, Dad, why are you closing your eyes? You won't be able to see where you're putting the sunscreen.

Libby builds sandcastles with the younger two and tickles Harry till he begs her to stop. She is good with them and this makes Thom smile. These days when he's with his kids it is down to him to entertain them, to make them laugh, to give them The. Best. Time. Ever!!!, as well as thinking through all the logistics, cooking, making sure Harry doesn't throw himself off the couch onto the sharp corner of the coffee table. He never gets to just watch them have fun any more, to sit back and appreciate them without having to be right there in the centre of things, and he appreciates that Libby takes some of that pressure off.

The more he gets to know her, the crappier he feels about arriving late at the airport to pick her up. He didn't even have the excuse of traffic. A handy one in the Los Angeles area, usually, but he'd come from Ebba's house, and Santa Monica was right by the airport. Bottom line: he forgot, was all. Plain and simple. Which did not exactly make the whole thing any less crappy. He'd had it in the back of his brain, knew that day was the day, but then Ebba called and everything else got relegated to the 'less-important-than-this' file in his brain. And it was only because Ebba asked about Libby, about when she was arriving, that he had remembered at all.

Most days, when they start work around ten out in the garden before it gets too crazy hot, one or the other or both of them has usually had some kind of overnight revelation: what if we started the scene this way? He types, and she drinks coffee and looks over his shoulder. Sometimes it's the other way around. Sometimes they work completely separately, each of them writing the same scene and then comparing the versions, combining the best parts of each. She is good at the melancholic stuff; he is good at making it funny. There is a lot of laughing some days. Some afternoons, they riff on possible plot developments, riff until they reach and then delve right into the realm of the absurd and then give up, go out for dinner and continue riffing over glasses of wine. (He cringes when she is ID'd, as though it were a public admonition for his spending so much time with someone considerably younger than him.) Thom likes having his house ringing with laughter again. It was a risk to ask to her come this summer, but so far so good, and so enjoyable.

When he'd written to Libby, she'd replied *let me think about it*, but he realises now that there was no way she was actually thinking about it: she was trying not to seem too eager. She is not the type to be able to shrug at such an offer, take it or leave it, whatever. She is the devoted type, the passionate type, the type to go online and look at flights the instant she finished reading his email. The type who, arriving at an airport an ocean and a continent away from home, in a city already sagging under the weight of a million unfulfilled dreams, would be devastated if there was no one there to meet her.

On the way to the airport he had called his maid and asked her to put some flowers in the room, to do what she could to make it look homely in the space of an hour or so, and she'd done a good job, but still, he'd had some ground to make up.

Hence, the day at the Huntington. His favourite place in Pasadena, or possibly in the world. A hundred and twenty acres of carefully tended gardens of many different kinds. Rows and rows of roses with intriguing or poetic names, like Daybreaker or Sheila's Perfume. Lilies. Cacti. Everything. Even a Shakespeare-themed garden: he sits here sometimes, breathing in the thyme and violets from *A Midsummer Night's Dream* or the fennel and rosemary inspired by *Hamlet*, and thinks about his younger self who would have seen a sign there, his destiny as a great stage actor made plain before him. Here, he can forget he is anywhere near a city; forget there is such a thing as traffic. He loves to come here to think, or to read. He has the kids every second week, but on the weeks when he doesn't, he and Libby could sit at the café tables in the Chinese Garden and work. They serve all kinds of tea there; she's British, she is bound to appreciate that. And of course, she would like the sunshine. She needs to make the most of the sunshine. Her skin is almost unbearably white, though improbably the traces of a watch mark suggest she was once whiter still. She will burn easily, he finds himself thinking. I should make sure she has sunscreen.

Libby

It's A Level results day back home. Libby had not forgotten exactly, but not remembered exactly, either. Coming to America has felt like breaking the fourth wall, like stepping into the Narnia wardrobe, like entering a parallel universe: she struggles to wrap her head around the notion that life is carrying on as it always has back home. She doesn't, actually, even try: it is oddly painful to imagine London going on without noticing her absence, and there is no room for pain in this new life of hers. But it's A Level results day, and if her Facebook feed weren't enough to remind her, she gets emails about it too, from friends and colleagues asking how her students have done. Mr Flint has emailed, too, congratulating the teachers on another record-breaking year and listing the names of the students who have met the requirements of their conditional offers to Oxford or Cambridge and will be, in what even Libby recognises as the unbearably pretentious parlance of those places, 'going up' to 'read' their subjects there. Gemma is among them – English, Clare College – and Libby lets out a breath she did not realise she was holding.

Back in the old days, when Libby got her own exam results, there was so much more ceremony about the whole thing. You didn't check online or get an automated text: instead, you went to the school office, queued, gave your name, waited for the envelope, tore it open, and cried or yelped or hugged the nearest person after asking them to check that the piece of paper inside really did say what you hoped it did. At her own school, where, jubilantly reading *English: A; Sociology: A; Psychology: A; History: A*, knowing she had amply fulfilled the Cambridge criteria, she had to content herself with a smile, with muted congratulations from the teachers. It didn't do, at her school, to boast about being a swot, to care too much about anything other than passing your GCSE maths retake. She couldn't expect hugs from her classmates who were delighted with their three Bs and a C, with their places at Lancaster or Warwick or Oxford Brookes. It didn't do for the teachers to appear to be too impressed by her, either, even if hers were the best set of results the school had had in three years. Libby had to wait until she got home for the hugs, for the appreciation, and even that was dampened by Michaela's thanks a lot, Lib, now I have to live up to that.

Thom, she knows, would have celebrated with her. He will celebrate with her now when she goes downstairs and shares the news that Gemma will be 'going up' to Cambridge. She won't tell him about that mortifying morning when she overslept, or that Gemma, it turned out, did completely fine at the interview without Libby's help. She will tell him, instead – she is less embarrassed about these things now – how she wanted to inspire her students the way Callum inspired his. How she wanted to spot the talent – the writing talent, the acting talent, the hidden, undefined talent of the student whose shyness masks more intelligence than others realise and whose passion for music or science or history needs a nudge in the right decision to find the place where it must be channelled in order to thrive. Time and again, *The Classroom* spotlights students who stand taller, who find an outlet for their skills, because of Callum. There is something very American about this, about the dogged and intractable belief that we can do anything we set our minds to, but it calls to her, resonates inside her, despite the best efforts of people like Vicky, who says things like, but the thing is, Lib, not everyone does grow up to be president, do they?

Still, it doesn't matter that Vicky doesn't get her. Thom gets her. They are kindred spirits; she recognises herself in his infectious enthusiasm; she wants to recognise herself in the idealistic passion of someone who strives to make the world a better place. You are conflating Callum with Thom, Vicky would say. You met Thom for ten minutes. You don't know what he's really like. But Libby did know: call it gut instinct. You can know something in your gut in a split second. The warmth of a person, their authenticity: these are things you sense, and that can happen in an instant. And Libby was right about Thom. This summer is proving her right.

Dan

Forewarned is forearmed, and all that, so Dan can't understand why his friends didn't just spring these women on him, allow nature or whatever the heck they thought would take its course to, well, take its course. But a week goes by, then two, and he begins to relax. He has never known Charlotte to make empty threats, but perhaps that is why she is now wielding that very tool with such power. An unexpected play. Nice work, Lottie. He calls her Lottie in his head because he knows – from bitter experience involving bruised arms – that it infuriates her, and at the moment he badly wants to infuriate her, even if he does not quite dare do it face to face, where there would be actual consequences.

He has relaxed just enough that when Liam emails round a dinner party invitation, it does not occur to him that the dinner party is also a blind date, that every social engagement stretching out into for ever now carries the threat of a blind date.

Tonight at Liam's table, her name is Natalie. She's wearing an emerald dress slightly off the shoulder and she is a very attractive woman and he has to admit that in another life, maybe. But this is not another life and in this one he is perfectly content to be single, thank you very much.

'Really?' Charlotte looks at him dubiously. 'Perfectly content? So if Libby asked you out you wouldn't be interested?'

'I don't deal in hypotheticals.'

'Since when?' The hand on her hip says, do not mess me around, Daniel.

'Since you ridiculous people have been on this ridiculous mission.'

'Okay,' she says. 'Fine.'

But it is not fine. It is not fine at all. Charlotte is just getting warmed up. There are, apparently, plenty more girls where Natalie came from. Olivia he likes, but she doesn't laugh at his jokes. Clémentine is his favourite, but there's no way he's going out with someone who's moving back to France next month. Stephanie's nose is huge, and he hates himself for saying this, but that's a no-no. And then it's Liam's birthday. And inexplicably (except, not at all inexplicably) Liam has invited his sister's best friend to the party.

'Listen,' Dan says to Caroline. He's had a couple of drinks too many. 'You know why you're here, I take it?'

'Yes,' she says. 'You.'

'I'm a poor lonely single guy desperately in need of a woman.'

'It is a truth universally acknowledged,' she says.

'I hate to break it to you, but I am not in possession of a large fortune. Or any kind of fortune.'

'And you're not in want of a wife.'

'At twenty-six years old? No.'

'But your friends are worried about you.'

'They've taken me on as their project, and I've had it. I can't take it any more.'

'I can help you out,' she says. 'Why don't we pretend to get on very well and get them off your back?'

Brilliant. He can't believe it has taken them so many glasses of wine to come up with such a simple plan. 'Okay. Let's leave the room and when I come back in I'll have lipstick on my shirt collar.'

'That's a little tacky,' Caroline says. He likes the fact that she has a sense of class. She takes him by the hand and makes eye contact with Charlotte as they leave the dining room, head for the kitchen.

'So we pretend we've kissed?'

'Or,' she says. 'We actually kiss.'

He considers this. Then he sees himself considering it, and sees who he has become, and is horrified. A woman is offering to kiss him, a woman with flowy blonde hair and long legs – and he has to think about it? Because of a silly girl halfway around the world who is saving herself for a fictional character?

'You don't mind being used like this?' he asks as he leans in, his voice low.

'You're doing me a favour, actually,' she says. 'I've been wondering what it would be like to kiss you.'

'Oh,' he says. 'Well, in the interests of science.'

She wears that strapless dress very well, and it turns out she kisses rather well too. She kisses with her eyes closed and he notes appreciatively the hint of glitter on her eyelids before he closes his eyes too. This is the first time in a very long time that he has kissed anyone. He has clearly been missing out.

'I think we should do that again,' he says, when she takes him by the hand to lead him back into the party room. 'Just, you know. Science. A controlled experiment.'

'Walk me home after?' she says, and just like that, he is in a relationship, and she's not Libby, and he is okay with that, he is more than okay with that. It also gets his friends off his back and he is okay with that too. It surprises him how okay he is with it all. This, he supposes, is what freedom tastes like.

Libby

One of Libby's favourite things about her new life, her charmed life, her life with Thom, is his swimming pool. Outdoors, of course; pleasantly warmed by the sun, of course. She likes to start the morning with at least twenty lengths: tiny lengths, and she usually stays in the water a lot longer than that, but she makes herself do the twenty first. She wears a tankini, which she likes to think hides her bumpy stomach a little, but she is never quite sure whether she wants Thom to see her or not, with her increasingly tanned limbs, with her not unattractive curves. She has caught him looking at them, or rather, trying not to look, concentrating a little too hard on her face, and part of her wants him to see her in her swimsuit, which is after all only glorified underwear, a flimsy piece of material separating her soft skin from his. She wants him to be tempted, but she is also terrified that he won't be. So she has waxed meticulously and eventually comes to the conclusion that the best moment for him to come out of the house in the earlyish mornings would be when she has just climbed out of the pool and is dripping wet and wrapped in one of his thick, fluffy white towels. That way, he can imagine a more perfect body than hers and by the time he has started to kiss her and the towel has fallen off, he will have ceased to think about such things as the roundness of her stomach.

Some days, she nudges this plan forwards by stepping inside before she goes upstairs to shower, just to switch on the coffee machine so that it will be ready for his breakfast and the start of their day. She thinks this is probably an adequate excuse for being in his house, in his space, in just a towel, waiting to be discovered by him just like back when he had her novel and her email address and did nothing with them over those long, excruciating weeks. But some days, she sees her life as if she were outside it and is shocked at what she has become. Today is one of those days and so after taking two steps into his house, she stops, though it is possible that is not so much because of a prickly conscience as it is because she hears voices.

'I'm just saying,' says the woman, and it sounds like Jenny, which of course makes sense, because it's Monday, the start of Libby and Thom's fourth week together, and Jenny is dropping off the children. 'She's spending a lot of time with my kids, and I don't know anything about her.'

'They like her, Jenny.'

'That's what worries me.'

Libby holds her breath and imagines Thom rolling his eyes.

'What is it that you want to know?' he asks Jenny.

'Who she is. Why she's here.'

'I told you those things already.'

'Yes, yes, screenplay, blah blah. I know. But you know what I'm asking. Don't play dumb with me.'

'You think that the screenplay is some kind of elaborate disguise for my getting to have daily sex with someone half my age?'

'I've seen the way your fangirls look at you, Thom. And I know that you like sex a lot. Or at least that you used to. And that fame and wealth and talent are powerful aphrodisiacs.'

'It's nice that you still think I'm talented.'

Jenny's turn, Libby suspects, to roll her eyes.

'I don't see what right you have to ask me those kinds of questions,' Thom says. 'She's good with the kids. They enjoy her company. Nothing inappropriate happens in front of them. Whether or not I'm sleeping with her is absolutely none of your business.'

'I wouldn't say *absolutely* none.'

'Well,' he says. '*I* would.'

'So long as she realises she's just the rebound girl.'

Libby already has her hand on her mouth, a physical reminder to herself to keep very, very quiet, so she doesn't gasp. She knows, anyway, that Jenny is lashing out. Libby is not the rebound girl; they are soulmates, she and Thom. She has always known this, since the first interview that she saw, and the rather miraculous chain of events that has led her to his house this summer is further proof of their joint destiny.

As, too, is the fact that he has stood up for her, for their relationship. She feels proud that what they have, such as it is, embryonic and not yet fully formed, is worth defending. She feels proud of a man who will do just that: defend it. He has not said it, but he doesn't need to: he loves her. Libby backs away silently. She is going to need a long shower to process this information.

Ebba

Ebba is writing inside today, downstairs in the living room. It has been a few months now since she sent in the final edits of her second book – a novel, this time – and she needs to get going on this one, her third. She has tried mood music. She has tried scented candles. She has tried pulling her hair tightly back in a high bun as she did in her ballet days, a signal to her body that it should enter creative mode. And now she is trying people-watching, but instead of inspiring her all that does is distract her. She is distracted, in particular, by a girl who has walked up and down her street twice now. As if looking for something, and yet also as if not looking for anything in particular. What is that about? Is there a story in there? There is a story anywhere if you just know how to look: the favourite saying of one of her writing instructors. What reasons could this girl possibly have for walking up and down her street like this? It reminds Ebba of being fourteen and cycling up and down Carlo Rodriguez' street, hoping he would come out and she would somehow magically have acquired the guts to introduce herself.

But this girl is not fourteen. She looks to be in her twenties, early to mid, and as far as Ebba has noticed there are no particularly hot guys on this block, though it's true that there is the ambitious director a few doors down and it is also true that she is perhaps too old to even notice eye candy that is age-appropriate for the girl. She continues to watch, and sure enough, the girl passes her window a third time. Ebba can no longer stand it; curiosity gets the better of her. She opens the door.

'Excuse me,' she says. 'You look lost. Can I help you?'

'No,' the girl says. 'Thank you. I'm not lost.' The round 'o' of a British accent.

Now that she is facing her, Ebba recognises the girl from her Facebook profile. 'Libby?'

The girl visibly cringes. Embarrassed, no doubt, to have been found out. 'I wasn't stalking you or anything, I promise.'

Ebba is amused by this, amused at the suggestion that she is important or famous enough to warrant a stalker, but it also occurs to her that for someone who is not stalking her, Libby has done an excellent job of finding her house.

'Well,' she says. 'Seeing as you're here, you want to come in for coffee?'

'Yes please. That would be nice.'

Ebba holds open the door. Shaking Libby's hand feels overly formal, but she does it anyway, because what else is there? It's way, way too soon for hugging. She doesn't know yet if this will ever be the kind of friendship where you hug. Anyone can write a kind review; anyone can seem nice on social media. But she is intrigued enough to take the risk of a coffee, even a coffee in her own house. Ebba coaxes answers out of her eventually: Libby was trying to psych herself up to knock. She wasn't sure if actually meeting Ebba was the best idea, and she wanted to, but she also sort of didn't want to, and walking up and down the street was helping her decide. (Only, Ebba wants to add, not very effectively.)

'What brings you to LA?' she asks after small talk, as she sets the coffee in front of Libby at the breakfast bar in the sun-dappled kitchen. Of course, she knows the answer, but she is not sure she wants Libby to know how much she knows of Thom's life, how often they speak now, how their rekindled friendship has her wondering.

'Well, you're not going to believe this,' Libby begins, and she tells the story that Ebba already knows. Ebba is grateful for her acting training, the training which has her convincingly feigning surprise and delight and excitement for Libby. But it's not feigning, not exactly. It's imagining herself as Libby, inhabiting her, Method style. So she finds that she is, in fact, surprised and delighted and excited for her, with her. You have a crush on an actor and you get to live in his house and spend all day with him, every day for an entire summer? No wonder she is unable to keep still as she speaks. No wonder she cannot hide her grin, her face which telegraphs how deeply she is in love. This is Thom they are talking about, after all: quirky and funny, articulate and brilliant, kind and charming in a boyish way that Ebba is glad the years and the divorce have not taken from him. Of course Libby is in love. Any girl worth her salt would be. (Ebba's acting training, it turns out, is also useful for masking jealousy.) And it is contagious, this joy: Ebba, despite herself, wants to be around it. It's been nine years since Ethan left her for the last time, six years since his death, and through the love of her friends and the writing of her memoir she has begun, finally, to heal. But joy has mostly eluded her this past decade. She wants to be around this girl who exudes it. This girl, with whom she shares an odd but compelling history, this girl whose novel she has flicked through, whose talent is evident, who wants so very much to make it, who reminds her, she realises suddenly, of a younger version of herself, before Ethan, before everything. After the coffee Ebba says to her, we should do this again sometime. She is intrigued. She wants to know Libby better. She wants to see Thom through her eyes too: it will be like falling in love with him all over again. The joy of it will do her good. She wants to catch this joy.

Libby

'Look,' Ebba has said. 'I get it. I wouldn't want to leave the house either. You've got a beautiful bedroom, an enormous TV, a swimming pool, and you've got Thom.'

Libby's stomach flipped over itself. 'I wouldn't say that I've *got* him, exactly.'

'You know what I mean. I just think, live a little! Meet some people.'

It's not that Libby never goes out. She does, relatively often, letting Thom have some time alone with his kids or out with some friends, not wanting him to think he has to constantly entertain her. Not wanting to be work for him. But Ebba has a point: she hasn't met anyone, made any friends of her own. She goes to the beach and she browses in bookshops; she reads in the shade of the Jungle Garden at the Huntington and brainstorms ideas for her next novel behind Vroman's Bookstore as the jazz plays on Sunday afternoons; she thinks back to her usual Sundays in another lifetime, piles of exercise books on her desk, red ink all over her hand, and she doesn't miss them in the least. She people-watches from coffee shops and convinces herself she recognises various minor celebrities. But as far as friends go, her time with Thom and her frequent coffees with Ebba feel like enough to her. She is only here for twelve weeks, but if she stays longer, when she stays longer, Thom will introduce her to people. She wishes he would do that now, but at the same time she doesn't want to share him. She likes that their time together is one-to-one time, just Libby and Thom, or family time, him and her and the kids. Besides, if they go to parties, he will have to introduce her, to put a name on what it is they are, and he is not ready for that, and she doesn't want to rush him. But sometimes he goes out, meets friends, and Libby finds herself alone. The internet is no fun in the evenings – the middle of the night back home – and it feels weird to watch *The Classroom* in Thom's house. And Ebba is so wise. She likes her advice, delivered gently and from a place of compassion, but firmly, the way Iona sometimes – too rarely – did back home when she was growing up.

And so, after browsing meetup.com, she finds herself eating dinner with eleven strangers at Sushi Roku. Cute accent, they tell her. Where are you from? they ask her. She enjoys the attention. Tells them about London. Isn't sure how to respond when they ask her what she is doing here, what brings her to Pasadena.

'Work,' she tries. But she knows this is feeble. She knows there will be follow-up questions.

'Acting work?'

'No. Screenplay.'

They nod in recognition. The food arrives and Libby is safe. Why doesn't she want to tell them about her life? Is she afraid they will laugh at her? That they won't believe her? That their lack of belief will pop the bubble of her illusion? But it's not an illusion. It's real. She's really here. She really lives with Thom. They are really falling in love. She refills the glass from the shared wine bottle and listens to the chatter around her. Asks others about their jobs. Nannies, some of them: they have stories that make for excellent anecdotes but no doubt less-than-amusing days. All of them, though, every single one of them, has Hollywood ambitions of their own: writing, acting, directing, acting. Mostly acting. Back in London, Libby's students were so excited for her. Her colleagues, too, those who weren't mortally jealous: I love that you're pursuing your dreams, they said. Go for it, we're right behind you. Remember us when you're rich and famous. But sitting here, eating seaweed and salmon and listening to these confident Americans, she begins to wonder: is it all a delusion? Are they all chasing ethereal, uncatchable dreams? She feels vulnerable, suddenly, as though a cloak of invincibility has been removed.

Dinner is over more quickly than she expected, each plate whisked away as soon as the last mouthful is swallowed. There is no lingering. The waitress brings separate bills for each of them, but Libby is only briefly wowed by the efficiency of this: it is quickly eclipsed by her bewilderment as the credit cards are taken away and then brought back for a signature. Libby can't remember the last time she signed a receipt in a restaurant, though she vaguely recalls her parents doing so back in the early 1990s. America, so bright and shiny, so full of newness and promise, seems tarnished somehow. Old-fashioned, but masquerading as forward-thinking. Fake. She shakes her head, drains her glass of its last dregs. She does not want to feel this way about this magical place.

'Anybody want a ride?' the girl next to her asks, and Libby thinks, in her light-headed state, that maybe this is not such a bad plan. It's nice of Alicia to offer, and it will save a few dollars on her cab fare.

'If you're sure...'

'Of course. My car is just around the corner.' She puts the address Libby gives her in her sat nav. 'Fancy street.'

'It's not too bad.'

They laugh. It feels like the easy laugh of friends.

'How did a British girl end up staying in such a fancy street in Pasadena?'

Libby loves telling this story. Her happily-ever-after in progress. The Plan that is turning out to be almost a blueprint.

'It's a long story,' she says.

'Got it.'

Libby is disappointed. She wanted to tell it. She wanted Alicia to be a little more interested.

'I'm working on a screenplay with an actor.'

'Oh.' Alicia indicates left. 'Who?'

'Thomas Cassidy,' Libby says, and as soon as the words are out of her mouth, her stomach drops. Alicia is dropping Libby off outside Thom's house and now she will know it is Thom's house and there is a reason his address is not plastered all over the internet and his Facebook profile is virtually unfindable and he gave up tweeting as soon as his last show was cancelled.

'From *The Classroom*? I loved that show.'

Ordinarily, this would untie Libby's tongue immediately. Finding another fan, getting to ask her what her favourite episode is, swapping quotes. But not now. Not now that she has made this mistake. Thom has never told her not to give out his address, not to tell people she is staying with him, because of course, these things go without saying.

By the time she has walked up the driveway to the front door, she thinks she might throw up. She has let him down. She has failed. She has proved she doesn't belong in his world. She can't tell him. She won't tell him. But she has to tell him. This is it. Their first fight. He will know she is an imposter. A silly little girl who just doesn't get it. She can't do it. She won't do it. Not tonight. She'll decide tomorrow. After she's slept on it.

Ha.

Sleep.

Sleep is clearly out of the question.

Thom

It's weird in the house without Libby. It shouldn't be so weird. But this is the first time in around a month now that he has been completely alone: not with the kids, not out with Ebba or other friends, not lying in bed reading, knowing that Libby was doing the same just a few feet away, beyond just a few walls. They watch movies together sometimes. He cooks for her. They play games, sometimes: Scrabble, mostly. She always beats him, she knows all the tricks, all the silly two-letter words that aren't words in any other context and he has instituted a rule that she is not allowed a word unless she knows what it means and can use it in a sentence. And the sentence cannot be 'Xi is a great word for Scrabble, not least because it really infuriates Thom when you get such a great score with just two letters', or any variation of it.

She has never gone out like this, by herself, in the evening, on weeks when the kids aren't around. He should probably applaud it. It is a good thing that she is not so dependent on him. A really good thing. But still, as he channel-surfs in his bedroom, he finds himself looking up, out his window, to see if the light above the garage is on, if she is back yet. It's a nervous twitch; maybe a dad thing. It occurs to him that he will be doing this for years with his four kids, with his three daughters especially. And when he sees Libby, before he can process it, before he has consciously decided to go anywhere, he finds himself downstairs, opening the front door in his boxers and ancient Juilliard t-shirt. She was heading straight for the annex; she wasn't going to come say hi, and this saddens him.

'Hey,' he calls out, and she stops. Almost frozen. She turns around and waves. There is something forced in this gesture.

'You okay?'

'Yes. You?'

'I just opened some wine,' he says. 'Come tell me about your evening.' She is still frozen, but eventually she says okay. The gravel crunches under her feet as she makes her way toward him. Her dress has slipped a little, shows more cleavage than she usually allows.

Thom is not opposed to this. But her face – it looks pale. She looks almost as if she is physically in pain.

'Are you okay?' he asks again, with greater intentionality this time, locking eyes with her.

She nods but halfway through the nod she changes her mind, and shakes her head instead.

'I have something to tell you,' she says.

She's pregnant. What? No, she's not pregnant. Of course she's not pregnant. Where did *that* thought come from? He has watched too many predictable movies. He has, perhaps, indulged too many unchaste daydreams. But there is no way she is actually pregnant, so he allows himself to joke, because the mood could use lightening, because he hates conflict and awkwardness, because he wants to delay the moment when she will say the thing he might not want to hear.

'Who's the father?'

Libby barely cracks a smile. 'No,' she says. 'That's not what it is.'

'Too bad,' he says. 'An American-born baby could come in useful. You know, for Green Card purposes.'

This time she really does smile. He has not, after all, lost his touch.

'I did something,' she says, and he waits, because surely a more thorough explanation is forthcoming. 'You're gonna hate me,' she says. This does not sound good.

'Spit it out,' he says. He regrets it immediately. He should have said, don't be silly, I'm not going to hate you. I the-opposite-of-hate you. Libby's face falls further, which Thom didn't realise was even possible.

'Someone gave me a lift home. And I accidentally told her you live here.'

'Accidentally.'

'Well. I—'

'Okay.' It is crucial that she stop speaking.

'I'm sorry,' she says. 'I'm really, really sorry. I just—'

'Okay,' he says again, and she looks at him hopefully, as if this okay might be an absolution. But it is not. Thom pictures his assistant, the told-you-so face she will be wearing when he calls her tomorrow with a casual heads up. Libby is waiting. She knows there is more. She wants him to shout, he can tell. She wants the air to be clear. She wants this to be over. So he does the mean thing. The cowardly thing. He turns his back on her and walks away.

***

And then of course – of course! – he feels guilty. Not right away. Libby: invited into his life, so much more than a fangirl, and, it turns out, behaving exactly like a fangirl. He feels betrayed by this. And disappointed, so disappointed: he thought they had more than that kind of relationship. A friendship, a partnership, chemistry. Not *that* kind of chemistry, obviously. He is almost certain, not that kind. Because that would be weird. Or, would it? There's the age thing, obviously. Not insurmountable. But not insignificant. It is all so confusing. He will focus instead on his disappointment, let this fuel his anger. This seems simpler. Simpler, and definitely safer. A couple of hours' worth of anger. Not fury; not enough to make him want to throw things. Just this low grade, 4.5 out of ten niggle that makes him unable to concentrate, that means he rips the pages of *Wired* when he turns them too hard, trying to occupy his mind with other things. He knows he won't sleep if he doesn't calm down, so he tries to tell himself it is not that big a deal. And it isn't, not really. Whoever it was that she told is hardly going to take a full page ad out in the *LA Times* to broadcast his address. And the sad thing is that even if this person did, he is pretty sure hardly anyone would care. His is not the face that sells magazines. He can't be that hard to find as it is, out there on the Internet. It only takes one person to have their location enabled on Twitter when they brag about being at his house for a party. It only takes one loose-lipped realtor, or her one usually trustworthy spouse or best friend she could not wait to tell because they'd been fans of *The Classroom*, back in the day. So the information is probably out there already, and yet no one has used it.

Thom's anger is irrational: he knows this, he tells himself this, and still, it niggles at him. Maybe because he is tired of all this. Tired of living a life where these things matter, or might potentially matter. He knows he chose this. He knows he shouldn't complain. But he wants to complain, sometimes. He misses that about Jenny, that they could vent about these things in the midst of their privilege and they understood each other: the frustration, but also their shame at feeling this frustration, and also their realisation on a rational level that this was all part of the deal, their beautiful house and the great school for their kids and their ability to raise thousands of dollars for worthy causes, and, most of all, the fact that they got to do what they loved, what made them feel the most alive they ever felt, that they got paid to do what others would willingly pay to do. It was all part of the deal, part of the sacrifice, and all things considered and weighed it wasn't much of a sacrifice at all. He misses being understood without having to explain himself and he realises, oddly, that part of the anger he feels toward Libby is about the fact that she doesn't understand him the way Jenny did. He and Jenny belonged in the same world; they were married fourteen years. They had four kids together: middle of the night diaper changes, the frustrations of not knowing what this tiny pink creature could possibly want, pinker and pinker as she screamed and screamed, the anxiety through various illnesses and the parental guilt of the post-immunisation cry: all these things Thom and Jenny shared. Hundreds, thousands of moments that bound them together incrementally, slowly, or sometimes in great leaps: labour, birth. She did all the hard work, of course, and yet somehow those were team efforts. Partnership. A revelatory experience in which both of them lacked the energy to be anything other than completely themselves. Of course he and Jenny know each other on a level so deep that it requires another verb, a much better verb than knowing or understanding. Libby has been in his life for five weeks. He is a fool to expect this kind of depth from his partnership with her.

He thinks about going to the annex, knocking. Saying he's sorry. Maybe, if he can summon more courage than he could a couple of hours ago, trying to explain some of this. But it's late now. She might be asleep. This is why technology was invented. For moments like this. He can text her; she will see his message when she wakes up. Before she has to face him. Before he has to face her.

Libs, he types. *I'm sorry.*

There is no answer. He pictures her, lying on her side, curled into herself, in shorts, a tight t-shirt, fresh faced, no make-up. He has always loved this look on women, the intimacy it implies.

But then there is an answer after all. He sees that she is typing, and then not, and then typing again.

You've got nothing to be sorry about.

In the strictest sense, this is perhaps true. He did not raise his voice to her, much less his hand. He stayed perfectly calm. But he lacked the courage to address the issue. He didn't care enough about her to overcome his discomfort with conflict. He didn't let her see his vulnerabilities. He saw her guilt, her mortification, and he let her wallow in them. He wanted her to wallow in them. He is a terrible person.

I should have stayed and talked it through with you, he says.

I was just so excited. About all this. It slipped out. I'm sorry. If she were speaking these words, she would be saying them in a small voice. Avoiding eye contact. He would be trying to make her smile.

Of course you were! I'm kind of a big deal.

This would, he knows, work better face to face, with the appropriate self-deprecating smile to show he is joking. But he is gambling on the fact that she will be able to picture it. He adds a winky face just in case. He thinks of her smiling. Of her maybe laughing through her nose the way that Ebba—

Ebba.

He has not thought about Ebba all night.

Libby

They have discovered a hole in the plot. The kind of hole that, if you pick and poke at it, unravels the whole thing. Like the time Sophie pulled and pulled on the scarf Libby had been lovingly knitting for her grandmother, and that was that: no Christmas present for Granny that year.

'It doesn't make any sense,' Thom says. 'We lost a year somewhere along the line.'

Libby chews her pencil, tries not to mentally blame Dan for not having picked up on it. Upstairs, a Disney song she can't quite place indicates the kids won't need entertaining for a while, that Libby and Thom have time to work through this. 'It shouldn't be that hard to fix.'

'Yet here we are, day three of trying to fix it, and nada.'

'More coffee?' Behind them, in the kitchen, the machine gurgles as if in acquiescence.

Thom bangs his head on the table. 'We tried that already. We've tried wine. We've tried everything.'

'You don't strike me as the type to give up so easily.'

'Oh,' he says. 'I'm not. You don't make it as an actor unless you're a pretty determined kind of person.'

'Impervious to rejection.'

'Impervious is impossible. But you grow a thick skin.' He shows her a callus on his heel. 'See?'

She laughs to cover her disgust. 'Attractive.'

Thom picks up the index cards they have carefully laid out, each one of them with a scene summarised on it. 'Don't watch,' he says to Libby, and so of course she stares at him when he shuffles the cards.

'Hang on a minute,' she says. 'What are you doing?'

'I told you not to look. I knew you'd freak out.'

'I'm not freaking out. I'm totally calm.'

'Do you even *do* totally calm?'

She stretches out her hand. 'See?' she says. 'No shaking. Totally calm.'

'Nice try,' he says, chuckling. 'I know you better than that by now.'

Her stomach somersaults. He knows her. Whatever happens with this movie, even if they never fix this plot point, they will always have that. He knows her, well enough to tease her. Well enough to see through her. Into her soul.

He lays out the cards in their new order and she watches.

'There,' he says. 'I think that works.'

She looks. She isn't sure about the plot changes, the difference in the order of things. But he has fixed the problem: the Juilliard audition, the pregnancy scare, they all fit into the timeline now.

'Yes,' she says. 'It works. But we're going to have to rewrite a fair bit to accommodate the changes.'

'Then I guess you'll just have to stay longer.'

For ever, Libby thinks. I will stay for ever if you will just ask. His eyes are asking that now, she is sure of it. Locked into hers. Searching her out. Reading her.

'We did it,' he says. 'We're a great team.'

She raises her hand to high-five him, but instead he pulls her into a hug. One of his famous hugs, his tight hugs, his hugs that make you slightly unable to breathe but in the nicest possible way. And then, more unexpectedly still, he kisses the top of her head. She pulls back and looks at him. So handsome. Her hero.

'You're a genius,' she whispers, not sure herself if she is serious or teasing him or some bizarre combination of the two, but not thinking about it too hard because he has not let go of her and her arms are tingling where he is holding her. And his eyes, his beautiful green eyes, they're looking right into her. Later, she will say, I know this is cheesy, but it's like time stopped. Stood still. He leans down and closes his eyes, and touches her lips with his, just barely, a skimming, like an invitation. He opens his eyes, as if looking for permission, and in response she grazes his lips with hers. The kiss deepens gradually, incrementally, like a crescendo. Passion. Sensitivity. Artistry. Libby has never been kissed like this.

They pull back for breath and he laughs, softly. 'Well,' he says. 'I did not see that coming.'

'Didn't you?' The signs were all there, Libby thinks.

'Crap,' he says, under his breath, and her heart lurches, whiplashed. From overwhelming joy to devastating heartbreak in, what, 0.5 seconds? Seriously?

'What?' she says. She wants to ask, that wasn't good for you? But the answer might not be what she wants it to be.

He nods towards the doorway to the living room. Clara leans against the wall, arms crossed.

'So I guess the whole don't be silly Clara, we're just friends thing is over,' she says. 'If it was ever true.'

'It is true,' he says, and Libby's heart sinks further. 'We were just celebrating is all.'

'Dad. *Hi*. I'm not four years old. That is not how co-workers celebrate.'

Thom is looking from daughter to, well, what is she? Co-writer, girlfriend, lover, future wife, random conquest? 'Can you give us a minute?' he says to Libby, eventually.

'Sure,' she says. Like this is normal. Like this is okay. She leaves the room and pulls the door but does not close it. She needs to hear this.

'Listen,' Thom says. 'I don't know what this is yet, okay? I need you to not freak out.'

'You don't know.'

'No.'

'So you're saying you just make out with anyone now?'

'I don't *make out* with people, Clara. I'm not one of your middle school friends. I'm a grown man, trying to figure out my life. I'm not just your dad. I'm a person too.'

If Libby had closed the door completely, it would have made little difference: she would have heard Clara's response loud and clear.

'Is that why you and Mom got divorced? So you could kiss women half your age?'

'Clara,' Thom says. Libby wills him to stay calm. 'Your mom and I divorced because we didn't love each other any more. There will come a time when we love other people.'

'So you love Libby? Is that what you're saying? You're going to marry her and have lots of baby brats with British accents who can't even say my name right?'

Yes, Libby thinks. Yes, that is the plan. Tell her that is the plan.

'Clara. Please.'

'Well? Are you?'

'I think I want to discuss this with Libby before I discuss it with you, if that's okay.'

'What if it's not okay?'

'It will have to be okay.' He has raised his voice, and now lowers it again. 'Look, Clara. I'm sorry that you saw that. I'm sorry that you're confused and hurting, but if it helps, I'm confused too.'

There's no snarky response this time. Just a slammed door on the other side of the room.

Thom

Oh crap.

Oh crap oh crap oh crap.

These are the only words that Thom can correctly form in his mind after Clara slams the door and he is left standing alone in the sunlit room. He doesn't even have the stronger words available, banned as they have been since the birth of that headstrong daughter of his.

Oh crap.

None of this was meant to happen.

Kissing Libby was never part of the plan. He said those things to Jenny to rankle her, to assert his independence, to remind her what divorce actually meant. He has assured Ebba—

Ebba.

Oh, crap.

Why this morning? Why today? The kids were in the house. So irresponsible. Proof to himself, he supposes, that he didn't pre-plan anything. Because if he had pre-planned it, he would have done it on a week with no foreseeable interruptions. But he didn't pre-plan it. He didn't even realise he was attracted to her.

Only, he realised it a little bit.

It's why he avoids looking out of his bedroom window when she goes swimming in the mornings. Also, sometimes, why he doesn't avoid it.

It's why, if he thought about it, he wants this screenplay to be all she wants it to be. He would have changed the ending weeks ago. He gets it, the need for realism. The message of the book: the girl doesn't get the guy, yet they both go on to lead fulfilled, meaningful, relatively happy lives. He gets it. He does. He also gets you've got to have your Hollywood ending. But this is Libby's baby. He doesn't want to say to her, what happens if we yank its arms this way? Dislocate its shoulder so we can better reset it? He doesn't want to cause her that pain.

The door swings open. How much of his conversation with Clara has Libby heard?

'Thom,' she says. Then she stops. She probably doesn't know what to say, and who can blame her? She looks at him with eyes that say, you are my whole world, eyes, he realises, that have said this all along, every day for five weeks, eyes that have begun to win his heart. Because how often can you look into eyes that say those things and not fall in love a little?

'Libs,' he says, and stops too. He needs time. To process. To make decisions. To get his head together. 'I want to say—' What? What is it that he wants to say? He could start with something that is unquestionably true. 'That kiss was quite something.'

She smiles, and this reassures him somewhat. 'It really was.'

'In a good way.' It is important that on this point he is absolutely clear, if only because on the others he will not be. She bites on her lip, and he panics. Please don't cry, he mentally begs her. Please. That won't help anything.

'I don't know what to say, Libs.'

'I'm sorry,' she says.

'What are you sorry for? I'm the one who should be sorry.'

'I'm British. It's what we do in socially awkward situations. We apologise. And then we make tea.'

He wants to laugh, but it seems inappropriate. The humour: another reason he has been attracted to her. Also, and he hates to admit it, the shallowness of it, but it is undeniable: also the Britishness. Probably a Pavlovian throwback to a film he did with Emma Thompson once, fell in love with her a little.

'Okay. Well, I'm the one who's sorry. For dealing with all of this so badly. My daughter, you know…' For not processing my attraction to you, he should probably add, if only he could face that conversation. For allowing it to go unchecked. For not listening to Ebba when she warned me you had convinced yourself you were in love with me and it was all going to go horribly wrong.

Ebba.

Oh, crap.

'You're not sorry we kissed, though?' Thom hopes he is imagining the pleading in her tone. He considers the question. What does sorry mean, exactly? He enjoyed it immensely. He does not regret it, though he does regret its aftermath. He regrets its interruption, which suggests to him that without the interruption things may have progressed. Which would have been an even bigger mess. So maybe the interruption was a good thing. It follows, then, that the kiss was a bad thing, and that he's therefore, maybe, sorry for it?

'It was inappropriate,' he says.

'Inappropriate,' she repeats, like a student of a foreign language twisting a word over and over in her mind, attempting to guess at its meaning.

'You're twenty years younger than me.'

'Nineteen,' she says.

He wants to laugh at this, too. 'Right. That's still a lot of years.'

'It's just a number.'

'A big number. And I have all these kids and I'm still trying to figure out the divorced thing. And—' And, he wants to say but he can't, there's Ebba.

'I get it,' she says, but she is biting her lip again. He is half-expecting the clichéd arguments of long-ago breakups. *But we're so good together! We're meant to be!* And she'd be right. It wasn't just the kiss. It was the way she laughed at his bad jokes, half at him rather than with him, as she shook her head. It was their mind meld, how they sometimes went off separately to work on a scene and then when they compared them they were almost identical. It was the way he felt easy with her, comfortable. Able to be himself. It was the kiss too, though. If the kiss was any indication, they *were* good together. Very, very good.

'I'm sorry,' he says again, and finally he knows what he is really sorry for. 'I'm sorry that I'm just not in the right place for this right now.'

'I get it,' she says again. Not, it's okay. Because it's not okay. He is crushing her dreams with these words. He sees that now. They are crazy dreams, ridiculous dreams, and she is young, and she will get over it, but he knows that doesn't make this moment any less painful for her.

'Maybe you should take the kids out for lunch. I'll go swimming or something.'

It's only eleven and she already swam this morning (not, you understand, that he keeps tabs) but he is hardly in a position to argue.

'Sure,' he says. He lifts her chin with his finger. 'Are you going to be okay?'

'Don't,' she says. Don't what, it is not exactly clear. He aches to hug her. He is not this guy. He does not want to become this guy. He *is* sorry for the kiss, because before the kiss it was fun between them. It was easy. It was deliciously crackling with what he now can't deny was sexual tension. Now it's just a mess.

Libby

She doesn't go swimming, of course. She just wanted him out of the house. She wants them all out of the house. She isn't sure that when she starts to cry and throw things, up there in the garage annex, she won't be heard from elsewhere. She needs this whole horrible thing out of her system: she wishes she could puke it up somehow, flush it away, be done with it after a glass of water and an Extra Strong Mint. She pummels her pillow first, but that is most unsatisfying. She needs to hear her pain echoed back to her: she needs noise. She slams doors. She punches tables.

Now the pain is distributed more evenly: in her wrists as well as her stomach. Then she screams. She allows herself this relief: to scream. Her mouth open wide, wide, as wide as it gets, to let the frustration out. She remembers shouting to angry music in her teens, how that was always cathartic, but sadly these days all she has on her iPod is of the ilk of Norah Jones and Ella Fitzgerald and Newton Faulkner, and they are not shouty people. She wants, badly, to call Vicky. (Although, if we're going with impossible wishes, what she actually wants is a hug from Vicky, a shared evening in front of *Friends* with a tub of Ben and Jerry's Cookie Dough flavoured ice cream.) But she can't call Vicky any more than she can do the other things with her. She can't, because if what she hears is *told you so* she will say some horrible things to Vicky, things she will regret and apologise for but never be able to take back, because you can't, can you? That's the reality of it. (One more reason why reality is overrated.) She can't call Vicky, because she hasn't called her all summer. She doesn't know how things are at work or how Vicky's mum is coping with the chemo. She has walked away from everything and everyone in pursuit of this dream, this dream which has turned out to be made of nothingness. She has been self-centred and selfish, and she has known this all along but pushed it to the back of her mind, promising herself that things will be different in a few months, that this time is for her, for her and Thom, for living her dream. But she is not selfish enough, not self-centred enough, to fail to realise that calling the instant she wants something will not endear her to anyone.

Libby lies on her bed, her king-sized, clean and ironed-sheeted bed, and cries, the ugly kind of crying. The loud kind of crying. The non-film-worthy kind of crying. She cries until she is too exhausted to cry any more. Until her eyes physically hurt and she has to listen to an episode of *The Classroom* rather than watch it because she can't keep them open. She falls asleep halfway through the episode and wakes with a start, jet lagged all over again. Where is she? And then she remembers.

The thing is, though: she wants to finish this screenplay. And she also doesn't want to hate Thom. She doesn't want things to be weird between them. If she can handle this with grace and maturity, maybe he will come to his senses, realise that nineteen years or no nineteen years, he should not just dismiss her out of hand. There are plenty of films, plenty of TV series, where this happens. In *The Classroom*, case in point: Callum finally kisses Sarah, the head of his department and technically his boss. And what does he do? He freaks out. He avoids her. Eventually, he apologises. And two seasons later, they finally get together for real.

So.

She will have to brave-face it.

Teeth-clench it, if she has to.

She will impress him with her poise.

Eventually, he will see sense. Would she have written it this way? Of course not. This setback was not part of The Plan. But what kind of true love doesn't have obstacles to overcome? Stories to tell at the wedding? *I never thought we'd work it out, but…* She can see that it makes a much better story. A better film. A better memoir.

Thom

'Ebba,' Thom says. 'I did something really stupid.'

He was not planning on telling her. He was emphatically, resolutely, definitely not planning on telling her. Yet here they are, at their table on Santa Monica's Third Street promenade, looking at their menus, and he has told her. He said it the way you might say, I think I'll have the bruschetta, half to yourself, while you keep perusing the list for other options, not really to the person you are with but rather in their general direction.

'Tell me you didn't sleep with her.'

He wants to be offended. He really wishes he were justified in his offendedness. But the truth is, if the kids hadn't been in the house that day, then who knows. Now, though, instead of offence he opts for relief. It could have been worse. It could have been so much worse. Or, you know, better, depending how you look at it. Because, really, honestly, it's been a while, and he—

'It was only a matter of time,' Ebba says. She is looking at the wine list. He really should have made sure they both had wine already before he started this conversation. If he'd planned it. But the thing is, he did not. He emphatically, resolutely, definitely did not. He wasn't going to tell her today; he maybe wasn't going to tell her ever. Sure, once upon a time they promised, no secrets. But that was before: before all her Ethan secrets. It was also when they were young and naïve and idealistic and not fully aware of the complexities of life. It was when they were in love, which—

'I'll have the Sauvignon Blanc from New Zealand,' Ebba says at last. She always has the Sauvignon Blanc from New Zealand. It baffles him that she spends so long looking at the wine list and then always picks the same thing. In another life, he might have found that grating. Not in this one. In this one it is endearing. It is one of the things he loves knowing about her.

'I didn't sleep with her,' he says. It is important to clarify. She is being impressively calm, but still, there are degrees of stupidity. He wants to make sure she knows where on a scale of one to ten his own personal brand of stupidity falls. A seven, maybe? Not a ten, though. That is the important thing.

'Oh,' she says. She does not seem particularly repentant for her erroneous assumption.

'I kissed her is all.'

'Oh,' Ebba says again. She is the one on the back foot now. This is going remarkably well, all things considered. 'That's all.'

'Yes.'

'Because it's been a really long time for you,' she says, working her way through the entrée section of the menu now, following each line with her finger. 'So I wouldn't have blamed you.'

He sighs with inexpressible, unexpected relief. It has not been as long as she thinks, but now seems like an inconvenient time to mention this. 'Thank you.'

But she looks up from the menu and her eyes are not the eyes of someone who doesn't blame him. Her eyes are sharp with fury.

'What are you,' she says. Levelly. Without raising her voice. 'Some kind of idiot?'

'Some kind, I guess.' He is not really in a position to argue. But still, he is a little confused. 'You said you wouldn't blame me!'

'I changed my mind.'

'Woman's prerogative?'

'Exactly.'

He makes eye contact with the waitress. Save me, he tries to say with his eyes. Come quickly and save me from this conversation. She's college-aged, working a summer job to pay for acting school or her MFA in screenwriting, probably.

'Just your type, isn't she?' Ebba says, nodding towards the waitress as she walks away after they order. Ebba has asked for an hors d'oeuvre: joy of joys, this means a longer meal.

'She's blonde, so no.'

'She's young.'

'Ouch,' Thom says. He needs badly to regain control over this conversation. 'You didn't used to be this snarky.'

'You didn't used to be this lecherous.'

'C'mon,' he says. 'That's not fair.'

Ebba arches an eyebrow.

'Okay, it's a little bit fair. But I hate when you're mad at me.'

'Oh,' she says. 'I was doing it for your enjoyment all this time.'

'Ebs,' he says. 'Look.'

The waitress brings the wine; this is blissfully fast. Ebba takes a sip, then another. Thom waits. He waits because he isn't sure what he is going to say, but also he waits for the wine to work its magic. Its mellowing magic, he sincerely hopes.

'Yes?' she says at last.

'Help me out here,' he says.

'Why would I do that?' The edge has gone from her voice.

'Friendship.' This is remarkably restrained of him. What he really wants to say is, because you still love me. Look how jealous you are. Another time he might have said that. To tease her. To test the waters. To watch her blush: she was cute when she blushed. But not today. Today is definitely not the time for that. 'The thing is, she's being totally normal. Like nothing happened.'

'And it's freaking you out.'

He considers this. 'It's freaking me out a little bit.'

'Because you keep expecting her to lose it.'

'Yes.' He knew Ebba would be good at this.

Ebba shakes her head and takes another couple of sips. 'Thom,' she says. 'Thom, Thom, Thom.'

'Um,' he says. 'Yes?' He is not sure of the proper response to this inexplicable repetition of his name.

'She is trying to impress you.'

'Impress me.'

'With her mature reaction. Yes. Writers are nothing if not epic daydreamers. And, you've read the novel, right? The one you're making into a film?' He nods. This seems to him like an entirely superfluous question, but he is a little afraid to interrupt. 'The impossible relationship in it? I assume you realise it's basically a love letter to you?'

'A love letter?'

The bruschetta has arrived and she begins to tear at it with her knife and fork, aggressively pushing the topping back on when it slides off. With your hands, is the only way to eat the thing. That much is glaringly obvious. Still, he decides he will pick his battles.

'She probably thinks, that was the plot twist. A kiss everyone regrets. Like in *The Classroom*, remember? Then everything gets sorted out before the end and everyone gets to be happy ever after.'

He ponders this.

'Wait,' she says. 'You kissed her and then what? Because that doesn't make sense. You just stopped? You told her it was inappropriate?'

'Yes,' he says. He'll maybe leave out the part about Clara until Ebba's second glass of wine.

'That's straight out of *The Classroom*,' she says. 'You are not making it easy for her to distinguish between fact and fiction.'

'It's not like I planned it,' he says. Weakly.

'Uh huh.'

Over entrées, he tells her about the latest complication: Jenny. Well, technically, Juliette, but he isn't about to blame his seven-year-old, who was innocently playing with her Barbies in the living room. Or, maybe not as innocently as he would like. She banged the faces of Barbie and Ken together in a vague approximation of a kiss – with, of course, the required sound effects – and then put on the lowest voice she could for Ken: 'Oh, crap.' Clara was only too happy to enlighten their mother as to what it was, exactly, that Juliette was re-enacting. Clara, of course, was the one to have told Juliette what had happened in the first place. Jenny was furious. 'I want her out of the house,' she said. 'I'm not sending you the kids if she's there. What kind of an example is that to set them?'

'And now you want me to help you out,' Ebba says.

'Yes.'

'How, exactly? You want me to explain the inner workings of a woman's brain?'

'Well, if you could, that would be extraordinarily helpful.'

'Extraordinarily is a very long word,' she says.

'You're drunk,' Thom says.

'This is only my third glass.'

'You always were a lightweight.'

'Things change.'

'Some things don't.' He squeezes her feet between his under the table. Ebba looks at him: a question. A slightly inebriated question, and he wants to answer it, and tonight could have been the night for just such questions, for just such answers, if he had picked the conversation topic a little more wisely.

'She's in love with you,' Ebba says, looking into his eyes. 'It is not complicated.'

'It is a little complicated. Given, you know, that she lives in my house and that we spend all day every day together.'

'And given her age.'

Thom looks at his watch. 'It's been a while since you mentioned that. Like, at least ten minutes.'

'It's an important part of the equation.' Ebba closes her eyes and rubs at her temple. 'Are you attracted to her?'

Here is where it gets tricky. Or, you know, where it would get tricky if it weren't already.

'She is not an unattractive young woman.'

'Young.'

'And vivacious and smart.'

'And she admires you and adores you and that's a little attractive too.'

He might as well admit it. 'Yes.'

Ebba shakes her head. 'Men.'

'Yeah, yeah.'

'She can stay with me on the weeks when you have the kids, if you want.'

'You're drunk.'

'Nope. Third glass.'

Already some of the weight has lifted from Thom's shoulders. 'We'll talk about it in the morning,' he says.

'In the morning?'

He realises too late what he has said. That all week he has been thinking tonight was going to be the night, that he has even told Libby that he will be gone till morning for an 'event', and despite how it has gone, this night, his subconscious was still there, in that place, ready. His subconscious is not the only part of him that is ready.

'I'll call you,' he says. 'Is what I mean.'

'Oh,' she says. 'Of course.' Thom thinks he can hear disappointment in her voice, but he is probably imagining it.

'I should take you home,' he says after dessert. If he needed proof that she is too drunk to drive, he has it when the check comes and she doesn't protest at his paying all of it.

In the car, leaning against the window and closing her eyes, she says, 'Remember our make-up sex? Our make-up sex was the best of all the sex.'

Yes. He remembers. But he has to focus on the road. Focus, focus, focus, he says under his breath. Down, boy. The focus gets him to her street. It gets him to her door. It gets him just inside.

'I'm not so drunk that I've forgotten how I feel about you,' Ebba says, and that's it, he can't take it any more. Leaning against her front door with her, the two of them like teenagers who just can't wait, just can't help themselves, he kisses her. Furiously. Passionately. She tastes of wine and garlic and tomatoes and deliciousness.

'Are you still mad at me?' he asks her.

'I'm really, really mad.'

'Good.' He leads her to the bedroom. 'That's the best way.'

Libby

The name Annabelle Harrison sits in Libby's inbox that morning. A name that is vaguely familiar, that reminds her of hope, the way a splash of perfume brings to mind a family gathering from long ago, perhaps a favourite great aunt you haven't seen since you were five. Libby clicks on the message and remembers as she does so: Annabelle Harrison, yes, of course. Ebba's editor.

In the excitement of everything, in the heartbreak and the rollercoaster of everything, the actual bookishness of the book has slipped her mind. It is not that she has given up on it, exactly, nothing as active as that. But her dreams now are of her name across a screen, alongside Thom's. Of a glittering première in an expensive ball gown, arm in arm with her tuxedoed hero. She doesn't think, any more, about the tables at Waterstones. She doesn't imagine the spines of books, her finger running across the faintly embossed titles.

Still, the email is not nothing. Annabelle apologises: she went on maternity leave, got behind, has struggled to keep up with submissions. And she says that she has to be honest that when Ebba asked her to take a look at the novel, she wasn't overly enthusiastic. But now that she has, she is pleasantly surprised. She likes the ending, she says: it is full of hope.

'See,' Libby says to Thom when she tells him. 'Hope! She gets it. It's not all about whether she gets the man.'

'I never said I didn't get it, Libs. Just that Hollywood doesn't. This is wonderful news.'

'I know,' she says, and she feels herself breaking into the kind of grin that will later make her jaw ache.

He raises his coffee mug to toast her. 'Congratulations,' he says.

'Nothing's definite yet.' She wants to be cautious, to protect her heart. She is learning that this summer. Re-learning it.

'She read your book to the end, Libs. Editors just don't do that.'

'True.'

'Did you tell Dan yet?'

'Dan?'

This is a word that does not belong in this universe. It is not a California word. It is a London word. It jolts her, the way mistakes jolt you out of a film or a book: Cockfosters isn't in Zone Four, the Central Line isn't blue, and suddenly you are aware of the author, of the author's fallibility, aware that what you are reading is just a story, and the magic is interrupted. Damaged. Broken. She has never mentioned Dan to Thom, not once. It hasn't been a deliberate omission; Dan has just never been relevant.

'I didn't realise I'd mentioned Dan to you.'

'He didn't tell you that he'd emailed me?'

Libby shakes her head. This makes no sense.

'After I emailed you that first time. He emailed me to check I was legit.'

'Oh.'

She is thinking, what? He did *what*? She remembers the email she forwarded to him. She remembers the certainty with which he told her that she should go, that it was all fine. She didn't question it at the time: she had so wanted to believe in the fairy tale. She can't decide if she is touched or annoyed. Touched by the way Dan has looked out for her. The way he has always looked out for her, carrying her stuff after she'd broken her leg skiing over the Christmas holidays, risking – and incurring – the wrath of the Powers That Were for taking the lecturers-only lift with her when they had their ten o'clock up on the top floor of Lecture Block A. Annoyed at him for going behind her back, for not telling her he had been exchanging emails with Thom. But touched again because he did it with the best of intentions. He has always been kind to her. It is in his nature to be kind.

'Dan,' she says. 'Yes.'

'He seems to care about you a lot.'

'We've been friends for a long time.'

'Just friends?'

Libby hesitates. Not because she and Dan are anything other than just friends, but because she wonders why Thom has asked. Is he jealous? Can she make him jealous? But no. She is not that person. 'Yes,' she says. 'Just friends.'

'You should email him,' Thom says. 'You should forward him the message from Annabelle. He'll be so happy for you.'

'Yes,' she says. 'I'll do that. He works in publishing, so he'll get what a big deal this is.'

But she doesn't. Her fingers hover over the 'forward' button and she thinks, maybe later. I'll tell him in person. Later.

Ebba

This is awkward, having Libby stay with her. Ebba should probably have foreseen the awkwardness of it. If she's honest, maybe she did. Maybe she just wants Libby out of Thom's house as much as possible. Which is ridiculous, right? To be jealous of someone who could (just about, at a push) be her daughter? Yes, it's ridiculous, of course it's ridiculous, but that doesn't make it any less real. It's not like *nothing* has happened between them. Sure, it was just a kiss, just (he swears) that one time. But things are so new between Thom and Ebba still. She doesn't want to jinx anything. Breathe on a relationship wrong at this stage and it could disappear as if it had never existed, and that's because it hasn't, not really.

It's odd, the newness. That something, that someone, could be so familiar and yet so new. It's what the passing of time does, she supposes, the passing of time and the things it throws at us, the way those things test us and make us stronger. The children we have or don't have, the ones we briefly have before they die inside of us, taking a part of us with them, a part of us that gets replaced with this curious alloy of grief and guilt, the guilt everyone says you mustn't feel but you somehow can't let go of because it's all you have left of this child, this child you wanted so much. Then there are the children we watch our partners, our ex-partners now, bring into the world with someone else and the long path to accepting the fact that it wasn't exactly that they didn't want a baby, but that they didn't want one with us.

And you don't know until it happens to you whether you will be strong enough for both of you when your talented partner discovers he needs amphetamines to write, and then just to be. When he finally breaks free of them, but finds he has forgotten how to write without them and seeks comfort in the arms of another woman. Another woman, who is not the one who has stood by him over many years of insomnia, of mood swings, of paranoia, of rehab. When he finds that even the comfort of this other woman is not enough, that he can no longer choose between addiction and writing on one hand and emptiness on the other, and takes one final overdose of the drug that destroyed him, that destroyed his life and now claims it.

But when you find out that you are strong enough, or that somewhere along the way you have become strong enough, it changes you. That is what Ebba wanted the message of her memoir to be. It is a love letter to Ethan, to the Ethan she loved before fame and success and infidelity and drugs took him, but it is also an encouragement to her readers: you are stronger than you think you are. You can survive more than you think you can. So she is not the same Ebba she was in her sophomore year when she worked in the video store on the Upper West Side that Thom came to every week until he finally worked up the courage to ask her out, to see a Shakespeare play: you'll see, he said, Shakespeare in Central Park, there's nothing like it. And Thom, she guesses, is not the same either. Money and relative fame do not appear to have changed him, but she is on the lookout for signs, because that seems unlikely to her. Marriage and fatherhood have deepened his thoughtfulness, his capacity to listen, which she loved in him even way back when that thoughtfulness did not quite extend to the practical details of life. He looks tired, permanently tired, but he is still funny. Some of the humour is self-deprecating, born, perhaps, from the sting of failure and from bitterness, but she still laughs with him more than she has ever laughed with anyone else.

But they have to be careful. They don't want Libby to know. They have agreed on this, each of them unable to articulate exactly why. Fear, mostly, of various kinds: of confrontation, of hurting her, of being the bad guys, of messiness. She is passed from Ebba to Thom as though she were herself the child of divorced parents, each of them circumspect when they are seeing the other, referring to each other as 'a friend'. *I'm having dinner with a friend tonight. I'm going away with a friend this weekend.* Libby has no reason to suspect. Of course they both have plenty of friends in the LA area, where they have lived for years, close to two decades, almost as long as Libby has been alive. With Thom she is still putting the finishing touches on the screenplay (how long does that take, exactly, Ebba wants to ask), and they are trying to sell it. On the weeks she is with Ebba, Libby goes for long walks on the beach and works on her second novel. Ebba works on her third book; the launch party for her novel is just a few weeks away and she is nervous and excited. Libby and Ebba talk about life, about writing, about books: Elena Ferrante, Colum McCann, Toni Morrison. Stay, Ebba sometimes finds herself about to say. Stay with me and we can be writers together and I can give you the love and affection I was never able to give to a daughter. But then she remembers the mess, she remembers the irrational but very present jealousy, she remembers that she is hiding the deepest and one of the most defining parts of herself from this young woman. This young woman who has so much life ahead of her, but who will feel as if that life has ended when she learns of the secret. So it's awkward. And Ebba wishes it weren't.

Libby

Promotion!

That's all the status update says on Dan's Facebook wall. Ever the man of few words. Underneath, eighty-seven likes and twenty-four comments. *Congrats*, they say, and (from his mum), *Finally!* and *Tell us more!* But of course, because it's Dan, he doesn't tell them more, at least not there, not in public, not where Libby can read it. She wants to know; of course she does. He is part of her DNA – they all are – Vicky and Nicola and Matthew and Ollie and Liam and Charlotte, and the others who have come and gone through the years, attached and detached from the group according to which staircase they lived on or whose supervision partner they were or who they rowed with. They're part of what makes Libby the person she feels she is. They have formed each other, shaped each other. They don't need to be in constant touch. News filters through the various connections eventually; nobody is going to forget you just because you go off-radar for a few weeks. And yet, Libby feels uneasy. She feels a twinge of regret for, of all places, the Chandos. She wants to toast Dan with the others, to congratulate him. But she also imagines herself nudging him, saying to him, you did it without me, then? You didn't need to discover me in order to make it. It would just be a joke, she is almost certain. Of course he doesn't need her: there are hundreds of Hot Young Authors out there, waiting, desperate. She googles his agency, clicks under 'News'. Nothing there yet. Dan is still listed as an agent's assistant.

Message me, she types under the Facebook update. *I want to know everything!* Then to silence the voice in her ear, Charlotte's voice, for some reason – it's not all about you all the time, Libby – she edits the comment so that it starts *Congrats! So proud of you!* And then she waits and she waits, checking Facebook more obsessively than usual. She has hardly been online since coming to California – because of the time difference, because of the cognitive dissonance, because she wants to be fully present in each moment, taking in every detail, every word Thom says, every subtle change in the way he smells. But now she finds herself picking up her phone when they take a break from writing, or when Thom goes to make coffee, or in the car on the way to lunch in Old Town Pasadena. It bothers her that she can't seem to stop herself checking, even when she knows that it's night time in England. It bothers her that Dan is intruding, somehow, on her Thom time. Eventually, after two days, she messages him. *Hey, stranger! Tell me about the promotion!* She sees that he has read the message almost instantly, but it's another day before he responds. This is so unlike him. Too busy for her already now he's moving up in the literary world? Now his dreams are becoming reality?

I found us a great client, he writes, eventually. *And there was an auction, and we got a BIG advance for her book.*

That's great! Libby writes, forcing enthusiasm with the exclamation mark, but she is thinking, that was supposed to be me. She doesn't write it, of course. She hates herself for even having this thought. *Who is she?* she types instead, not even sure if it's okay to ask, okay for Dan to tell her. But he sends her the link to her website. She is stunning, of course, curly black hair framing a face of high cheekbones and ridiculously straight teeth and Libby wonders if he has slept with her and then is appalled with herself for wondering. Dan has integrity, too much to mix the professional and the personal like this. He has never been the type to sleep around. So this girl is gorgeous: so what? He knows good writing. Her looks aren't why he picked her book off the slush pile. They certainly aren't why there was a bidding war. She wonders briefly what it says about her that she would suspect his motives like this. Only briefly, though: to linger there would be uncomfortable.

You found your Hot Young Author? she writes, trying to bring the playfulness back into their relationship.

She's really talented. I couldn't put her book down.

Again, a twinge of something in her gut. She considers telling him about Ebba's editor. I'm a real writer now too, she thinks. But she'll wait. She'll wait until it's final and she can really wow him.

You have a good eye. Thanks for everything you did for me and my book.

He doesn't respond. Libby isn't ready for the conversation to end yet.

How's life otherwise? It frustrates her that he posts so little on Facebook. His life is going on without her, he's making new friends, like that Caroline person, smiling in a sundress in a picture with him, and she feels shut out. She knows she is being ridiculous, that Libby and Dan are Libby and Dan, that they will always be Libby and Dan, Caroline or no Caroline, and Caroline can't possibly be his girlfriend, can she, someone would have told Libby? She wants to say, I miss you, but this is not exactly true. She has really only messaged him to quiet her unease.

Good, he says. *Life is good.* A pause. *You?*

She has become an afterthought.

Great, she says, because obviously. Everything is going according to plan. They've had their hiccup, she and Thom. Now it's just a matter of time.

Ebba

Thom calls to say he has made reservations for dinner, and after Ebba puts the phone down the word echoes in her mind. Reservations. Reservations. Reservations. Like a warning. Like an omen.

'I have reservations,' he said, and paused to sneeze, so that in the horrifying intervening second she thought he was breaking up with her. She debated, a few sentences later, whether to tell him this, whether they could or should laugh together at the thought of it. The thought there is anything at all to hesitate about when life has so clearly given them this, their second chance, and that is surely all the evidence they need. She decided against telling him, but perhaps as punishment the word chills her even after she puts the phone down.

Reservations. She'd had plenty when he'd Facebooked her out of nowhere, two summers ago, wanting to talk about her book, wanting to catch up. She'd had them and silenced them, out of curiosity, maybe, some sort of challenge to fate, some sort of tribute to her former self. She had wondered if, after the divorce, he would be broken, bitter. She had wondered if he had forgiven her for leaving him all those years ago, for choosing the path that was not only the harder one but also, she sees now, the wrong one.

Now she has other reservations. He has all these kids – four kids! – and to go from zero to four without even babyhood years in which to get acclimated to these new people seems terrifying. Small people, yes, but they take up so much space. Thom talks about them, sometimes incessantly. Clara's viola playing, Rosie's devouring of books, Juliette growing up so fast, how can she be seven already? Harry, most of all Harry, his mischievousness, the way Thom can't bring himself to scold him quite as much as might be appropriate.

Dive in, her favourite aunt used to say, as she stood at the edge of the swimming pool, all in one go, don't think too hard. But she always ended up climbing down the ladder instead, getting progressively colder instead of freezing all at once. It felt more comfortable that way. It felt kinder to herself. There would be nothing comfortable about walking into Thom's life, now, his fully formed if slightly disjointed life as the kids came and went between their two homes, between their two real parents to whom she could never compare, this club of two not open for new admissions. Jenny has succeeded where Ebba has not, in romance, yes, in her life with Thom, in the producing and bringing up of these children of whom he is proud, but also professionally. Jenny has made her name on network TV. People have heard of her. Ebba loves the stage. She feels, truth be told, slightly superior about it as a medium, about the acting that is required there, the roles that seem somehow worthier of her training from the Yale School of Drama. But outside of the narrow theatre world and the few people who recognise authors from the pictures on their book jackets, she is an unknown. Most of the time this suits her fine: she can have a life, go about her business, sit in coffee shops and write. But sometimes, when she sees Jenny's name on a TV screen she feels a pang of something she is not proud of. Unworthiness. Inferiority. Jealousy.

Reservations, maybe.

Dan

Libby has been commenting on Dan's Facebook posts. This he finds unhelpful. He would prefer not to think about her. For the first time in his adult life, he actually wants to forget her, he thinks maybe he can, and she will not let him.

He wants to because Caroline is beautiful, and sexy, and interesting. She is also what he has always believed to be a creature as mythical as the unicorn: a low-maintenance girlfriend. She does not – or at least not yet, let's not get ahead of ourselves, he tells himself – make unreasonable demands of him (unless you count plentiful sex, which is hardly unreasonable, and he takes gratefully as his due after all those barren years). She has a life outside him, and he likes this. Wednesdays she has fencing, Fridays she plays badminton, and every other Monday she has one book club or another. She lives in Fulham, just a couple of stops from Putney on the District Line or a walk across the river, so it's easy to see her during the week, and they spend Saturdays together, reading the paper at Costa or going on day trips to places like Hampton Court or Windsor: dreamy places, slightly magical places, places he always said he would go to with Libby, but Libby is far away and has forgotten about those plans, though she clearly has not forgotten about him.

The problem with a low-maintenance girlfriend, with a girlfriend who does not demand to be included in all of his activities or make him feel guilty for not taking part in hers, is this: it leaves him with a lot of free time, still. A lot of thinking time. Far too much thinking time. He goes to the gym a couple of times a week like he always has, but that, of course, does not stop him thinking. Even when he listens to podcasts, *Books and Authors* by the BBC or *Guardian Books*, his mind wanders back to Libby. It is probably Pavlovian: he used to come to the gym a lot to try to rid his mind of her, to burn up some of the frustration that seemed to accumulate in every muscle of his body when they would meet up and still she would not say anything about that night on the Tube platform, and yet again neither would he. He didn't know who frustrated him the most: himself for his cowardice, his fear of rejection, his eternal over-caution and risk-aversiveness, or her for just ignoring him, for not at least thanking him or giving him recognition for baring his soul. Instead she ripped that soul right out of him when she got on the Tube that night, and the gym gave him somewhere to attempt to heal, which he realises is a bit absurd; you don't heal a heart by building up muscle. It turns out you don't quieten your mind that way, either. But you do get fit and toned and he likes his new body. He likes running to the bus without being out of breath. And he likes Caroline's appreciation of it; so there's that, at least.

But the moment he gets on the treadmill he thinks about Libby. He thinks about her, how tanned she must be by now, like she was at the end of the group holiday to Greece after their second year at Cambridge. She wore a white top then – a halterneck, he thinks it might be called – at their last dinner and she looked golden to him. Honey-coloured. He so wanted to taste the honey. But then the conversation turned – as it always, somehow, did, when she was around – to the latest episode of *The Classroom*, and the fresh courage he had begun to talk himself into feeling seeped away as she talked about Thom, that it was a shame he was married, because she wouldn't kick him out of bed, and had they all seen his latest literacy advocacy video, and wasn't he great. One day, Dan was sure, she would snap out of her dream world, this teenage world of the celebrity crush and that would be the time to tell her how much her skin looked like honey. But look where that strategy has got him. He is still waiting.

Well, except not, he reminds himself. He is not waiting any more; he has found Caroline. Low maintenance. Sexy. She will be waiting for him when he gets back from the gym. She will have bubbly anecdotes about her actual life, which beats excited daydreams about some ridiculous hypothetical future. Beats it hands down. He will pour glasses of wine for the two of them and he will, again, forget about Libby, for a few hours, maybe even days. He is sure he could do whole days if she would just stop reminding him she is there. In California. Honey-skinned.

Libby

Ebba's house is not as luxurious as Thom's, not by a long shot, but Libby likes it there. There is no swimming pool, but, even better, the beach is fifteen minutes' walk away, and so her morning swims have simply been relocated. She misses Thom, but it's a relief to let her guard down. To not feel as if she has to plaster on a mask each morning, pretend everything is just dandy, as they say over here (don't they?), when she has this mass of emotions swirling inside her that she doesn't know how to name, much less deal with. She can't talk to Ebba about them, not yet, though she wishes she could, that it weren't so potentially awkward. Sometimes she laughs at the absurdity of her own situation: she's living with the long-ago ex-girlfriend of the man she has been obsessing over for her entire adult life. Which is not weird. Not at all. But for longer and longer stretches of time, she forgets this about Ebba. Ebba becomes a person, the way she did when Libby read her memoir and wanted to climb inside the pages and hug her. The two of them spend long evenings together drinking wine and eating olives and cheese on the porch, talking often about books, sometimes about Europe, sometimes about Thom: Ebba tells Libby stories from long ago, and because it is long ago, it is not threatening. It does not twist her gut into knots but rather makes her smile, makes her love him a little more.

In the daytime, they sit at Ebba's dining room table and write. Ebba's second book comes out in a couple of weeks and Libby can't wait for the launch party: another new thing to be excited about in this improbably charmed new life of hers.

Libby is sketching out ideas for her second novel, but mainly writing about this summer, a memoir of her own, because when all this is resolved everyone is going to be curious about the young woman who won the heart of (in her, of course, totally unbiased opinion) the most desirable man in Hollywood. About how she did this despite not fitting the traditional image of the blonde and beautiful trophy wife. It was the accent, she will joke at parties, Thom's tuxedoed arm resting around her waist. He never really stood a chance. She's just charming, isn't she, they would go away saying to each other, Matthew Perry and Lauren Graham, I hope it lasts, I hope he gets to be happy again. He seems pretty happy now.

Things are always a little strained on those Mondays when she returns to Thom's. There is, firstly, that moment of greeting, condemned to awkwardness by Anglo-Saxon culture which has given its members no universal norm for approaching it: do we hug? Shake hands? Just stand there uncomfortably and murmur, hi? Thom and Libby almost always opt for this last choice, and her heart sinks when he suppresses what she knows to be his natural instinct for touch. How was your week, they each ask, respond in generalities. But the break from each other, from the awkwardness of the situation, has done them good, and by lunchtime they are laughing again, self-consciously at first and then more freely. By the time she leaves at the end of the week and makes the trek across the city, there is sadness in her voice and she sees affection in his eyes. It is okay. It will be okay. The next kiss will not be too long coming, and this time there will be no interruption. There will be no apology. There will no false start.

It probably won't be this week, though, because this week, Clara is around. Around, and miserable. Her mother has taken the others to Disneyland for Rosie's tenth birthday and she's had to stay because of stupid orchestra practice. Thom has not hidden from Libby that he is raging at the unfairness of it, too, but tries not to show it to his daughter. Still, doubtless this very unfairness gave him the moral upper hand when he argued that Libby should come work with him this week, because this was the appointed week and it wasn't his fault that Jenny had messed up the system she herself had imposed. He may not have mentioned to Jenny, though, that he has asked Libby to keep an eye on Clara when he goes out to play tennis. It seems pointless to hire a babysitter.

'Clara hates me,' Libby points out to Thom. The words have tumbled out of her mouth before she is able to think about stopping them. They are not in keeping with her resolution to be the low-maintenance girlfriend.

'I wouldn't take it personally,' Thom says, lightening the mood.

'She hates everyone at the moment. You don't have to entertain her or anything. Just make sure she doesn't burn the house down.'

Libby has a vision of the curtains in flames, the house engulfed, like in the fire safety video they had been forced to watch in freshers' week, which had effectively ensured she never used a scented candle for the rest of her life.

'It's a figure of speech, Libs.' Thom seems amused; she must have looked horrified. 'You'll be fine.'

When he leaves there is, predictably, uncomfortable silence.

'So it's no fun being left behind, huh?'

Clara shrugs. 'You talking about me or you?'

'What do you mean?'

'You wish you were going out with Dad tonight.' It's not a question. Oh, to be twelve years old again and so sure you know how the world works.

'I meant you,' Libby says.

'It's kinda pathetic the way you look at him,' Clara continues, undeterred. She walks to the fridge and helps herself to Coke. She is not allowed Coke at her mother's and Thom is determined to be the fun parent. Libby ponders how to respond.

'How was orchestra practice?' she tries eventually.

Clara shrugs again. 'It was okay.'

'Violin, right?'

Oh, the look of disdain. 'Viola.'

This is not going well.

'You like playing?'

'I like Disney more.'

'You know what I think?' Libby doesn't pause long enough for Clara to inform her that she doesn't particularly care what Libby thinks. 'I think you're too old for Disney.'

'Nobody's too old for Disney.' She might as well add, shows how much *you* know. Some step-mom *you*'d make.

'Well, of course.' She won't cry. She won't. She won't be defeated by a twelve-year-old. 'But the others, they're going to want to do the little kid things. You're much too cool for those now.'

Clara considers this. 'You do maybe have a point there.'

'Thank you.' Libby sounds triumphant in spite of herself.

'No problem.' Automatic politeness. Nothing more. But a civil exchange. Progress.

'Listen,' Libby says. 'I was going to watch *High School Musical* tonight. Want to watch it with me?'

'You?' Clara raises her eyebrows and it's almost shocking how much she looks like her father in that moment. 'Aren't you a little old for that?'

'I have gaps in my cultural knowledge,' Libby says, attempting to sound dignified and probably failing.

'You mean you want to bond with me.' Clara air-quotes the 'bond'.

'I just know that if my parents and siblings went to Disney without me, I'd be feeling pretty rubbish. And I'd want a fun movie and ice cream to cheer me up.' She even says 'movie'. She has to get credit for speaking American, surely.

'We're out of ice cream.'

'I have ice cream. Upstairs. If you want to share. Or I can just let you have it if you want to be alone.'

'No, it's okay.' Libby has long suspected that ice cream has actual magical powers, and this seems to confirm it. 'Let's do it. Plus, I think we have some popcorn somewhere.'

'Okay. You get the popcorn and the soda' – she mentally collects the brownie point for the American word here too – 'and I'll get the ice cream and the nail polish.'

'Nail polish?'

'Well, sure. Isn't that what you do when you watch a movie? Once you've eaten all the popcorn and ice cream?'

'I guess it could be.' She is smiling. She is actually smiling. Libby has got Clara to smile, and it takes every ounce of self-control to wait until she is upstairs in her apartment, collecting the ice cream, to do a little victory dance. She does the dance again at the end of the night after Thom comes home to find them laughing, blowing on their nails to dry them faster.

'You know,' she hears Clara say to Thom, loudly enough that she is pretty sure it is intended for her ears too, 'she's not as bad as I thought.'

'You guys had fun together?'

'It wouldn't be so terrible if she stayed around for a while.'

'We'll see, Pumpkin.' That's the last Libby hears of the conversation. She hears it over and over in her head before the sugar rush and the high of victory eventually wear off and sleep starts to creep up on her.

We'll see.

The way you do in another chapter, the one at the end of the book where everything is resolved: we'll see.

This isn't over.

Thom

This is just what Thom needs. Clara deciding she likes Libby and wants her around. One more person he will have to comfort when she leaves, as if it isn't bad enough that he will be hurting himself and can't even quite pinpoint why. Mostly he is angry with himself for not seeing this whole saga coming and for failing to adequately safeguard against it. A little, too, he worries that he did see it coming, that he wanted it to happen, that if it hadn't been for Ebba… He is grieving, perhaps, for his lost youth, for the twenty-five-year-old who would have enjoyed Libby's company and been able to take that enjoyment further. Grieving, too, for the way life takes you down one path to the exclusion of all the others. And then he feels guilty, because he should not be having these thoughts. This early in a relationship, especially, he should be besotted, obsessed. And he is. He is those things. Really.

It will be easier once Libby has gone. But perhaps the other thing he feels is fear, because what if it isn't? What if he misses her? What if this was all a gigantic mistake and it was Libby he was meant to be with? She appeared in his life the way a fairy godmother does at the darkest moment in children's stories. It could have been a fairy tale for him too. Maybe he missed it. What if he missed it?

And the strangest thing of all is that Ebba will miss her too. He knows this because of the way she talks about Libby: with tenderness, with affection, almost as if she were her daughter.

Ebba has not met his kids yet. For the most part, he is not worried. They have not told anyone about their relationship: it's still too fragile, it's too miraculous, and they worry about Jenny. They worry about Clara. They worry, most of all, about Libby. They know they should tell her before they tell anyone else, and they dread this. The lump in Thom's throat in anticipation is the same lump that sat there until he told the kids about the divorce. That night turned out to be every bit as bad as he imagined it would be, slammed doors and endless tears, so is there any reason to imagine this will be any different? What are they supposed to do, take Libby out for a milkshake and begin, we have something to tell you, hope she fills in the gaps herself so they don't have to watch her face fall as they say the words?

No. He can't do this again, so soon: have his words destroy someone else's world, watch her shoulders slump and her face cloud over. He can't do it. He is pretty sure Ebba can't do it either, and that is why she has said to him, we'll tell her together or we won't tell her at all.

And now, as well as doing this to Libby, he has to do it to Clara too? It was going to be hard enough for her to accept Ebba as it was. Now Ebba will not just be replacing her mother, but also Libby, whom she clearly likes more than she is letting on, because that is her way.

Thom wants to sleep through the next six weeks. Wake up to find the knots untied and an email from Libby telling him she has a boyfriend, maybe the friend who emailed him that time. But that is not how life works. He will have to drink the milkshakes. He will have to watch the faces fall. He will have to hate himself for a while.

At least this time, he won't be alone.

Libby

For once, Libby's sister Iona has Facebooked Libby. A private message, of course, waiting for her when she comes out of the shower after her morning swim. Iona isn't much of a Facebooker in the traditional way: she is much too self-effacing, much too discreet. One of the many ways in which they are opposites of each other. Libby has repeated the mantra for years now: we're different and I respect that. But she isn't really sure if she has ever respected it, much less understood it. Still, though, Libby wishes, sometimes, even now in California – perhaps especially now – for those too-rare nights when she would sit on Iona's bed and tell her about the boy she had a crush on or the meanness of the girls who always picked her last for teams in Games. Iona always seemed to know what to say, though now that Libby thinks about it she doesn't remember much of her advice. Perhaps it was simply her listening that Libby craved. To be understood. Her Cambridge friends: they understood her best, Dan especially. There were times when, debating this or that political issue, Libby would feel too passionately to be able to effectively explain her point. Instead, it would come out as a rant, as a series of emotions. And often Dan would take this series of emotions and translate them into coherent arguments, so that Libby felt that she had contributed more to the discussion than was actually the case. He made her better. They were a team.

She does miss him, after all.

Libby and Thom have an easy rapport, but it is tiring each day to put on a mask, to strive for perfection, as she did back at home so that Iona would choose her, give her time and confide in her. With Dan – with the rest of Libby's King's friends – there is none of that exhaustion, because there is none of that charade. They accept her. They've pooled money together to send her off in the direction of her dreams. And now she has left them all behind. It is a sacrifice. A worthy trade-off, of course: Thom is Thom and she loves him. But staying here for ever won't be without cost.

Lib, Iona's message says, *I've read your novel. I know you sent it to me ages ago and I feel like a bad sister for only just getting around to reading it now, but you know me and books, and anyway, better late than never and all that. I liked it.*

Lauren reminded me of you a little. A lot. It made me sad to think of you in ten, twenty years, still single, because of a guy you can't get over. I don't know who the guy is, Lib. I've always wondered if you like Dan, your Cambridge friend. You talk about him a lot. Or maybe the guy is Thom. Maybe you're worried that if it doesn't work out with him, it will somehow leave you broken. He's just a guy, Lib. There are other guys. I thought I would never be happy again after Jeremy. I thought he was the love of my life. And in a way, maybe he was. You only get one first love. But you know what? Eventually it gets better. Eventually you can look at other guys. Maybe you go to your younger sister's wedding and you flirt with one of the ushers. Maybe he asks you out and then a few months later he asks you to move in with him. (It happened yesterday. You're the first person I've told.) I'm happy, Lib. Happier than I ever thought I could be again. I wanted you to know that. I wanted you to know that sometimes life gives you second chances.

Libby, of course, is crying by now. It is unthinkable that anything other than joy should be moistening her eyes. And yet the joy is tinged with other things. Frustration and jealousy and homesickness. And anger. Anger that Iona is selling out: Jeremy was supposed to be the one for her, the only one. She is offended on his behalf, offended by this betrayal. Is it really possible that she wanted Iona to pine, always loving him and only him, defiantly turning down other suitors, like in some Jane Austen novel, or maybe a Jane Austen novel set in the twenty-first century when unmarried women are allowed and expected to live full, satisfying lives?

Libby splashes her face, re-does her make-up. She is being ridiculous. Enough of this. She will go downstairs, start the day's work with Thom. In the end, Iona can do what she likes. It is none of Libby's business. She has a new life here; she will soon have a new family. Step-kids who love her, finally. She is thinking already about what film she and Clara should watch together next.

'You okay?' Thom asks her, when she joins him at the table.

'Yes,' she says. 'Why?'

'You look, I dunno. There's no spring in your step today.'

He is so attentive. So caring.

'I've just had an email from my sister,' she says. As if that should explain everything. To some people, it would. To Dan, it would. These few words would be enough to clue him into her conflicted emotions. He might not be able to name those emotions, but he would know they were there. He would know to put his hand on her shoulder. To ask, *you okay?*

'Which one?' Thom asks, and Libby realises she is going to have to explain. *The one I love the most. The one I always wanted to be like. The one I gave new life to in my book.*

'Iona,' she says. 'The oldest. She's pretty happy. About to move in with a new man.' She avoids his eyes as she says this, because she doesn't want to blush. She is also pretty happy, also living with a new man. In a manner of speaking.

Thom fails to pick up on this. 'You don't like this guy?'

'He's fine,' Libby says, though she has been absent from the family dinners this summer. She barely remembers this guy's name, never mind what he looks like. 'It's just—' It is going to take so much explaining. And is she going to sound callous and bitchy? Probably. That is best avoided. 'It's fine,' she says. 'It's just hard being away from home.'

This is not in the least bit true. Though it is true in one particular way: she wants to talk to someone from home. Someone who understands her. Someone to whom she doesn't have to explain the complexities of her family and her past. To whom she doesn't have to explain anything. With whom she can just be. Someone like Dan.

She catches herself thinking this thought and makes eye contact with Thom. Look where you are, she tells herself. Look who you are with. It is only natural that Thom doesn't yet know her as Dan does. It is simply a matter of how much time they have spent together. Of facts about her that he hasn't learned yet. On a fundamental level, he *gets* her; that's the most important thing. She will have the intimacy, the mutual understanding, with Thom one day. One day soon.

Ebba

Libby asks Ebba almost every week if she has read anything by Colum McCann. She loves *Let The Great World Spin*, won't stop talking about the poetry of it. It was my favourite book, she has said, until I read yours. This effusive admiration makes Ebba cringe a little, but it is so genuine that it is hard not to find pleasure in it.

Browsing the fiction shelves at Santa Monica's Barnes and Noble, Ebba finds the Colum McCann section. Libby's favourite isn't there, but something else catches her eye: a novel called *Dancer*. She picks it off the shelf, flicks through and reads until her feet ache, then she sits down on the floor and reads on. She reads until tears surprise her and the words blur. Ebba loves the theatre; she loves writing; she has told herself for years that even without her injury, even if she'd made it into a ballet company, her dancing career would be over by now. She would be looking for another passion, another way to fill her days, express herself, give meaning to her life. She found acting and writing much sooner than she would have found them if she had been dancing all her life; she has saved herself years. She has saved herself, too, decades of hunger even beyond that of an actor, the agony of all her friendships being built on competitiveness, the manifold horrors of ballet school. She tells herself these things, over and over, and she is usually able to conclude that life has turned out for the best.

If she had followed the ballet path, she would never have met Ethan; she might never have met Thom, except, if all the stars had aligned, maybe at Juilliard if she had been good enough to get her BFA from there. She might have been good enough. It was certainly looking that way: her picture in the dance magazines, her name singled out by the *New York Times* review of the Summer Intensive performance. Not meant to be: the title of her book, the theme of so much of her life, it seems. It's what she tells herself, everything happens for a reason, these platitudes that for so much of her life have been vital to her emotional well-being or at least her emotional survival. But deep in her belly, stored with all the other pain, is the absence of dance all these years, the death of a dream. Heartbreak sounds to her like the snapping of an Achilles tendon; hope like the applause of a riveted crowd at Lincoln Center.

These things, Ebba knows, sound different to Libby, but her soul is no less fragile. Deep sensitivity is one of the things they have in common, one of the things that sometimes makes Ebba want to wrap Libby in cotton wool and sometimes makes her want to sit her down and give her a preview of life's hard truths. Libby and Thom have a meeting set up with Ricky Jamieson, the hot-shot studio exec. Maybe this is it, Libby has said. This might be it. And Ebba wants to say: yes, but probably it isn't. It would be like expecting to marry the first person you date. To say so, though, seems unnecessarily harsh; instead, she shares Libby's excitement, cheers her on. She finds such joy in this, in cheering her on, in watching her grow as a writer, in mentoring her.

As Ebba stands, waits in line to pay for the book, an idea begins to form: what about another kind of mentoring: ballet teaching? What about helping others to discover what she herself has so loved? Her friend Gareth runs a studio; she could contact him, see what he thinks. They have known each other their whole lives, danced together a hundred times. He always jokes she turned him gay. My kiss in Romeo and Juliet? she asked him finally a few years ago. It was really that bad? He looked into her eyes; they were drinking gin and tonics, it was a moment of searing honesty. No, Ebba, no. But it is when I knew: if I could kiss a woman as beautiful as you and feel nothing, then, well...

It's true, Libby said when Ebba told her this story. You *are* beautiful. Which was embarrassing and predictable and touching all at once, and not dissimilar to her response when Ebba shares the teaching idea. I think you would be good at that, Libby says. I think those kids, those adults, whoever, they would be lucky to have you. Just like I am.

Thom

Thom can see that Libby is nervous. It doesn't take a psychology expert to ascertain this. It never does with Libby; her emotions are right there on her face. And in her body, the way she holds herself: slightly slumped in her seat, tracing the chain of her necklace with her index finger. And not talking. This not talking, it unnerves him. It is so unlike her.

They are at the bar at Dan Tana's in West Hollywood, waiting for their table to be cleared. Ricky Jamieson is meeting them here. For an early dinner, yes, but dinner just gives them all something to do with their hands while they wait for his verdict on the screenplay. Thom is nervous, too, though he would never say so and thinks he is concealing it well. His training as an actor has been so useful for so many things in life. But what acting has not prepared him for, oddly, is the fear. He has spent most of his life doing things that terrify normal people: public speaking, for one, and yet writing messes his mind up in an odd way. He and Libby have spent the summer trying to come up with a list of sober male novelists.

'There is a reason for this,' he tells her, every time she suggests someone new for the list who isn't sober at all. 'Writing is hard.'

She always laughs at him. 'What makes you think I don't know that?'

'The fact you do it so well?'

He means it, too. It is not just a line. He doesn't need lines. She is putty in his hands; she would be, at least, if he were that kind of guy, which he desperately doesn't want to be. But he wants her to realise she is gifted. He wants to see her grow in confidence. To be able to sit up straight, look people she thinks are more important than her in the eye. She is a good writer; she can be better still, and confidence, Thom thinks, is key to this. She needs to believe in herself enough to keep pushing for better, to keep working at her craft. She smiles now, looks down at her fingernails, no doubt wishing she could chew them. Today she has gotten a manicure, to stop herself.

'You're too nice,' she says when he tells her these things.

He wishes that were true. There are so many things about this summer – about life – that he would have handled differently if it were.

'Writing,' he says. 'It screws you up. It messes with your mind in a way nothing else does. You want to write this great story, using beautiful language, and you want people to love it, and think you're the best for producing it.'

He knows it because of *The Classroom*. He had an idea for a storyline and pitched it to the director, who said, 'Okay, sounds good, have a draft to me by Tuesday?' and left the room before Thom had the chance to stammer out, 'What? I didn't mean—'

The fear paralysed him for a day but then he had no choice but to put words down.

'It's always so much better in your head,' he says to Libby. 'Then you put it all on paper, and—'

'Yeah.'

In those moments she looks at him as though she can't believe that he is human, that he feels those things she's felt a million times. That was before, though. Now she is fully aware of his weaknesses, his humanity. And though her awe for him made him uncomfortable sometimes, now that it's obscured by all of the other crap he finds he misses it.

Finally the table is ready. They are led there, to a booth with those red leather seats, continue to wait. Ricky is known for his perennial lateness in that Hollywood way of people who know that others will wait as long as it takes because he holds the key to their dreams, their future. Power can be such an ugly thing. But they are on time anyway, just in case. And because Thom knows him a little, because they drank at the same bar after their respective divorces, he hopes some of the act – if it is still an act – will be redundant.

Ricky is only, in fact, fifteen minutes late: just long enough for Libby to notice the wine bottles on the ceiling, the minor celebrities at another table; just long enough for Thom and Libby to choose their food, not to have to waste time with such things once he sits down. He shakes hands with them, gets straight to business in this dimly lit restaurant. His floppy blond hair gets in his eyes; Thom has warned Libby that he can come across as a lovable buffoon, that she should not be fooled by this.

'So,' Ricky says. 'I really liked it.'

Thom looks at Libby. To check she is breathing.

'Let's order,' Ricky says. 'Then let's talk about the ending.'

Thom was expecting this.

'I like it,' Ricky says again once he's told the server he'll have his usual and hors d'oeuvres have been brought. 'But not the ending. She has to get together with him at the end. If this was some deep, artsy foreign film crap then yeah, sure. Have it be miserable. Have it be' – and his chubby fingers draw exaggerated air quotes – 'like life. That's what people expect when they go to see that stuff. But this is basically a rom com. Let's not try and be smart about it. Let's not try and make it more than what it is. There has to be a happy ending. Write me a happy ending.'

Thom feels kicked in the stomach on Libby's behalf, at this verdict delivered with no feeling, no subtlety, no nuance. He looks over at her: silent, chewing, a little pale. A rom com! Sure, it's funny: he has seen to that. Humour is his thing, has been what he's brought to the table, though she's vetoed some of his puns. But it's not just a rom com. It's deeper than that. He knows Libby has worked hard at its being deeper than that. They have worked at it together.

'We were hoping to give the audience something a little different,' he says.

'The audience doesn't want different.' Ricky runs his fingers through his hair. 'The audience wants the tried and tested formula. So do we. Works for them, works for us.'

'But if they aren't given the choice—'

'Are you saying the ending's a deal breaker?' Libby asks. Her first words in what feels like a long time.

'Action movies with a twist are one thing. Rom coms not so much. So pretty much, yeah.'

She looks at Thom. Her eyes, he is almost sure, say well, maybe we should do it. I don't know, Thom. I thought artistic integrity was important to me, but I want this, and I want this really badly. I can't bear to see another dream smashed. He wishes he could lean across the table, take her face in his hands, remind her of all the things that matter to her. The world doesn't need another bland rom com. What the world needs is for you to be you. Fortune cookie wisdom, he realises. And yet somehow also true. This Hollywood glitz, it's not even real.

'It's really important to us that the movie has a different message. That you can live a meaningful life even if you don't get the guy.'

'Suit yourselves,' Ricky says. 'But you'll probably need to find a different studio for that.'

Libby has stopped pushing her food around the plate. (Not eating: also uncharacteristic. Also worrisome.) She has stopped tracing the checks of the red and white tablecloth with her finger. She excuses herself, heads for the restroom. He hopes she is okay. That she is just going there to think. The dead weight of her dreams is bearing down on him too. He thinks it would be easier if this were his own script. Less complicated. Fewer emotions involved.

'Look,' Ricky says, once Libby is out of earshot. 'Ditch the girl. Rewrite the ending. We'll option it no problem.'

'Ditch her?' he repeats.

'Yeah. You know how these things work. She's sweet and young and earnest and that's all lovely and everything, but "like life" doesn't sell movies.'

'She wrote the book, Ricky.'

'Sure. But you know you can't copyright an idea. Your name across a screen, imagine it. Just yours. Written by Emmy-award winning actor—'

'My name's been across plenty of screens.'

It should not be working, this blatant appeal to his vanity, but Thom is picturing it now. He can even see the font. Trajan, maybe.

'I'm sorry,' he makes himself say. 'No.' He doesn't even know what it is he is supposed to be sorry about. Maybe Libby's Britishness is rubbing off on him.

'Okay,' Ricky says. He gives Thom a look that says, you're making a mistake.

He stands to leave. Just like that. Doesn't wait for the check, doesn't leave cash. Thom should not be surprised after all these years in Hollywood. And yet.

Libby

'Where did he go?' Libby asks when she comes back from the loo.

'He left.'

'No deal?'

'No,' Thom says. 'No deal.'

'I was thinking in there,' she says. 'I was thinking maybe we should give the story a happy ending.'

'I know.'

'You know?'

'I know you pretty well by now.' These words, as always, they do something to her insides. He knows her. She is easy to know, she realises this, but still. There is tenderness in this acknowledgement. Intimacy. She dares not jinx things by thinking of love.

'But he's gone.'

'I told him no.'

Is she angry? It is difficult for her to be angry with him. There is something in the depths of her stomach that feels like anger, jostling with all the other emotions. Thom is searching out her eyes, maybe wondering, too, if she is angry.

'You didn't want to check with me first?' She hears accusation in her own voice. She didn't plan for this. She meant to be playful. Or curious. Not accusatory.

'I know how you feel about this story, Libby.'

Oh, mortification: she can feel the tears welling up. This must not happen. She must not cry. She doesn't even know why she would cry. What it is in the cocktail of emotions that would be making her cry? Or is it the cocktail itself? Too much emotion, overflowing, leaking out of her? Anger? Disappointment? The end of a dream? Yes. Yes, that's it. She knows this because she can feel her chin is trembling. Stop it, she tells herself. Stop it stop it stop it. But it doesn't work. It never has worked, and today is not the day for miracles.

'Libby,' Thom says. 'Are you okay?'

She can't let him see what she knows to be her impending meltdown. She takes a deep breath, hopes she can get through a sentence. 'I just need some air,' she says. She attempts a smile, maybe a reassuring smile, if that's how he wants to read it, though she isn't sure yet if he deserves it. If she wants him to be feel reassured. She knows, nevertheless, that it is a rather feeble smile.

Outside, she leans against a wall, closes her eyes. She knows she will need to cry this out later. But for now, she has to compose herself. She can't let Thom see her as a blubbering mess. Have those first impressions from the airport confirmed.

'Libs,' he says, and she jumps. He is standing right next to her, his hand on her shoulder. 'It's okay to be upset.'

She feels her chin go again. Damn it. It is so not okay to be upset. It is not okay to be anything other than fun and easy-going. Thom has enough hassle in his life with the ex-wife and the kids. The last thing he needs is a girlfriend who can't hold it together in a restaurant.

'I know you're disappointed,' he says.

I'm angry, she thinks. I'm angry that you took away my choice. My chance.

'I'm—' she starts to say, but of course speaking was a mistake. Of course she can't get through a sentence.

'C'mere,' Thom says, and she lets him hold her. She lets herself cry. 'It's okay,' he says into her ear.

She is still trying to be angry. 'We should have discussed it,' she says. 'The ending. Because maybe—'

He pulls away from her a little and waits for her to look at him. Into his eyes. 'You would have hated yourself for making that compromise.'

He's right. Of course he's right. He has understood her better than she could understand herself. He knows her. He holds her tightly again. She fits so snugly in his arms. She feels so safe with him, with someone who knows her well enough to protect her from herself.

'It's okay to be disappointed,' he says again. 'You have to let yourself feel it so that you can move on. Don't be in a hurry to move on. Let yourself feel.'

He doesn't want her to be perfect. He wants her to be real. This whole time, that was what she should have been. Real. Thom runs his hand through her hair. He is messing it up, but her hair doesn't need to be perfect either. She can smell tomatoes on his t-shirt, tomatoes and herbs of some kind, maybe thyme, blending with his familiar aftershave.

'It's going to be okay,' he says. 'I believe in you. I believe in your novel. There'll be so many other opportunities. There are so many other studios. It's going to be okay.' His breath tickles her ear as he whispers these things. He wipes the tears pooling under her eyes. His skin on her skin.

'Nice job with the waterproof mascara,' he says, and she smiles. 'That's better,' he says.

He knows her so well. He leans in to wipe away another tear with his thumb, though she isn't even sure there is another one. She can feel his warm breath on her cheek. She closes her eyes, waits for him to kiss her.

'Come on,' he says, instead. 'They have Baileys cheesecake for dessert on special. You love Baileys cheesecake.'

So well. He knows her so well. They are so close now.

Libby

Libby sees.

As she walks into the shop with Thom for the book launch, she sees Ebba pausing mid-conversation. She sees the way Ebba looks at Thom. She sees Ebba's distraction, her inability to focus on the conversation she has been having. She sees her excuse herself and come towards them. She sees how long the hug between Ebba and Thom lasts. She sees him lean in as if to catch a better impression of her perfume. She sees Thom's awkwardness as he says something like, this is nice, isn't it? The three of us together. We should hang out more often. She sees Ebba's frown that seems to say, get it together, Thom. She sees eyes in the bookstore turning to Thom and people readying their notebooks for autographs and formulating questions in their minds, and none of those questions are about the young British woman Thom walked in with, because they have all read Ebba's memoir and they all know what the real question is here. She sees Thom whisper something as he brushes her arm, eat 'em up, Ebs, or I'm so proud of you, or go get 'em. She sees Thom catch himself on the arm of the chair where he is aiming to sit because he can't take his eyes off Ebba, and this is less funny than it would be in different circumstances. She sees Thom start the applause that spreads throughout the room when Ebba steps up to the microphone. She sees Ebba's eyes wandering around the room to make the audience feel welcome but resting on Thom before she starts to speak. She sees Thom positioning himself at the back of the book-signing queue so that he will be able to take as long as he wants to talk to her. She sees Ebba catching her seeing. She sees that Thom doesn't notice when she slips out. She sees, more clearly than she ever thought she could, how foolish, how ridiculous, how blind, how utterly stupid she has been.

Ebba

Ebba's heart plummets when she sees Libby walk out. She thought they were being discreet. She thought that, like an early pregnancy, they weren't showing yet. But she forgot about the glowing. She forgot there are some people who always notice, who are attuned to these things.

She signs the books, because that is what she's there for. She signs the books, and makes conversation, and smiles at the compliments, and meets interesting people – a professor who uses her memoir as an example in his non-fiction class, an actor who went to elementary school with Ethan – but her heart is heavy.

'Thom,' she says, when he hands her his copy of her novel. Smiling. Oblivious. 'You brought Libby.'

'Of course I brought Libby,' he says, failing to grasp the subtext, the self-rebuke, the accusation. Of course he brought Libby. She is trying to tell him what the stakes of that are. To say, we should have discussed this. Strategised. How did we not see this coming? 'She loves you,' he says.

'And do you remember who else she loves?' When Thom doesn't respond, Ebba corrects herself. 'Thinks she loves.' She waits.

'Oh.'

'She's not stupid, Thom.' Unlike you, she wants to add.

'But we're being—'

'She has eyes.'

He stands, blankly. Unsure of what to do or say. And though Ebba does not know what to do or say either, this exasperates her.

'What do you want me to write in the book?' she asks him.

'Whatever you like.'

She is so irritated with him in this moment that she is tempted to do just that, write *whatever you like*. But she looks up at him from the signing table and she remembers how she feels about him when she isn't misdirecting her frustration, her guilt, her anger at herself.

To Thom, she writes, *My inspiration*. She signs, and adds *xoxo*. What she really wants to write, what she decided last night that she would write, is *My love*, but it feels strangely public now. It feels out of context, and wrong. Love feels like a word that should be whispered between them, not imbued with the ugliness of this particular victory. It is a word they have not used yet, this time around, and she does not want the first time to be today, to be in the middle of this conversation.

'I'm so proud of you,' he says as he takes the book. 'I know it's not a very original thing to say.'

'I don't mind unoriginal,' she says. In this case, at least. She minds it in people. The more quirky they are, the better. 'Thank you for coming. Really.'

'Of course,' he says, as though staying away were unthinkable. As though his love for her has become a reflex. Like breathing. And then, 'What are you doing now?'

'Lunch with my friends who came from out of town for this. Do the two of you want to come?'

'The two of us?'

Ebba waits, again. She is almost certain he is not always this slow.

'You make it sound like Libby and I are a couple.'

'I'm willing to bet that's how she still thinks of it. She's persistent. She's a dreamer. You can't talk someone like her out of feeling that way.'

He looks a little scared, and Ebba is glad she has gotten through to him.

'That's crazy,' he says.

Ebba laughs. She remembers Thom telling her about Libby after his visit to Cambridge: she wasn't one of the crazies, you know?

'Women get like that sometimes,' she says. Possessive. Delusional. Jealous.

'Men do too,' he says, as though lightly, but there is nothing light in this phrase loaded with meaning and memories.

Over his shoulder, Ebba sees Libby at the counter, buying the book. Soon, she'll be coming over to the table for a signature. 'Make yourself scarce for a while,' she tells Thom. Ordinarily she might go for something more subtle, but subtle doesn't seem to be cutting it today.

'Got it,' he says. He walks over to the non-fiction section, where he is swallowed by a group of women who ask for his photograph. 'We were secretly hoping you'd be here,' she hears one of them say. She wants to hear more, but there isn't time: Libby is walking towards her. Ebba smiles at her, as if nothing has changed. *For a great writer,* she writes. *And a great friend.* She is so tempted to leave it. To go on playing this game, living this double life.

'Listen, Lib,' she says, as she gives her the book back. She sees Libby stiffen. 'We need to talk.'

'It's okay,' Libby says. 'I get it.'

Ebba can see she is putting superhuman effort into keeping her voice even, into the smile that does not reach her eyes.

'Still,' Ebba says. 'We need to talk. Not now. Not here. Come for lunch with us. Then you and me can go for coffee, okay?'

The smile is still on Libby's face. Frozen.

'Okay,' she says. Wishing, no doubt, that this coffee would be a normal coffee. Wishing she could unsee what she has seen today.

***

'It's too beautiful here,' Libby says when Ebba hands her the latte. They are sitting in front of one of the coffee huts on Santa Monica beach.

'Too beautiful for what?'

'For me to cry.' Before she has even finished the words, before Ebba has begun to reply, Libby is wiping her eyes. Ebba feels like a bitch, but she also thinks it isn't fair that she should feel this way. She saw him first. Twenty years first. Yes, yes: very junior high. But this whole thing feels very junior high. Maybe that's how it always feels when you both love the same man, even when you are both grown, articulate, smart, mature women. Maybe you always feel that the other person cannot possibly love him, loves instead some fictionalised version of him. Like the character Libby has created – out of the roles Thom has played, and the perfect answers he has given in interviews, and the version of him in her novel, and of course, out of Mr Darcy.

(There is always a little bit of Mr Darcy in every girl's fantasy, and that's what this is for Libby. A fantasy.)

'I'm sorry,' Ebba says. Not an apology. Categorically not an apology. If this or anything like this ever takes places in one of her books, she will make sure the readers know that it is categorically not an apology. But she's sorry the way you're sorry when someone you know is grieving the loss of something precious, even if that thing was only a dream, was never really real, never really belonged to them.

'I am an idiot,' Libby says, cradling her coffee, as one might in the middle of the winter, somewhere winter exists. For warmth. For comfort.

'You're not. You were bewitched by him.'

'I am in love with him.' Libby waits for Ebba's eyes to meet hers. 'I know you don't think that's possible. No one thinks it's possible. Fine. I can admit that before, it was an infatuation. An obsession. But now, it's something else. We've spent hundreds of hours together this summer. I know him, Ebba. Not him as I might imagine him. Him. I know him, and I love him.'

'I know,' Ebba says, though she wants to shake Libby until she sees sense. You see what he wants you to see, she wants to say. You see the guy playing the guy who played Callum. You don't know that he's lost himself under layers of roles he's played. Why do you think he's so indecisive, so unsure of what he feels? He needs someone to script his life for him. And she wants to know something else, too. 'Did you think he felt the same way?'

'I thought he might.' Libby studies each of her fingernails in turn. 'Which, now, just makes me feel incredibly stupid.'

'He has a way of looking at you, doesn't he? Like he can see right into your soul.'

Libby nods. 'And like he likes what he sees there.' She chooses a fingernail to chew and begins the work. Ebba resists the urge to snatch her hand out of her mouth. This whole conversation, it turns out, is one long, challenging exercise in self-control.

Ebba puts as much kindness as she can into her voice, into her eyes. 'Your fairy tale was so close to coming true.'

'I had this dream I'd meet him. And I met him. And it was every bit as amazing as I wanted it to be. And then I wanted him to read my novel. And he read my novel. I wanted him to email me. He emailed me. All these impossible things kept happening. So then I started expecting the impossible. This was the last hurdle. And you—'

'It wasn't because of me,' Ebba says. She wants this to be true, and she also wants it not to be true. 'It's because you're twenty years younger than him.'

'Nineteen. And there are plenty of people with huge age gaps in his world.'

'His world.' Ebba fights to maintain an even tone, a gentle tone. 'His world, exactly. I know you want to be part of that world. But—'

'I know,' Libby says, and this surprises Ebba. She was expecting, yes. She was expecting, but I could be.

'And maybe it is because of me. I was stupid all those years ago. He's a wonderful man. I don't have to tell *you* that. It isn't often you get a second chance like this.' She is surprised to hear her own voice begin to crack. 'That's a kind of fairy tale too.'

'Yeah.' Libby starts chewing a different finger. 'When I read your book, I thought, you know, if Ebba got back together with Thom, that would be okay. There are like three people in the world that I'd be okay with him dating, and you were one of them.'

'But now that it's not hypothetical?'

'Yeah. Still. You've been through a lot. You deserve a chance to be happy.'

'I'm not sure that it's a matter of deserving, but thank you, Libby.' Ebba takes Libby's hand, the one she is not destroying, and squeezes it gently. 'Thank you for not scratching my eyes out.'

'Yeah, well. No promises.' She smiles. Ebba is almost certain she is joking.

'Name a villain in your next novel after me, if it helps.'

'Deal.'

'You're a wonderful writer, and a wonderful young woman. I want you to find something real with someone real.'

Libby wipes her eyes. 'I want you to be happy too,' she says.

Too bad this has to be a zero-sum game.

Dan

Dan's phone lights up and Caroline stirs next to him.

'I wish you'd turn that thing off at night,' she mumbles.

'I don't think it has an off switch.'

'That's funny.' Instead of laughing she shuffles closer to him. 'You're a funny man.'

'That's why you love me,' he says. He kisses her shoulder. As long as they're both awake…

'Early start tomorrow,' she says. 'Sorry.'

'You can't blame a guy for trying.'

Sleeping Caroline is, if anything, hotter than awake Caroline. He loves the way her blond not-quite-curls tumble across her face. He loves the stillness of her. When she's awake, it's perpetual motion: sport, or a restless leg, or pacing while she thinks. But in bed she allows herself to stop. She allows herself to be held.

The phone flashes again and she makes an unappreciative noise. He reaches over to turn it off. *Libby America*, it says. Libby? At 2am? It must be urgent for her to make a cross-continent call like this. It must be important for her to wake him up at 2am. Except, no: what is he thinking? This is Libby. She hasn't done the maths. She hasn't thought about the fact that it's the middle of the night where he is, that he has work tomorrow. She needs him, or has decided that she misses him, or wants to discuss some trivial change to her novel, and she has not stopped to think. He checks her Facebook page: photos of sunny beaches. Her cover photo changed to one of her and four children, Thom's, he supposes. Well, good luck to her. She's made her choice. She has forfeited any right she may once have had to middle-of-the-night phone calls.

***

But of course, his conscience doesn't allow for such conclusions. His conscience? Maybe not his conscience. He has nothing to feel guilty about. His heart, then, maybe?

It's 2am here, Libby, he writes.

I know. I'm sorry. It's just I'm having a pretty crappy day.

What does she want from him? Is he supposed to get involved somehow?

What's happened?

Found out that Thom is dating Ebba.

He snorts. Caroline sighs.

'Sorry,' he says to her.

'You will be.' She punches him, playfully, but it hurts a little, and he suspects she intended this.

He brings the phone under the covers so the light from the screen doesn't disturb her.

Wow, he writes. To give himself time to think of a fuller response.

I don't know what to do.

Do?

I think I should come home.

Uh oh, Dan thinks. This is trouble. He much prefers life now that she is on the other side of the world, practically. When she comes back, as he knows she eventually must, his heart may be in peril. He hopes not. Caroline is amazing. And, most importantly, not delusional. Not hysterical.

Have you finished the screenplay?

I was going to stay to help sell it. But it's going to be weird.

It's only going to be weird if you make it weird.

She probably doesn't like that very much. It's time, though, for people to start telling her the truth. Tough love, and all that.

You went there to do a job. I think you should finish it.

Okay.

He knows what she is thinking. She is thinking, you don't get it. Only, of course he gets it. Of course he gets that living and working with a guy you're obsessed with and have just realised – finally – doesn't, can't, won't ever love you is, well, a little on the awkward side. Of course he gets that all of this means her dreams are lying in pieces on the floor. Of course he gets that she needs to curl up on the sofa and eat ice cream with friends who have known her all her adult life but who are unavailable to her right now. He just doesn't think it's fair of her to drag him into it. He should say, call me any time. He should say, I'm sorry. He should say, I know it's hard. No, he should say, probably: look, you broke my heart, you can't come waltzing back into my life and expect me to clean up the mess you've made with your crappy decisions. Crappy decisions which, might I add, have never included me. Are, in fact, the reason for the broken heart I mentioned. But instead he writes:

Vicky might have some wisdom.
It's 2am, though.
It's 2am for me too, Lib. I'm in the same country as her.

But of course, he knows what she is thinking. That his devotion to her was such that a 2am phone call would barely bother him. May, in fact, be welcomed. That he cares about her more than her best friend does. That he always drops everything for her, does not consider it so much a sacrifice as a reasonable trade-off. Well, that's over now.

I'm sorry to wake you.

There is an American accent in this, in the phrasing of this, but even the momentary irritation of this does not suppress the pang of something he is feeling. Guilt? There is no need for guilt. No justification for it whatsoever. It occurs to him that she might be crying. Which is precisely why he can't call her. If he hears her crying, that will be the end of his tough guy resolve.

Tough guy?

Yeah, okay, he doesn't buy that either, the Cambridge English graduate, but still.

'Okay,' Caroline says, pushing the covers back. 'I'm awake. Which, now that I think about it, does have some plus sides.' She runs her hand through his hair. He loves it when she does that, but he can't. Not now.

'Early start tomorrow,' he says, finding the off switch on his phone. What do you know, it was there all along. 'We should sleep.'

Libby

Libby wants so much to talk to Dan. He has always been there for her – always – from carrying her bags for weeks after her skiing accident to listening to her talk about *The Classroom* for hours and hours to helping her with this novel, this novel that is what it is – almost a Hollywood movie! – because of him. He has always been such a good friend, and she has come to expect it of him. To demand it of him, even. To be upset when he refuses, quite reasonably she now realises, to take a call in the middle of the night. Would she have done it for him? Yes, of course she would have. She would have done it for any of her friends.

Oh, really? Unbidden, a mental image of Charlotte comes to her, hand on hip. Oh, really? That's what you used to be like, I'll give you that. But when was the last time you cared about someone other than yourself and following your dreams and all that rubbish?

That isn't fair. She cares about Thom, for a start. She would walk across broken glass for him – though under what circumstances that would be necessary, it is not quite clear. And his kids: she is so fond of his kids. She can see herself, in a few years' time, hauling herself out of bed at 3am to go and pick up Clara from a party she should not have been at. Holding her hair back as she once did for Vicky and Nicola and Charlotte. Or if Rosie catches the flu and wants to be read to, hour after hour, she will do that too. She will do it all. The essence of motherhood. Or step-motherhood, or whatever. Selflessness.

Except.

Except that dream is over now. Lying in pieces like shards of glass there is no point walking over because even if she did, it would not change the fact of Thom and Ebba.

Except that selflessness, now, means accepting, even encouraging, their happiness. Accepting that the fairy tale wasn't hers after all: that she is just the supporting character in someone else's story. If it was anyone other than Ebba, she would fight. Cast her in the role of villain and look around for some poisoned apples. Believe and believe and keep believing that she and Thom were meant to be. Fight to make it happen: lose that weight, have those teeth whitened, learn to walk in heels, be everything that he needs. She wants the best for him, and that's what love is, isn't it? To want the best for someone. So it would not, under any other circumstances, be selfish to fight for him, because the best for him would be her.

But there is no way to argue, no way she can even believe, that Ebba is not the best for Thom. Being with him back when they were so much younger, Ebba has told her, it reminded me of ballet lifts. I wanted to lift him, I wanted to say to the world, look, look how beautiful he is! Look how talented. Look how *good*. Not a good actor, no, that isn't what I mean. He is a good actor, a great actor, but I mean a good person. It sounds so trite. *Good* is such a flat word. But it's him. Right at his very foundation there is goodness. I wanted people to see that.

Libby remembers the knot of emotion at the back of her throat when she read of Ebba leaving Thom. She remembers drawing a sad face in the margin of the book. She remembers feeling wronged on Thom's behalf, wanting to put everything right for him. She imagined that she would be the one to heal him. I feel so sad for him, she said to Vicky, after she read the chapter. She seems like such a great person. They should have been together. And Vicky had, just for a few minutes, entered the game. Yes, she said, except that in your dream world the fact that they broke up means that you get to be with him one day.

Well, yes.

Silver linings.

But Libby was right about Ebba. Right about her loveliness, her elegance. She can't and she won't wish heartbreak on her, much less seek to achieve it. Libby wants the best for Ebba and for Thom, and the best for both of them is each other, and hey, maybe she'll be invited to the wedding, get to dance with B. J. Novak or Matthew Perry?

See, she mentally addresses Charlotte. See how unselfish I'm being. How reasonable. But Charlotte has disappeared and Libby cannot conjure her back. Because, of course, she has her own life. They all do, her Cambridge friends. They have moved on without her and she doesn't blame them. She doesn't deserve them, these fabulous people.

She opens an email and begins to type.

Hi gang,

I realise I've fallen off the planet since I came to California. I'm sorry – you all deserve better than that. It's been – what, exactly? Brilliant, heartbreaking, sunny, eye-opening? – such an adventure, but I'm ready to come home. I miss you all. And I want to try and be a better friend. Also, I wanted to say again – thank you, thank you, thank you, for the amazing gift of money that's made it possible for me to do this. Dinner's on me as soon as I get my advance cheque (yes – I've sold the book!). Love you all more than words can say or actions have recently indicated.

Libby xxx

She presses send, scrolls through Facebook for a bit. Likes some posts, feels a pang of disappointment for the group holiday she has missed, for the birthday celebrations she has not been part of. And then, an email notification. Matthew.

Lib,

I'm glad you're coming home. We all miss you. The Chandos isn't the same without you complaining about the temperature of the wine!

Listen, we've all been sworn to secrecy, so you definitely didn't hear this from me, but: the money. It wasn't from all of us. And I'm not comfortable taking the – ahem, no pun intended – credit for it. It was from Dan. He borrowed the money from Liam. It was all Dan, okay? He doesn't want you to know he's been in love with you this whole time. As if you didn't know! Of course you know. We all know. But he's worried, I think, of being hurt, or of messing up the group dynamics, or something. I don't know. It's never really made any sense to me. Just – and I can't believe I'm saying this, I sound like such a girl – just please be careful with his heart, okay?

Cool. Now hurry up and get on the plane.

Matthew.

In love with her? What? No. It's just Vicky's silly theory. It makes no sense.

It makes perfect sense.

This whole time, she has been contorting herself into mental knots to convince herself of her own selflessness, when the truly selfless one is Dan. Dan, who sent her off to follow her dreams at considerable personal cost. Dan, who has loved her enough to encourage her love of somebody else.

Dan, who doesn't answer her Facebook messages except under duress. Who doesn't pick up the phone any more. Dan, whom she might have lost for good.

Thom

Libby can't look at Thom. She can barely look in his general direction. They are sitting at his kitchen table, where they so often sit, but everything is different. The air is charged with heaviness. Gone is the ease of their rapport. Gone, her easy smile. Gone, any smile at all.

'We're basically done, right?' she says.

'I think so. Since we're agreed on the ending.'

She looks at him, as if to say, the last few weeks have hardly been an advertisement for happy endings. As if to ask, so this is it, you and me? This is our ending too?

'I hope we can be friends in future,' he says, answering her unspoken question. 'I've enjoyed working with you.'

She finally holds his gaze for a brief instant. 'Me too,' she says. 'You're very talented. And living in this house has been amazing.' He knows it takes a superhuman effort for her to say this. He also knows that she means every word.

'I was hoping we could sell this screenplay together,' he says. He wants her to stay. Not for always. But just a little longer. He wants her to stay until he can make her laugh again. Until he has shown her all the beauty of Southern California.

'You're the one who's going to sell it, Thom. You've got the name they care about. I'm just some random British girl who happened to write the book in the first place.'

There is an ugly hint of bitterness in her voice. It doesn't suit her.

'Writing the book is the hard part,' he says.

'You're right,' she says. 'You know it, and I know it. But Hollywood being so self-centred…'

He knows she is including him in this accusation. He feels the sting of it and he wants to argue. But he also knows there is no point. She wants to be mad at him; maybe she even needs to be mad at him. Maybe he deserves it. He should have been clearer from the start, or from the time they kissed, at least. He should have said, 'Look, I know we have great chemistry, and maybe in another life, but I am not capable of much love right now, and all the love I am capable of is for Ebba. I'm sorry I can't give you your happy ever after. I'm sorry there's only one of me.'

She is so young: a life ahead of her. If she stays, he will introduce her to all the single men he knows. The ones who aren't too messed up, at least. There aren't a whole lot of those, but she only needs one, right?

'Stay,' he says. 'You should get to experience Hollywood. Not just the kitchen table of some has-been actor.'

'I don't belong here,' she says. And then she says it again, with what sounds like pride. 'I don't belong here. In the shallowness. Swanning around in expensive ball gowns when there are actual people with actual lives that I could help to become better versions of themselves.' This is a line from *The Classroom*, a line from the soul-searching moments of a character deciding he was going to leave his glamorous Broadway life to become a teacher. A line she has also quoted in her novel.

'Swanning around,' he says.

'Exactly.'

'You're going to go back to your old teaching job?'

'If they haven't replaced me.' *Replaced* seems so brutal a word. 'But it's not like there's an over-abundance of English teachers in London. I should be okay.'

'We might get a decent amount for the screenplay if we sell it.' *Decent* being relative. He knows the amount will make a much bigger difference to her life than it will to his. He will barely notice it. He could let her have it all. Penance.

'If.'

'Yes.'

'I've lived the last five years in the shadow of an *if*. I need something real. I want something real. If we sell it – that's great. If they actually make it into a film – even better. I might even come to the première.'

He smiles. He senses she is starting to soften.

'Swan around for just one night?'

'I think I could manage that. Plus, imagine the street cred with the kids I teach.'

'Okay. So is that a promise?'

'Yes,' she says. 'Okay. It's a promise.'

He will do his best with this. He wants to see her again, even if it's in many months' time. Maybe with a boy on her arm. And if there isn't a boy, then just for that night, he will be her date. The fairy-tale ending. He can at least give her that.

Dan

Libby is coming home.

Oh, how he wishes she would stay in California. Out of the way. Out of his head. Awake mainly when he is asleep. Harmless. As harmless, at least, as she can be while still posting to his Facebook wall enough to make his girlfriend notice. Caroline is not the jealous type (low-maintenance, remember?) but she is suspicious of Libby. You have nothing to worry about, he tells her, but he is a terrible liar and for this reason it would probably have been better if he had said nothing at all. Caroline is bubbly, energetic, fun, intelligent, and, best of all, extremely fond of sex. He is almost sure that he loves her, or at least that if he doesn't yet it will be just a matter of time. The lights were off when they said it to each other for the first time and so perhaps his fibbing – his wishful thinking, as he prefers to call it, his trying-out of the words – went unnoticed. Or perhaps not, and perhaps that is the true source of Caroline's suspicion.

Still, Libby is coming home. She is coming home soon. She is coming home in one week, two days, six hours, and fourteen minutes, to be exact. She has told him this in the most innocuous way possible, seemingly the most undemanding way possible, by tagging him on a Facebook post along with the rest of the King's gang. But he knows what she is expecting.

Are you going to go and pick her up at the airport? Vicky has texted him.

I don't know. Maybe. You think I should?

I don't know.

Well, thank you. This has been most helpful.

You're welcome xx

He knows what this means: a conflab at the next Chandos meet-up. He wouldn't be surprised if they took a vote. All those in favour... He will try to get Caroline to come to the pub that time, though she almost never does: they can't corner him with that stuff if she is there.

But Saturday rolls around and of course she claims she has a migraine.

'They all like you, you know,' he says.

'That's nice, but it doesn't change the fact that I have a migraine.'

'Would it change the fact that you have a migraine if I promised you we won't talk about Cambridge?'

'You always promise me that, and then it's never true.'

'But it doesn't matter anyway, because you have a migraine.'

'Exactly.'

He kisses Caroline in the darkened room before he leaves, and mentally gears up for the confrontation.

'Here's what we think,' Charlotte says, before he's even made it to the bar for a pint.

And by *we*, you mean *I*. He does not actually say this. He is too afraid of her displeasure, and nothing displeases Charlotte like the implication that she is somehow bossy or domineering. It's not my fault I have all the good ideas, she said once in the second year, and they teased her mercilessly about this line until she cried. Charlotte, actually crying! So now they only quote her to each other when she isn't around and the decision on the restaurant or the film proves particularly difficult. Turns out, this group does need an organiser after all.

'We think,' Charlotte is saying now, 'that if you go and pick her up, it will be perceived as a Grand Romantic Gesture.' He can tell she is capitalising the words in her head. They sound neon pink to him. 'Welcome back, all is forgiven, oh and by the way, I'm still in love with you. So, if that's the message you want to send, you should pick her up. If not, that's what the Tube is for.'

'I have a girlfriend,' he says. 'Remember?'

'Oh, do you?' She makes a show of looking around at each of the faces in the group, then all the faces in the pub, in booths, leaning on the bar, squeezed onto a brown leather sofa.

'She has a migraine.'

'Also, your Facebook profile doesn't say anything about a relationship.'

'And it's not a real relationship if it's not on Facebook?'

'I suppose that would depend on *why* it's not on Facebook.'

'It seems as if you're angry with me for some reason, Charlie.' Charlie is not quite as bad as Lottie. Not quite as worthy of her fury. But it is enough to get her lip twitching in irritation. 'You told me to find myself a girlfriend. I've found myself a girlfriend. And now you're angry at me because I've found myself a girlfriend?'

'We want you to be happy, Daniel. And it doesn't seem as if Caroline has made you happy.'

'So is that why you're angry? Because I'm not happy enough?'

'This might help,' Matthew says, handing him a beer. 'With the happiness thing.'

'We want you to get over Libby.'

'I have a girlfriend,' Dan repeats, lamely.

'Yes. Yes, you've mentioned this.'

Liam and Ollie have been silent. Again. Where is the guy loyalty these days? He looks at them, appealing for rescue.

'So, anyway,' Liam says. 'Who wants to come and play on the quiz machine?'

'Me,' Dan says. 'I do.'

This is a plausible exit strategy. He likes quiz machines. He does not like conversations like the one he is having with Charlotte. And they need him for capital cities and obscure Sixties bands and cricket facts. 'It's Kiev,' he says now. 'Kiev is the capital of Ukraine.'

'But seriously, mate,' Matthew says as they collect the pound coins they have won and slot them back into the machine. 'What are you going to do?'

'I don't know,' he says. Matthew pats him on the shoulder in sympathy. Dan much prefers this approach to the problem, though it leaves him none the wiser. Even Charlotte, come to think of it, has not actually told him what to do. She has given him options based on how he feels, which presupposes that he knows how he feels. Which of course he does not.

Okay, well, that's a lie. He realises this after the fourth pint. He does know how he feels. He just wishes he didn't.

Ebba

Libby stands in the middle of the bright bedroom above Thom's garage, looking as if she cannot figure out which way is out. Looking as if, now that she has a chance to escape a week early, she isn't sure that she wants it.

'You okay?' Ebba asks. It's a ridiculous question. She wants the answer to be yes and that is why she has asked it, but of course it isn't yes, of course it cannot be yes, of course it will be months before the answer is yes. Still, Libby nods her head, though her eyes tell a different story.

'I'm ready,' she says.

Her suitcase stands imposingly in the dead centre of the room. An enormous suitcase, but not big enough to contain all the dreams and expectations she brought with her, and is taking home, crushed, broken, heavier somehow, like a precious vase that despite being meticulously wrapped in tissue paper and bubble wrap has suffered from the careless handling of airport professionals.

Ebba has convinced Libby to spend a few days with her before she flies home to the greyness of a London fall. 'I don't have a swimming pool,' she said. 'But I do have a beach. Well, not *have* have, but...'

'I love the beach,' Libby said. 'And it would cost a lot to move my flight forward a week.'

Ebba hopes that is not the real reason. She hopes that, like her, Libby wants to take the time to allow their friendship to return to something resembling normal.

'The beach will soothe your soul,' she says now, and the words sound pretentious out loud, but whatever. 'It always helps me when I'm feeling down.'

Ebba can see what Libby's thoughts are in her face, as she always can. She is thinking, I imagine that being with Thom also helps when you are feeling down. Or she is thinking, how can you possibly ever feel down when you get to be with him? She has so much to learn. Ebba wishes in some ways she could shield her from those things, but in other ways she doesn't. In other ways, she thinks, the sooner you can learn this stuff, the better. You will be more fully equipped for the things life throws at you. Being with a man does not erase the regret you feel at having hurt him many years ago. It doesn't erase the grief for the man who came after him, grief that still wakes you in the middle of the night. It doesn't take away the rest of the pain that comes with living, the absence of a beloved father, the way a wave might come up and wipe away all traces of a message scrawled in the sand with the heel of a foot: *Ebba loves Ethan, 1996*. But, like those waves, being with Thom does soothe her soul. She cannot deny that. She cannot deny that she has been extraordinarily lucky, luckier than she had allowed herself to believe she ever could be again.

'You want help with the suitcase?' Thom calls up, and she responds straight away, 'No thanks, we're good,' because to stand in the small space that is this room with Thom and Libby, however briefly, seems unbearable, unthinkable. And then she attempts to pick up the suitcase and changes her mind.

'Actually, yes,' she calls down.

And of course it is every bit as awkward as she imagined, this moment, but it is also over quickly, with cursory hugs and awkward platitudes. In seconds, they find themselves standing outside, by Ebba's car. The two of them drive away wordlessly, winding through the streets of San Marino. Ebba has chosen this prettier, less direct route, scenery rather than efficiency, to ease Libby out of Thom's life. She sees Libby wiping her eyes and she knows it is not theatrics and it is not a guilt trip. It is unmitigated heartbreak, or mitigated perhaps by her embarrassment at crying at all. But the drive to Santa Monica can be a long one, and so once they are away from Pasadena, once Libby has mentally said goodbye to all the places she has been with Thom, all the places she wishes she had been with Thom, Ebba finds a radio station that is not NPR and hums along to the upbeat tune of 'Brown-Eyed Girl'. She wants Libby to catch its breeziness, to sing along too, and it seems a very long time of just Ebba humming, but then there are two of them, and they make eye contact and smile for the first time that morning. Ebba has always known that Libby will be okay and in this moment it seems that Libby, too, catches a glimpse of this hope. She wants, over the week they will spend together, to give her many such glimpses, glimpses that are less and less fleeting. She wants to talk to Libby, really talk to her, in a few days' time, once the salt water has begun to heal her wounds. To ask, do you regret it? Regret coming? No, Libby will probably say. I had to do it. I had to follow my dream. I couldn't spend the rest of my life wondering what if. Exactly, Ebba will say. Exactly. And then she will want to add, but she is afraid it might seem mean: a dream was all it was meant to be. Sometimes that's all dreams are meant to be.

And hopefully, hopefully, Libby will nod into the wine. And they will talk about the life awaiting her, back home, the life that is only just beginning for her. Hopefully there is a boy – a man – waiting for her who will understand that she had to chase this impossible dream, see where it ended. A boy who will not have to wait two decades for her, because the dream has exploded in time and she will not spend those decades chasing the wrong thing, or the wrong person. Ebba hopes Libby will be able to hear that. That she will walk a little taller, stand a little straighter as a result. Maybe a week is a little ambitious, even with wine and sand and sea. But in a few months, maybe. And with the love of a good man. An age-appropriate man. Someone who will love her despite her questionable decisions, or perhaps because of them, because of the endearing devotion from which they spring.

Thom

The kids have insisted on coming, and Thom thinks it will be good for them, so despite Jenny's protests he takes them with him to the airport. Ebba has told him not to come at all; she thinks it will be easier with just her and Libby. She's probably right – let's face it, she's almost definitely right – but what the heck, he might as well admit it: he needs closure. His heart almost broke when Ebba came to pick Libby up for the last time, Libby and her enormous suitcase. Planning on staying for good? he'd joked when he picked her up, and it seems less funny now. Yes, whatever, he knows he is being melodramatic, blame it on the acting gene if you like, but he will miss her. He will miss the way she twirls her hair between two fingers; the way she hums the imagined soundtrack of a scene as they write it. He will miss her enthusiasm, and her naïveté, and her belief, unfaded, uncynical, that this movie could make it, that it could be good. So refreshing in his life, surrounded as he is by cynicism and products of repeatedly crushed hope, of competitiveness and the kind of friendship that mentally tallies your film credits and award nominations at the same time as it hands you a drink, as if everyone around him could be reduced to a set of stats and pitted against one another. If she stayed, no doubt she would lose the very ordinariness that so attracts him (he may as well admit it, now that she's leaving). She would acquire all kinds of insecurities, the desperation to be noticed that is both the driver and the downfall of so many people in his world. So it is better if she leaves now, intact (well, Ebba has pointed out, there is the small matter of her broken heart), goes back to the everyday life she is used to and prepared for, the friends from her own world.

Nonetheless, he will miss her.

So he needs to say a proper goodbye. To hug her, tell her she is welcome back any time, really, and maybe she has other novels up her sleeve? Because when she left with Ebba, all he was able to say was, 'It's been great, Libby, have a safe trip', and there is so much else he wants to tell her.

And the kids were horrified, too, that she didn't say goodbye, even though she left each of them a card and a thoughtful gift. He was reminded of *The Sound of Music*, the scene where the children return to the house to find Maria gone, incredulous that she didn't even tell them beforehand that she was leaving, wondering if she even loves them. He doubts that his kids would show quite the initiative of the von Trapp children to try to find her – hitchhiking a ride to LAX, stowing aboard a plane to London – but still, it was probably best that he take matters into his own hands.

He sees her at the check-in counter, recognises her Union Jack sweater from the back, recognises, too, the two sets of shoulder-length brown hair, hers and Ebba's. From the back it is surprising and almost creepy how much they look alike, how similar their gestures are. He watches them for a moment, watches Ebba put her hand on Libby's shoulder. He is glad Ebba is with her, glad she has someone; he is gladder still that she and Ebba seem to be close again.

'Daddy.' Juliette tugs at the hand that is holding hers. 'Daddy, I see her.'

'Who's the lady she's with?' Harry asks. 'Is that her mom?'

'Her mom's in England, silly,' Clara tells him, and he is glad for the pre-teen superiority that spares him from the uneasy task of explaining.

Juliette breaks away – there are never enough hands – and runs to meet Libby. She nearly trips a couple of people on her way over to the check-in desk and for some reason, today of all days, he finds this amusing. He watches Libby's surprise when Juliette tugs on her sweater and then the delight of both of them as Libby picks her up, all fifty pounds of her, and blows raspberries on her neck. Ebba turns in the direction Juliette has come from, catches his eye, shakes her head slightly, as if to say, of course you couldn't keep away, you are incorrigible, but her eyes are dancing and it is going to be harder than he thought not to let on to the kids who the lady is, who she might become. Ebba nudges Libby, nods in the direction of Thom and the other kids and Libby smiles, a sad smile, mascara already making its way down her left cheek.

'They wanted to say goodbye,' he says, by way of apology or explanation, or something, when Ebba, Libby and Juliette join them.

'*They* wanted to say goodbye,' Clara says. '*I* didn't.'

Libby's face falls. Thom is surprised, too. He understands that Clara is acting out, but this seems to be cruel to an unlikely degree; he thought Libby and Clara had bonded.

'*I* came to tell you not to leave,' she continues, and the smile returns to Libby's face.

She puts her arm around Clara. 'That's lovely of you,' she says. 'But I can't live here for ever. Visas, you know.'

'I have an idea,' Rosie says, and he thinks, uh oh. I think I know what is coming. She is the quietest of his children, but when she speaks, he often has the impression that she has been thinking about what she is going to say for a long time. 'My friend Esther got to stay in America because her mom married her step-dad. Marry Daddy, and you can stay for ever!'

'I wish I could,' Libby says, and catches herself. 'Stay for ever, I mean.'

Clara sniggers. They may be friends now, but that does not make her stupid.

'But you can't?'

'No.'

'But why?'

'Because,' she says, and Thom holds his breath. Because your daddy loves the lady over there, who's standing over to the side… 'Because sometimes life is like that. You've seen Narnia, haven't you? You can't stay in the wardrobe for ever.'

Juliette is unconvinced by Libby's explanation, and she crosses her arms to show this. 'I don't want you to go.'

'I know, honey. Maybe you can all come and visit me sometime?'

'You just cost me ten thousand dollars,' Thom says, and realises it is the first thing he has said to her since they arrived. Something catches in his voice.

'Sorry,' she says, not looking at him, and then she does. 'Well, I'm not *that* sorry.'

He laughs. She has made him laugh for the first time in quite a while, and it feels good. Behind him, he hears his name mentioned, but he does not turn. Now is not the moment for photos and autographs. Now is the moment for one last hug, each of them in turn, Harry wriggling, Juliette refusing to let go, Clara determined to be stoic, Rosie sensible but crestfallen, Ebba crying when it is her turn. Airport goodbyes: the very hardest kind. He holds Libby, breathes her in. He kisses her gently on the cheek.

He says, 'Keep in touch, okay? I really mean it.'

She wipes her eyes and says, 'It's been amazing.'

'Yeah. It's been real.'

She laughs. Finally, he has gotten her to laugh.

'No, it hasn't,' she says. 'It's been the least real thing ever. The opposite of real. But it's definitely been something.'

If it weren't for his kids, if it weren't for Ebba, if it weren't for the prying eyes of the curious who are almost sure they recognise him from somewhere, he might be tempted to kiss her again. But instead, he squeezes her arm.

'Come back soon, okay?' he says.

'Okay,' she says.

This still feels all wrong, somehow. He watches her go. The look back as she goes through security. The falsely courageous wave. Juliette's repeating, over and over, I don't want her to go. And then she is gone, and the attention shifts to the stranger in their midst.

'You're a friend of hers?' Clara asks Ebba.

'Yes. Clara, I'm Ebba.'

'That's a pretty name,' she says. What has happened to his snarky preteen? Where did she go? 'Dad used to date someone called Ebba. Before he met Mom.'

'Huh,' she says. 'That's interesting. I've never met anyone else called Ebba.'

'Yeah,' Clara says. She is impenetrable, this daughter of his. Has she guessed? Maybe she already has, or maybe she does when they get to the parking lot and she sees Ebba brush his hand and ask him, 'You okay?'

'I'll call you later,' he says to her. By later, he means, as soon as the kids are in bed. As soon as the weirdness of the day and of the summer is over with. They need to talk, Thom and Ebba. They need to plan how to tell the kids that this thing between them, it might be real.

Libby

Libby has requested a window seat, as she always does, and after Los Angeles has receded out of view she allows herself a daydream. Not about Thom, those are over; she is leaving behind that part of herself. Maybe it was inevitable that she should go after her dream. Did it make it right? Probably not. But who knows. She at least, once everything stops hurting, will have some fun memories, some stories to tell back home. But for now, she is thinking about the future, the immediate future, the in-just-over-eleven-hours future. Landing.

She doubts anyone will be there to meet her. Nobody has offered. A few have clicked 'like' on her Facebook post, but that is not exactly a commitment. Not that she blames them: it will be 7am in London when the plane touches down. Once, they would have gladly got up at five in the morning to meet each other at airports. It occurs to Libby that the rest of them might still do this for each other. But she does not deserve them. She walked away from them without so much as a backward glance twelve and a half weeks ago and if everything had worked out the way she wanted to believe it would, she would happily have given up a lifetime of Chandos wine and Pizza Express banoffee pies for the sake of her new exciting life of glamour with the handsome Hollywood superstar. (Fine: regular star.) Their lives have moved on without her. Dan has a new best friend, apparently; Libby has suspicions she is more than that, but Facebook has not informed her of any change of status and Vicky has sidestepped her casual questions. Libby ditched them all to go and chase her dream; she can't expect them to come running to Heathrow, even to the shininess of the still relatively new Terminal Five. She vaguely remembers the story of the prodigal son from school assemblies: he goes off to have fun, spends all his money, ends up feeding pigs and then comes home having lost everything. And still his father runs to meet him. Well, sure, but the father is God in that story, and you'd have to be superhuman to show that much undeserved love.

Still, the daydream Libby allows herself as she leans against the side of the plane is that the King's group, all of them, even Ollie and silent

Liam, would be standing at arrivals with Welcome Home banners. Vicky running to hug her: it's been so quiet and lonely without you in the flat. Charlotte would probably have organised it all, would have dragged along even Matthew – who back at college had regularly missed ten o'clock lectures on account of their being too early. And Dan, who wouldn't want to be there at all. Once upon a time, maybe. Before she made it clear that the life she dreamed of did not include him. He is kind, devoted, gentlemanly. He has always taken care of her. And she has lost him, because of a fantasy. Lost the closeness of his friendship. If Matthew is right, if Vicky has been right all along, she has lost, perhaps, the chance for more. Dan has always, she realises, been her insurance policy. He deserves so much better than that. So much more. She could have been happy with him, and she has thrown it away.

The reality, when she lands, will be what you don't see in *Love Actually*: the exhausted traveller, unnoticed by anyone, who heads straight to Costa to gather her strength for the trek home on the Tube with her enormous suitcase. She should probably sleep in preparation for this.

She doesn't, of course, other than an intermittent doze, and she finds herself finally dropping off to real sleep just as the lights are turned on and breakfast is served. She is not impressed.

Neither is she impressed, upon landing, by the welcome, or lack thereof, that she gets in the customs hall of the Heathrow terminal. Where are the flags, she wants to ask? Why is no one welcoming the Brits home over the tannoy? Americans would never stand for this. She makes a mental note to complain to whomever it is you complain to about these things just as soon as she is over the jet lag. Still, at least there is no interrogation at the end of this long queue, just a cursory glance at her passport photo, and her suitcase has even made it intact.

She is minutes away from the Costa: minutes away from being able to sit on a seat that is firmly planted on the ground and stretch her legs out as far as they will go. She can see it now, as she comes through arrivals; a medium latte and one of those cherry and almond slices, maybe, she has missed—

'Lib!'

She looks to her right and can't quite believe it.

He's here.

He hasn't shaved, and his clothes are crumpled, but she realises she likes this look on Dan. The dishevelled Cambridge boy. Her dishevelled Cambridge boy? He runs towards her. Actually runs. She pushes her luggage to one side and hugs him. She has forgotten how good it feels to hug him now that he is slightly less bony than he was in their first year at King's.

'Back to reality,' he says, and it's so good to hear his British accent. 'Welcome home, Lib.'

She pulls back and looks at him and he looks back at her, into her eyes. She can't believe he is here. She doesn't deserve him, and yet here he is. Waiting. All these years waiting for her to come to her senses. She might be finally there.

'Reality sounds pretty good right now,' she says, and kisses him.

Acknowledgements

As I finally hold my book in my hands after a decade of writing seriously, I'm deeply grateful to all who have made this endeavour possible. Among them:

Mel Flashman – thank you for believing in me as a writer, for all you've done to make this a better book, and for your advocacy on its behalf. Thanks, too, to Sarah Bush, for your enthusiasm.

Mary Chesshyre – it's always nerve-wracking to hand your book to an editor but I hit the jackpot with you!

Adelle Wadman – it still makes me giddy that someone whose writing I admire so much thought mine was publishable. Thank you for giving my fledgling author career just the nudge it needed at just the right time.

Karin Tanabe – thank you for having the confidence I would make it when I was just a baby author, and for all your feedback, for your soothing text messages, and for cheering me on.

Rena Rossner – how wonderful that we are hitting our writerly strides together. Thank you for the advice you gave me with your agent's perspective. I'm so glad that we bumped into each other on that Authonomy forum more years ago than I care to count!

Rebecca Kabat – my first superfan. Thanks for being the guy the guy counts on.

Sabine Sur – you are both an excellent writer and an excellent giver of feedback. Thank you.

Sara Kaiser Creighton – your input was selfless and invaluable.

And all my other early readers: Laura Brown, Liz Dawson, Laura Graham, Edward Holmes, Laura Maddux, Katie O'Rourke, Alessandra Scheiber, Craig Segall, Colette Victor, Juliet Wilson, Natalie Williams, and the anonymous reader at the Romantic Novelists' Association New Writers' Scheme. Thanks especially to those among you who've helped me process the various emotions that writing, editing, and publishing this novel has brought up – you know who you are!

Reif Larsen and my classmates at the Fine Arts Work Center in summer 2015 – thank you for helping me reshape the scene I most look forward to reading out publicly, and for giving me the courage to do so for the first time.

Caileigh Scott – thank you for answering my barrage of Hollywood- and theatre-related questions and for naming *The Classroom*.

Thanks to everyone on social media – friends and strangers – who has taken the time to help me figure out details and remind me of the differences between British and American English without shaming me too much!

Thank you to the Gotham Writers Workshop, whose Friday night write-in provided the impetus for one of the chapters of this novel.

Heartfelt gratitude to friends and professors from my MFA at American University, especially David Keplinger and Heather McDonald, my thesis advisers, for all your thoughtful reading, advice, comments, and encouragement, and Danielle Evans for taking me seriously and instilling quiet confidence in me as a result.

Blake Dennis – I'm so thankful that life has reconnected us, and so touched by your enthusiasm for my various projects and your willingness to listen to and help me figure out my abundance of feelings about them all!

Emily Travis Ribeiro – thank you for our endless discussions and for your friendship, encouragement and support in innumerable ways over these many years. I am deeply grateful for you.

Christina Haag – without your grace and kindness, this novel would have been neither written nor published. I am so thankful for you and for your achingly beautiful memoir *Come to the Edge*.

To my 'Thom' – my unwitting, inexhaustible muse: thank you for all that you are.

And, of course, thank you to Aaron Sorkin – without whom it is doubtful I would be writing at all.

Finally, and most importantly, thank you to my heavenly Father. To paraphrase Eric Liddell – God made me to love words, and when I write I feel His pleasure.

Note to the Reader

Thank you for reading *Unscripted*! If you enjoyed it, I'd be so grateful if you could post a review online on Goodreads and wherever you bought this book. It helps get the word out to other potential readers.

And if you'd like to make sure you keep in touch and up to date with my future books and other writing, head over to clairehandscombe.com/mailing-list.